A Knight of Battle

Knight Series Book 2

Candace C. Bowen

A Knight of Battle (Knight Series – Book 2)

ISBN-13: 978-0692483985

ISBN-10: 0692483985

Released through Seven Realms Publishing 2012

Re-Released through KnightTime Press 2017

www.knightseries.com

Printed in the United States of America

Dedication

This book is dedicated to my brave, determined, and beautiful cousin,
ANN MARIE VINCENTI PELTIER
Family is forever no matter how far apart they are.
Love you beyond measure.

Acknowledgments

Writing is lonely work. Fortunately for me, I am blessed with an amazing circle of friends who are always there to save me from myself. Jodi DeCrescito Recalt and Astrid Pfenninger Haldane are two of them. They are the sisters I chose for myself, and I cannot thank them enough.

I was under contract and faced a deadline when I wrote Albin and Lecie's story in 2012. The timing could not have been worse since I was going through a difficult divorce. While it was well received, I was never satisfied and promised myself to one day do justice to the story. It took five years but with love in my life, I finally did it. I hope you are as pleased with the story as I am.

When I released this book in 2012, I wrote the following to my son: 'As always, I have saved the best for last. To my incredible son, Clayton William: Words escape me when it comes to expressing how very much I love you, little man. Always live with love in your heart and there will be no limit to what you can do.'

Here I am five years later and while so much has changed, the love I feel for my now teenaged son is limitless. He is my inspiration, and I am so very blessed to be his mom.

Love and Light,
Candace

Candace C. Bowen – Novels

A Knight of Silence – Knight Series Book 1
A Knight of Battle – Knight Series Book 2
A Knight of Valour – Knight Series Book 3
A Knight of Defiance – Knight Series Book 4
Spur of the Moment
Wicked Embers (Sequel to Spur of the Moment)
Jack of Hearts
Voodoo Fire
Order of the Knightshades – The Stygian Stone

ANTHOLOGY CONTRIBUTIONS
Bump Off Your Enemies
The Darwin Murders
Tasteful Murders

COMING SOON
A Knight of Regret – Knight Series Book 5
Malevolence (Sequel to Voodoo Fire)

Cast of Characters

Sir Albin (Hero)

Lecie of Rochester (Heroine)

THE WOUNDED STAG INN AND TAVERN:

Anne (Staff)

Betta (Tavern Wench)

Clayton (Lecie's Younger Brother)

Edric (Lecie's Father)

Gunilda (Tavern Wench)

Hamon (Tapster)

Harsent (Tavern Wench)

Joseph (Stable Hand)

Mary (Staff)

Merek (Staff)

Osana and Sabina (Lecie's Twin Younger Sisters)

Simon (Staff)

Tugger (Family Dog)

William (Staff)

Winifred (Staff)

PEOPLE OF ROCHESTER:

Caine (Sheriff Richard's Son)

Dr. Rayburn (Village Leech)

Edmund (Sheriff Richard's Son)

Father Bartholomeo (Village Priest)

Frederick (Sheriff Richard's Son)

Justice de Glanville (King Henry's Itinerant Justice)

Leofrick (Sheriff Richard's Son)

Mylla (Sheriff Richard's Daughter)

Sheriff Richard

Emmaline (Sheriff Richard's Wife)

Chapter One

The Wounded Stag Tavern & Inn
Rochester, England
Autumn 1127

"You do realize the ale is on the inside, do you not?" Standing in the pouring rain, Talan glanced over at his fellow knight. "If your intent is to admire the sign all night I shall leave you to your musings."

"What was that you said?" Without breaking his gaze from the blue and yellow painted wood sign depicting a stag with an arrow through its haunch, Albin remained motionless.

Losing patience, Talan hoisted his leather pack higher on his shoulder. "Whatever is the matter with you? From the trice we rode into town you have been behaving oddly. As for me, I am drenched to the bone and parched after our long journey from Castell Maen. Are you coming in or not?"

Shaken from his musings, Albin ran a hand along his dark close-cropped beard. "We must look a sight, aye?"

"Since when have you given a whit about your appearance?" Albin remained still as if he had not heard. "Do try not to catch your death," Talan said sidestepping around his friend. "Fulke would be most aggrieved."

"Will do," Albin mumbled. Excitement for his most recent trip to Rochester had turned to indecision the instant he caught sight of their destination. Temptation in the form of the owner's young wife lay within.

He knew that he had no one else to blame for his quandary. It was he after all who had volunteered as proxy to oversee the building of

Rochester Tower for his liege and boyhood friend, Baron Fulke of Erlegh. It was too late now for second thoughts.

Half convinced to follow after Talan, he straightened when the tavern door opened and the object of his torment stepped out.

"Sir Albin." Lecie beckoned to him through the downpour. "You are soaked through. Come and warm yourself beside the fire."

Dropping his leather pack beside the door, Albin ran a hand through his dark wavy hair as he followed Lecie's instruction. Taking a seat beside Talan at a table closest to the hearth, he kept his eyes downcast.

"I shall get you both ale or if there is something else you would prefer—"

"Ale is fine," Albin blurted cutting Lecie off.

"And whatever fare you have would be much appreciated," Talan said. "I believe Albin here is in vital need of nourishment."

Lecie self-consciously touched her soiled apron. "I was unaware you would be coming so I must apologize for the paltry offering."

"Whatever you have is fine," Talan assured her. "We know you have your hands full with tending to Edric and the three young ones. By the way, how is our friend faring these days?"

"We are ever hopeful he is on the mend," Lecie said lowering her eyes. "Now if you both will excuse me, I shall see to your refreshments."

Albin kept his eyes fixed on Lecie's softly swaying skirts until she disappeared into the cooking chamber.

Following his friend's gaze, it became clear to Talan what was wrong with his friend. "You are in love with Lecie. Mon Dieu, I should have seen it afore now."

"Keep your voice down," Albin hissed. "You know not what you are talking about."

Propping his elbows on the table, Talan grinned. "Do I not? Come to think upon it, you have always acted oddly when we took up residence in Rochester."

"Cease your prattle, here she comes." Leaning back in his chair, Albin briefly flicked his eyes to Lecie.

Carrying a tray, she placed two bowls of unappetizing porridge before them followed by misshapen rolls and two cups of ale. "I truly wish that I had known you were coming."

"It looks delicious." Albin met her gaze for the first time as he sought to reassure her.

"Lecie, you are wanted above," the ginger haired tapster behind the bar called.

"Excuse me," Lecie said hastily before disappearing up the steps.

"She looks weary," Albin softly observed.

"No doubt she is." Talan dipped a roll into the porridge. "It cannot be easy for one so young to be burdened with so much responsibility."

Sipping his ale, Albin scanned the groups of men relaxing around rough-hewn tables after a hard day of harvesting rye and barley in the fields. "With Edric ill, she needs more assist with running the place. The harlots who work for their keep barely keep the tables clean. "

"We both agree on that." Talan signaled to the tapster with a raised hand.

Hamon gave a grunt of acknowledgement before bringing over a pitcher of ale to refill their earthenware cups.

Accepting the brew with a nod, Talan drew the ill-kept tapster into conversation. "How has Edric been faring since last we met?"

Hamon's calculating gaze slid to the steps leading to the upper level. "Coughing up blood for the past sennight, he has. I wager he has walked his last."

"From what I heard, Lecie believes otherwise." Albin could not stop himself from saying.

"What concern is her opinion to you?" Hamon narrowed his eyes suspiciously. "You asked for mine and I spoke the truth."

Lanky with wiry ginger hair and bowed shoulders, there was something shifty in Hamon's pale gray eyes that had always rubbed Albin the wrong way. "Be that the case, I suggest you keep to yourself about it when Lecie's around."

"What he means to say," Talan spoke to diffuse the rising tension, "regardless of the truth, Lecie is hopeful Edric will get better. Surely she does not need the additional worry of believing otherwise?"

"Always the peacemaker," Albin grumbled.

"Why cosset her when his death is a forgone conclusion?" Unflinching under Albin's cold regard, Hamon shrugged. "Lecie herself knows this which is why she fears leaving his side overly long."

"It saddens me to hear it," Talan said. "Has the village leech been tending to him?"

"Not since Lecie ordered him away," Hamon said with indifference. "Edric has been on the decline ever since."

"Ordered him away?" Talan glanced around at the packed tavern. "Surely, they can afford the physician's services?"

"It has naught to do with cost." Albin defended Lecie. "Rayburn's only treatment was to blood-let him. It did naught but make Edric weaker."

"Rumor has it, her refusal centers on somewhat more, Sir Albin," Hamon cut in with a sly smile.

"What is this more you speak of?"

"Lecie is young and tis well known in the village that she has been forced to care for Edric for some time now. Some believe it would be to her advantage to hasten his passing along."

Albin's hand tightened around his cup. "I am convinced I need look no further for the origin of these baseless rumors."

Oblivious to Albin's rising temper, Hamon said, "Twas not I who sent the leech away."

"I myself am the one who counseled Lecie to the futility of blood-letting." Albin glanced at Talan. "Lady Reina is vehemently opposed to it and believes it weakens the body. I completely concur."

Hearing a summons from a nearby table, Hamon's pale gray eyes glittered. "I shall be certain to pass along that information to anyone who inquires, Sir Albin."

"You do that," Albin sneered. "I care naught for what you do or say."

Talan leaned close after Hamon moved off. "I can now see why you have always had an aversion to him."

Scowling after Hamon, Albin forced himself to relax. "Nor do I trust him."

"What makes you say such a thing? He must have Edric's confidence for he has been the tapster here for as long as we have been coming to Rochester."

"Tis not any one thing in particular." Albin took a long swallow of ale before setting the cup down. "More like a feeling in my gut."

"Then we should pray he is wrong about Edric," Talan said. "Clayton is far too young to claim his inheritance and I have heard no mention made of any other male relations."

"One more thing Lecie will have to worry about," Albin said. "Tis not right women are barred from owning property."

"Do not let King Henry hear you say that. The inhabitants of Maen are already on the outs with him."

Albin looked up when a slight woman with frizzy dark hair came from the kitchen. Recognizing Gunilda, one of the tavern wenches who serviced the local men, he turned his attention back to Talan. "It still does not make it right."

Sauntering up to them, Gunilda concealed her rotted teeth behind a tightlipped smile. "Dare I hope tis I you have been seeking to keep you warm on this most foul of nights, Sir Albin?"

Running his eyes over the hardened young woman, Albin noted her stained kirtle and pox-marked face. "You know I am not one to pay for a toss."

"A lady can always try." Tossing her thin braid over her shoulder, she turned her attention to Talan.

Talan choked on his ale and coughed to clear his throat.

"Pardon my brother-in-arms," Albin said thumping Talan soundly on the back. "He is more accustomed to real ladies."

"A lady like me can do things to you that no prim noblewoman would ever do." Pressing her bosom against Talan's arm, Gunilda wiped a spot of foam from Talan's upper lip.

Leaning away from Gunilda, Talan ignored Albin's smirk. "Have the sheriff's sons been in of late?"

Disappointed by his lack of interest, Gunilda straightened. "If I tell you, will you buy me a cup of wine? I cannot stomach the ale Lecie makes and she forces us to purchase the finer brews."

"There is nothing at all wrong with the ale she brews," Albin said in Lecie's defense. "In truth, I prefer it above all others."

Gunilda threw her head back to laugh, exposing several missing teeth. "It sounds to me tis not only the ale you fancy. Given that you are a knight, you should aim higher than a lowly alewife."

"You are not fit to call other women—"

"What Albin means to say," Talan interrupted, "is that it takes knowledge and skill to brew ale. I know for a fact that Lecie's recipe has been handed down several generations."

"I was not born for such drudgery." Gunilda shrugged. "If the harvest were better this year the local men would have more coin to spend. As it is, I am forced to tend tables in order to make board."

"Then I suggest you go about doing it," Albin snapped.

"Suit yourselves." Running her hand along Talan's back, Gunilda sauntered toward another table.

"My, you do have it bad." Holding up his cup for a refill, Talan caught Hamon's eye. "And she did not answer my question about the sheriff."

"She would not have answered the question to your satisfaction anyway."

"Whatever do you mean?"

"Dare you deny your only interest is in his daughter Mylla?"

"Drink your ale," Talan groused accepting a refill from Hamon. "You know I am well acquainted with her brothers."

"Speak and they shall appear," Albin said when the door swung open.

"Sir Talan, what a surprise to see you here." A tall blond broad-shouldered man called, coming up to them. "When did you arrive?"

"Leofrick." Talan stood to greet his friend. "We still have the dirt of the road upon us. Join us for a drink?"

"Gladly." Dipping his head in greeting to Albin, Leofrick pulled out a chair. "Mylla has spoken of little else since last we saw you in London. It appears you have made quite an impression on my young sister."

"How has she been faring, if I may be so bold to ask?"

"Tis best you are bold afore my brother Edmund arrives. You know how he can be," Leofrick said rolling his eyes. "As for Mylla, she is well enough."

Albin stood when a man he assumed to be Edmund came through the door. "I will leave you to become reacquainted."

"I have yet to even introduce you to the sheriff's eldest son," Talan said.

"Another time." Albin acknowledged Leofrick. "It has been a long day and I am not fit company for conversation."

Conflicted, Talan was distracted when Edmund greeted him.

Taking a stool at the bar, Albin's gaze kept moving to the steps.

"Good eve, Sir Albin. I take it you will be in town for a while?"

Albin stiffened when feminine fingertips played lightly over his shoulder and back. "Hello, Betta."

Slipping onto the stool beside him, Betta plopped an elbow on the bar. "You do not seem your laughing self this eve. Something got you down?"

Running a weary hand along the back of his neck, Albin exhaled heavily. "All is as it should be."

"But not as what you would like it to be, eh?" Betta waved Hamon over for a cup of ale. "Care to talk about your troubles? I am a good listener these days."

"There is nothing to talk about."

"If there is one thing I know, it is the mind of men. You are brooding over a woman, are you not?"

Surprised she could discern his thoughts so easily, Albin took in the tavern wench that had been at The Wounded Stag for as long as he could remember. Time had not been kind to the aging harlot. Her lusterless graying-blonde hair hung in a limp braid reaching to her waist, and a life of hardship revealed itself in every line of her careworn face.

Changing the subject, Albin glanced once more toward the steps. "Have you two rooms available for us?"

"Lecie has lost much needed coin keeping your usual chamber empty for you," Betta admitted with a sly smile. "She has been anticipating your return for some time now."

"She has?"

"Aye." Betta studied his surprised reaction. "She figures the duration atween your visits in order to be better prepared for his lordship's arrival."

"Right," Albin mumbled with a sinking feeling. "Makes sense for her to do such a thing."

"I know not what she will do after the tower is completed. I take it once that happens we shall no longer see any of you?"

"I have not given it much thought, but I suppose you are right."

"When the time comes, I know Lecie will miss your visits."

"What makes you say that?"

"I have eyes, Sir Albin." Betta changed the subject when Hamon approached. "Is his lordship expected on this trip?"

"No, Fulke has become a doting father of late." Albin's smile was genuine when he added, "He and Lady Reina have a beautiful newborn daughter."

"With the things I heard him say in this very tavern, I never would have imagined it of him." Accepting a cup from Hamon, Betta held it high. "Here is to his lordship's continued good fortune."

"I shall drink to that." Knocking his cup against Betta's, Albin took a long swallow of ale.

"Do you not have a chamber to clean?" Gunilda rudely confronted her competition. "If Lecie hears of you shirking your duties, she will toss you out on your wizened arse."

"Lecie would do no such thing even with your forked tongue spreading falsehoods," Betta scoffed. "What has you so vexed anyway, Gunny? Your only interest is coin, and you know good and well Sir Albin is not one to pay for a toss."

"Well we both know he would not choose you if he did."

Betta shook her head with a sympathetic chuckle. "When will you give up? You always chase after the wrong men."

"So you say." Running her eyes over Albin's tall muscular frame, Gunilda's eyes settled on his dark brown eyes. "Every man boasts a mind that can be easily changed."

Albin choked down some ale while the women discussed him as if he were not there. Quickly draining his cup, he stood. "If you two ladies will excuse me, I feel the need to get some rest."

"Let me know if there is anything else you need." Gunilda seductively licked her lips. "'Tis been so long since I have set eyes upon you, I may be of a mind to give it away."

Clearing his throat uncomfortably, Albin refrained from responding. He ignored Talan's beckoning wave and retrieved his saddle-pack from beside the door.

His thoughts on Lecie, it took a moment for his eyes to adjust to the darkness of the upper level passageway. By memory he made it to the chamber he had used on his previous visits. With his hand on the latch, he stood staring at the closed door to the master chamber further down the corridor. Disgusted with himself for feeling jealous of a dying man, he tore his gaze away to enter his room.

Tossing his pack beside the unlit hearth, he pushed aside the russet woolen bed curtains to sit while he pulled off his boots. As if in response to his grim thoughts, loud wracking coughs drifted to him through the door. With an audible curse, he stripped down to his braies before crossing to the window to throw open the shutters. He stood staring up at the star laden sky determined to uphold his knightly vows at whatever the cost.

Mentally preparing himself for his next encounter with Lecie, he slipped beneath the woolen blanket on the bed to stare blindly at the canopy above him. Conjuring Lecie's golden-brown eyes and shining chestnut hair, he drifted off into a fitful sleep.

♥

In the hours before dawn, Albin woke with a start. Disturbed by the vestiges of a dream he could not fully recall upon waking. Having second thoughts about coming, he listened to the nocturnal creaking sounds of the inn. It was not until he heard a series of wracking coughs that he sat up with a curse to fling the bed-curtains aside. What kind of man was he to covet a dying friend's wife?

Giving up on sleep altogether, he dressed in his white linen chainse, black woolen tunic bearing the Erlegh coat of arms which consisted of three silver embroidered shells on a field of red, and his black breeches. Pulling on his knee-high black boots, he left his black woolen cloak behind and made his way below.

Intent on taking a walk, he noticed a flickering light coming from the kitchen and made his way toward it.

He drew to a surprised halt at the sight that met him in the overly warm chamber. Seated at the end of a long planked wood table, laden with half-chopped vegetables rested the object of his torment. Her arm outstretched, Lecie's flour dusted cheek rested upon it as exhaustion had clearly overwhelmed her.

Taking in the bruise like shadows beneath her eyes, Albin acted on instinct to protect her. Lifting her into his arms, she barely stirred.

Cradled gently against his chest, he ignored the feelings coursing through him and focused on avoiding the tables in the common room.

Guided only by the meager light coming from the kitchen, he briefly gazed down at the serene beauty of her face in repose. Her petite figure had grown gaunt since the last time he had seen her. Her long chestnut hair, usually pinned back in a snood, looked tousled as it flowed like a silken waterfall to her waist. Her high, delicate cheekbones were even more prominent by her recent weight-loss. The only thing that did not change was the perfect curve of her soft pink kissable lips.

In spite of the obvious changes, he found himself wanting to claim her more than ever before. He wanted to draw her into his protective embrace and lift the burdens of the inn from her shoulders even as it angered him to know that he had no right to do so.

Ascending the steps, Lecie's beautiful golden eyes fluttered open. "Sir Albin," she murmured softly, "these are always the best dreams."

Dumbstruck, Albin came close to tripping on the last step. Mentally replaying her words, he focused on her lips. Could it be that she was indeed as attracted to him as he was to her? "Mon Dieu," he whispered, "give me the strength to resist."

Pausing in the upper passageway, he faced a new dilemma. He could not very well carry her into Edric's chamber. Ill or not, a man would not take kindly to seeing his wife in the arms of another.

Seeing no other alternative, he carried her into his room and laid her gently down on the bed. His throat felt parched when he watched her curl on her side toward the very spot he had been sleeping.

His fingers lightly brushed against a full breast when he covered her with the blanket. Uttering a curse, he attempted to gain control of his traitorous body.

On his way down the darkened passage, he idly pondered how much longer Edric had left to live. Shame for thinking such a callous thing coursed through him when he heard yet another racking cough followed by a low moan of pain.

Albin rolled his eyes toward the ceiling. "I am doing my best." Rapping lightly on Talan's door, he began to fidget anxiously.

Muttered oaths and stumbling preceded the cracking of the door. "Albin, what is amiss?"

"You are more skilled than I so I need you to assist me below with some cookery."

Understanding lit Talan's weary gaze. "Did you return to the common room after I left to get soused?"

"I am not soused." Albin spoke in hushed tones.

"Then break your fast at first light with the rest of us," Talan muttered, attempting to close the door.

Pushing against the door, Albin scowled. "Tis not my stomach I am thinking of. With your noble nature, you will be pleased to discover I am here on behalf of another."

Talan opened the door wider. "Lecie?"

"Aye, Lecie," Albin whispered anxiously. "She fell asleep in the kitchen whilst cooking and I had not the heart to wake her."

"Give me a trice to dress."

Reappearing a moment later raking his hands through his tousled light brown hair, Talan followed Albin down the steps.

"By the looks of it, I would say Lecie was in the midst of preparing a stew," Albin said. "You know she only attempted such for our benefit."

Eyeing the untidy cook surface covered with root vegetables, Talan appeared perplexed. "I thought you said she fell asleep in here?"

"She did. I carried her up to my chamber so she could get some much needed rest." Albin lifted the lid off of a salted meat barrel. "Does this look like dried pork to you or mutton? I can never tell the difference."

Talan hesitated before peeking into the barrel. "You brought her to your chamber?"

"What would you have done under the circumstances?"

"Likely the same," Talan said. "You can share with me if we manage to finish afore morn. That is salted pork." Lifting the lid of another barrel, he found rabbit meat. "What should we prepare?"

"If I knew the answer to that, I would not have fetched you," Albin said with a trace of sarcasm. "Can you complete what she started?"

Eyeing the supply of garlic, onions, peas and beans, Talan pulled several rabbits from the cask and held them out. "Rinse the brine from these and cut the meat into bite-sized chunks."

"What are we making?"

"Apparently, we are not making anything," Talan said. "I am doing the cookery and you are lending assist."

Eyeing Talan's smug look, Albin mimicked his tone. "Very well, what are you making?"

Talan hung an iron cook-pot on the hook above the fire. "Twill be a stew of sorts."

"Sounds flavorsome." Rolling his eyes, Albin reached for a water pot.

The meat was cut and added to the simmering water while Talan had Albin chop onions. His eyes watering from the pungent vapors, he squinted over at Talan who was adding additional ingredients to the pot. "If you were Guy or Gervase, you would have plied me with queries by now."

"Why would I question you for doing a noble deed?"

Albin smiled, once again thankful for Talan's quiet nature.

"Besides," Talan continued, "I already know the reason behind it."

Albin's hand stilled but he kept his eyes on the task at hand. "Why do you keep saying that?"

"Deny it and I shall not mention it again."

"You should not encourage such a thing." Albin began chopping again.

"Whyever not?"

"You have missed far too many of Father Godfrey's masses," Albin said before changing the subject. "I take it you will see your Mylla anon?"

"I have been invited to call upon Leofrick," Talan said with a worried look. "I shall stop at day's end after checking on the tower's progress."

"Given you spoke of little else on the journey here, I would have thought you would be pleased."

"Tis not the thought of seeing Mylla again that troubles me," Talan admitted. "Leofrick confided that King Henry's Chief Itinerant Justice has expressed an interest in her."

"Ranulf de Glanville?" Again, Albin ceased chopping. "He is old enough to be her grandfather."

"I know," Talan said. "He is also a close confidant of the king. They have known one another since boyhood."

"What are you going to do?"

"Pray it is only a passing interest. What else could I do?"

They worked in silence until Talan added bacon fat and garlic to the pot. Nodding in satisfaction, he added wood to the hearth fire.

"That should see Lecie through the morrow. Let us make bread bowls to serve it in."

Following Talan's instruction, Albin kneaded dough into ball shapes. "It actually smells appetizing."

Stirring the pottage with a long iron ladle, Talan smirked. "Do not sound so surprised."

"I am nonetheless," Albin admitted. "Where did you learn to cook?"

"As a small lad, I used to watch my mother prepare meals." Talan smiled in reminiscence. "Finish the bowls whilst I soak a stock of barley. By the looks of it, ale is running low. Once the barley soaks, we can lend assist in making more."

"Ale is running low?" Albin asked in stunned disbelief.

Laughing, Talan shook his head. "I am of the belief you would rather starve than go without ale."

"In that you would be correct," Albin said with a grin.

Baked to a golden brown the bread bowls were lined up on the cooktop surface. With the barley soaking, Talan added more kindling beneath the cookpot before he gave a satisfied nod to Albin.

The sky was lightening when the pair tiredly made their way to Talan's chamber.

Spreading the coverlet on the floor beside the banked hearth, Albin fell asleep the second he closed his eyes.

Chapter Two

Lecie blinked awake at first light confused to find a russet canopy above her head.

Her eyes flying wide, she sat up and looked around. It was definitely not her small space in the garret. Worse yet, it was the chamber facing the garden that she reserved for Sir Albin's visits. Stumbling on her skirts in her haste to leave the bed she rushed into the passageway to check on her father.

Guilt assailed her when she slipped inside his chamber. Relieved to find him dozing, she took in his frail, sunken frame. A lump of emotion formed in her throat as she soaked a cloth in a bowl of water.

Dabbing at his sweat-beaded brow with the cool cloth, Edric slowly opened his pain-filled eyes. "Lass, you look weary."

"I am fine, Da." Concern etched her smooth brow when she heard the congested rattle in his chest. "Did you call for me in the night?"

"Did you manage to get some sleep?"

"You are not to worry about me," Lecie said. "Tis you who needs to rest more."

Reaching for her free hand, Edric gently squeezed it. "Rest assured I shall be resting soon enough. Forgive me for placing such a burden on your shoulders."

Tears flooded Lecie's eyes as she gazed sadly down at him. Having lost her mother and the babe she carried during delivery years before, Lecie was the eldest of four children. She would be lost without her father.

As if reading her mind, Edric wheezed, "I fear what will happen to you all once I am gone."

Seeing concern shadow his light blue eyes, Lecie forced a brave smile. "I am my mother's daughter, Da. I have been running the inn on my own for some time now."

"That you have, and your dear mother would be as proud of you as I am."

Thinking of the patrons who would go without a warm meal to break their fast, another wave of guilt brought a flush to Lecie's fair cheeks. "You have grown far too thin so I shall fix you a nice broth after I rouse the children."

A spasm of violent coughs seized him. Waiting for the bout to pass, she supported his shoulders so he could take a drink of water.

Easing him back onto the feather tick, he weakly clutched her arm when she turned to go. "You cannot deceive me," he wheezed. "Your eyes speak the truth. If you continue on as you are, you will collapse from the weight of it all."

"I am perfectly well." Patting his hand, she admitted, "Mayhap, just a tad weary of late. A good long soak in the tub would cure all that ails me."

"That sounds ever so nice." Edric closed his eyes as if imagining it. "Instruct Hamon to take charge of the tavern this eve. I would have you take that soak."

"Worry not, I shall see to everything." Bending to kiss his sunken cheek her smile melted when she stepped into the passageway.

Leaning against the paneled wall beside his closed door tears slipped from her eyes. She would have to try harder to conceal the strain from him.

Determined to get her many tasks completed by day's end, she entered the small chamber her siblings shared at the end of the hall. The seven year-old twins, Osana and Sabina slept in a bed across from five year-old, Clayton.

A fond smile lifted the corners of her lips as she gazed down at her sleeping sisters. Favoring their father in looks, they boasted flaxen curls reaching past their waists. So identical in appearance, it was only when one became acquainted with them were their differences apparent. Where Osana was bold and brave, Sabina was shy and reserved. The only similarity the three sisters shared were the striking golden-brown eyes of their mother.

Bending, Lecie gently shook Sabina's shoulder.

Her sister's eyes fluttered open. "Is it morn so soon?"

Lecie smoothed a wayward curl from Sabina's brow. "It is little one, time to wake and face the day."

Knowing Sabina would wake her twin, she moved over to Clayton's pallet. Blond like the twins, he boasted their father's blue eyes.

Kneeling, she leaned to kiss his rosy cheek. "The sun is up and tis time to wake, little man."

Without opening his eyes, Clayton groaned and rolled away from her. A morning person he most certainly was not.

Reaching over the bed, Lecie threw open the shutter, allowing the early dawn light to penetrate the cramped chamber. Large chambers were for paying guests.

"I shall see he wakes."

"Thank you, Sabina," Lecie said straightening. "I fear I shall need your assist in the kitchen this morn afore you begin your work in the garden."

"Do not fret so," Osana said. "We shall do what needs to be done."

"How swift you all have been forced to grow." Lecie turned away to conceal her sudden tears. "I shall await you in the kitchen."

Rushing down the steps, she smelled the enticing aroma of food. Puzzled, she made her way to the kitchen only to glance around in amazement.

The worktable held over a score of coarse rye and barley trenchers to hold the aromatic pottage simmering in the large pot above the fire.

Wondering if Betta had seen to the meal, she froze when she heard the deep resonant tone of Sir Albin behind her.

"Hello, lass."

Suddenly breathless Lecie turned to face the man that had so often entered her dreams. "Sir Albin." Gathering her unkempt hair, she pulled the thick mass over her shoulder. "I all but forgot you had arrived."

Albin hid his disappointment behind a grin. "I tend to have that effect on people."

"Oh, I did not mean…"

"Please accept my apology for my less than enthusiastic greeting last night," Albin said to fill the awkward silence that descended. "The weather was foul and twas an arduous journey from Hitchin near Dunstable."

"I did not notice anything untoward about your greeting." Shyly meeting his warm brown gaze, Lecie's heart began to beat faster. Tall and broad-shouldered, Albin's wavy black hair was parted in the middle and reached the collar of his black tunic. In lieu of the latest fashion consisting of ankle length tunics, belled chainses and striped hose, he and the Erlegh men wore short woolen tunics, linen chainses with tight-fitting sleeves, black breeches, and polished leather boots. She admired his strong jaw, close-cropped beard and wide firm lips, and knew if he were to smile or laugh, he would reveal a set of even white teeth.

"Again, I seem to have that effect on people," Albin said with a tinge of disappointment. "Fulke and the rest of the men tend to make better impressions."

"You have had your hair trimmed since last we met," Lecie blurted. "It suits you well." Covering her mouth with her hand, she briefly clenched her eyes shut. "That was very bold of me. I should not have said it."

"I take no offense," Albin said running his fingers through his curls. "Lady Reina was kind enough to trim it for me."

"Is her ladyship doing well? Last I heard she was soon to be expecting a babe."

"She and the wee lass are both doing very well."

"I am very pleased to hear it. His lordship seemed quite content with life the last we spoke."

"My Liege is a truly blessed man." Albin's eyes moved to Lecie's hands where she fidgeted nervously with her brown kirtle. "He has found a happiness most men search the whole of their lives for."

Noting his regard, Lecie slipped her rough, blistered hands behind her back. "Since I know not when to expect him, I keep his lordship's chamber ready at all times."

"I no longer think that is necessary," Albin said. "He is content to stay at Castell Maen with his family whilst Talan and I undertake his duty here."

Lecie's eyes flared as she recalled something. "You carried me up the steps last night, did you not?"

"Twas obvious to me you needed the rest. I apologize if you take it as an offense against your person."

"I would never perceive a kindness in such a way." Lecie gestured to the table. "Do I have you to thank for this as well?"

"I only followed instruction," Albin said with a grin. "Your thanks should go to Talan. He did the hard part."

Lecie's voice was choked with emotion when she said, "Twas very kind of you both. You are guests and should not have to prepare your own food."

"After all this time I had hoped that we have become more than guests," Albin said. "The men of Maen consider you and Edric our friends, and friends assist one another in time of need. Besides," he teased, "I had no other choice since I heard a scandalous rumor that ale is running low."

"Most scandalous indeed," Lecie said with a laugh. "I shall be sure to replenish the barrels afore the day is out. In the meantime, can I get you a bowl of stew to break your fast?"

"If you would be so kind." Albin dipped his head. "Talan and I are off to the tower to survey the progress once we have eaten."

"It looks as good as it smells, Sir Albin." Ladling pottage into a bread bowl, she placed it before him. "I shall get you a cup of ale to go with it."

He lightly clasped her hand when she made to move away. "After which, will you join me for the meal? It has been some time since we have seen one another."

Embarrassed, Lecie snatched her hand away.

"Forgive me." Albin was quick to apologize. "I do not know what came over me."

"You have done nothing to warrant forgiveness." Lecie's cheeks flushed red when she held her hands out to show him. "I fear I do not boast the hands of a gently born woman."

Taking her hands in his, Albin lightly caressed the chafed areas with his thumbs. "I only know of one other gently born woman that can even compare to you."

"Thank you," Lecie said. "I shall join you after I get you that ale."

Roughly clearing his throat, Albin said, "Then I shall await you in the common room."

Joining him soon after, she sat in the chair Albin held out for her.

Imparting the latest village gossip to him, they were halfway through their meal when they glanced up at the sound of small feet racing down the steps.

"Sir Albin," Clayton shouted, skidding to a halt beside them.

With a fond smile, Lecie pushed back her chair to stand. "Have a seat, little man. I shall get you a cup of almond milk to go along with your breakfast."

Glancing over at the twins when they took their seats, Lecie scolded, "Mind your manners in front of our guest."

"Sir Albin is not a guest," Osana quipped. "He is here far more often than a traveler passing through would be."

"Nevertheless, mind your manners, Osana."

"There is indeed truth to that, little lass," Albin cut in with a chuckle. "Since my chamber is held available for me, I suppose I am to be considered a bit more than a passing traveler."

"You always preferred a view of the back garden," Lecie responded softly. "'Tis far from being the best of the lot, yet I would see you enjoy your stay."

She held his gaze until Clayton drew Albin's attention by tugging on his tunic. "Has Tugger come to greet you yet? He is quite fond of you."

Rumpling the boy's tousled curls, Albin shook his head. "I have yet to be mauled by your dog this visit, Master Clayton."

When Lecie entered the kitchen to retrieve breakfast for the children, the outside door swung open.

Tugger, the family's large brown mastiff came charging in ahead of Hamon and Gunilda. His claws scrambling for purchase on the slate flooring, he raced past Lecie toward the common room.

Imagining the tongue mauling Sir Albin was in for Lecie shook her head with a soft chuckle.

Hamon dropped his arm from around Gunilda's shoulders when he spotted Lecie. "Something smells good this morning, love."

Ignoring him, Lecie filled bowls for the twins when Gunilda swiped them from her.

"You know," she whispered close to Lecie's ear, "if you let Hamon break you in, you would not have to toil so hard. He is more gentle than most."

Lecie reached for another bowl. "And what happens when your looks fade and no man is interested in what you have to sell?"

"You are talking about Betta." Gunilda glanced back at Hamon. "I am smarter than she. I have me a man to take care of me when I can no longer sell my charms."

"The laundress is due today for the linens." Lecie changed the subject. "If tis your wish, bring your bed linens down to be laundered."

"Whyever for when they are only going to get soiled again?"

Turning to conceal her look of disgust, Lecie addressed Hamon. "The laundress is due four jugs of ale in recompense. Please see that she receives her share and returns the jugs." Without waiting for his response, she swept from the kitchen.

About to take a seat beside Albin, Lecie looked up when Betta came down the steps.

"Lecie, I heard retching noises coming from Edric's room. I warrant he will soon be coughing up more blood if he has not done so already."

"I will see to him. Take my seat and eat whilst the stew is still hot." Lecie pushed back her chair to stand.

"If you will allow it, I shall see to Edric," Albin reached out to stop her. "You have not yet had enough to eat."

"You have come to my assist enough for one day, Sir Albin. Please extend my gratitude to Sir Talan for the meal as I have yet to see him." On her way up the steps, she called, "Betta, please see that the children get enough to eat afore starting their chores."

Lecie's empty stomach rolled at the stench of vomit when she entered her father's chamber. Lying on his side, he was too weak to reach the bucket set beside the bed.

"Forgive me," he wheezed, "I made more work for you."

"There is no need for that, Da." Eyeing the fouled sheets, she added, "I shall have to fetch Hamon to assist me. Do you have further need of the bucket?"

"No, lass. I pray the worst has passed."

Easing an arm behind his frail shoulders, Lecie propped him up so he could take a drink of water.

She placed a kiss on his sweaty forehead after he lay back with a sigh of relief.

Her smooth brow puckered with worry, she studied the deep lines etched into his grizzled, careworn face. "Does it pain you more this day?"

"No more than usual."

Opening the shutters to allow the cool morning air to enter, Lecie inhaled deeply. "Tis a beautiful morning, Da, I wish you could see it."

"No morn shall ever be as beautiful as you are my Lecie." Her father's eyes glistened with unshed tears. "You have the look of your mother about you."

Sobering at the mention of her beloved mother, Lecie fought back tears. "I miss her so."

"I shall tell her when I see her."

"Rest now, Da. I will hear no more talk of you leaving us." Fighting for control of her emotions, Lecie averted her eyes on the way out. "I shall return as soon as I locate Hamon."

She felt Sir Albin's gaze on her when she passed through the common room.

Entering to find the kitchen empty, she stepped outside to search for Hamon.

After scanning the yard and stables, she approached the small lad who kept the horses. "Have you seen Hamon about, Joseph?"

"He and Gunilda headed off toward the river. Shall I fetch him for you?"

"No, once again I shall make do on my own," Lecie said with a frown. "Take a break and get something to eat inside."

Bobbing his head, Joseph darted through the back door ahead of her to eat in the kitchen.

Passing back through the common room, Sir Albin stood. "Surely there must be something I can do?"

"I can manage, Sir Albin. Thank you kindly for the offer."

"You do not have to take everything upon yourself, lass." Moving around the table, Albin lowered his voice. "There is no shame in asking for help."

Lecie suddenly found herself close to tears. "You are not in Rochester to make my lot in life easier."

"Mayhap not, but I would like to lend you assist whenever I can."

"In that case, I will gratefully accept your offer." After retrieving clean linens from a cupboard, she led the way to her father's chamber. "I must warn you that it is bad, Sir Albin. He has taken to vomiting, and spitting up blood of late."

"Then let us get him cleaned up, shall we?"

Pushing the door open, Lecie stood aside for Albin to precede her.

"Sir Albin." Edric recognized his visitor and struggled to sit up. "It has been some time since I have seen you last."

"Rest easy, Edric." Despite the sour stench hanging heavy in the air, Albin moved closer to the bed. "I would like to have found you faring better, my friend."

"Without my Lecie, I no doubt would be faring worse." Edric spoke in a raspy whisper.

"She is indeed a Godsend." Albin glanced toward Lecie.

"Since I cannot locate Hamon, Sir Albin has kindly offered his assistance," Lecie said retrieving a clean tunic and breeches from the wardrobe.

"We cannot make a lackey out of a knight of the realm," Edric wheezed.

"You are doing no such thing. Would you perhaps like to bathe first?"

"It has been ever so long since I had a soak." Edric looked hopeful. "If it can be managed, I would like it above all else."

"Consider it done." Albin turned to Lecie. "Tell me how to make it happen."

"I just need a trice to heat the water in the cistern," Lecie said. "Normally we transport the tub into the guest chambers afore we fill it, yet twould be much faster if we could get him to the bathing room."

"Then that is what we shall do."

Nearly overcome with emotion, Lecie bit her lip. "Thank you, Sir Albin."

"Think no more of it." Albin brushed aside her thanks. "A man feels better after a long soak. Is not that right, Edric?"

"Aye, indeed he does," Edric sighed.

Leaving them, Lecie opened the shutters in the bathing chamber. Consisting of rough-planked walls, the room held a wood hipbath set beside a small hearth.

Swinging the suspended pot beneath the pipe coming through the outer wall, she twisted the iron spigot to fill it with rainwater. Collected in barrels on the roof of the inn it was a time-saving invention of her father's.

Lighting the fire in the hearth, all she would have to do is swing the pot over the waiting tub. To drain, a second pipe slipped into a plugged hole on the side of the tub to empty into the garden below.

Satisfied with her preparations, Lecie re-entered her father's room only to draw up short at the sight of him upright and naked. With a soft inhalation of breath, she whirled around to present her back to the men. "The bath is prepared, Sir Albin."

"Sir Albin," her father rasped, "would you be so kind as to hand me a blanket so that I may cover myself?"

"Aye, of course." Albin sounded perplexed by the request.

"If you assist me to stand, I am sure I can manage to walk the length of the passageway."

"How long has it been since you were out of bed?"

"It has been a while now," Edric admitted.

"That is what I thought." A rustling sound preceded a grunt of pain from Edric before Albin said, "Lecie, would you lead the way?"

Turning around, Lecie was surprised to see her father cradled in Albin's muscular arms. Seeing the vast difference in sizes between the men, she met Albin's concerned gaze with one of her own. "Follow me."

She stood by the bathing room door averting her eyes when Albin gently lowered her father into the heated water.

With a soft sigh of pleasure, Edric leaned back against the lip of the tub. "You shall forever have my thanks for this, Sir Albin."

"Will you be alright for a spell so I can lend assist to Lecie in changing the bed linens?"

"Aye, I shall be fine." Edric managed a weak smile as he studied the two of them standing together. "God willing, things will work out the way I have always prayed they would."

"Call if you need assist," Albin said following Lecie out.

"Sir Albin, I shall not keep you any longer," Lecie said in the passageway. "Hamon is never gone for long. I am sure he will be back by the time I change the linens."

"And if the lout is nowhere to be found?"

"If that is the case, I shall find a way to manage. I always do."

"Why are you so stubborn, lass?"

"I am not stubborn."

"Are you not?" Albin teased. "By consistently refusing my help, it gives credence to the fact that you are indeed stubborn."

"It has nothing to do with being stubborn," Lecie said. "I am unused to asking for help, and I most certainly never expected to be asking for it from you."

"I mind not and there is no one else who can lift Edric from the tub, Hamon included. Why it looks to me that a brisk wind could knock the oaf over."

Smiling at the visual of Hamon sprawled in the dirt Lecie relented. "In that you are no doubt correct."

"So accept what is sincerely offered." Albin's tone softened as he stared down at her. "And let us not say another word about it."

"On one condition." Staring at his slightly fuller lower lip, Lecie felt breathless.

"Anything," Albin whispered.

"You must not let it interfere with your duty to his lordship."

"I give you my word." Fighting the temptation to pull her into his arms, Albin took a step back.

"Then we have a deal." Tearing her gaze away, Lecie led the way into her father's chamber.

Albin watched her in silence as she began to strip the soiled linens from the bed. After a moment, he walked up behind her. "How long does he have?"

"I know not." Turning to face him, tears slipped from her eyes. "After I ordered him away, the village leech will no longer come to check on him."

"You love him," Albin stated without a hint of emotion.

"More than anything," Lecie's voice broke as she struggled to contain her sobs.

"Then I shall continue to pray for his recovery."

Brushing at her cheeks with the back of her hands, Lecie said, "We both shall."

They were finishing with the bed when Talan knocked on the doorframe. "Am I interrupting? I was hoping to pay my respects to Edric."

"Sir Talan." Lecie managed a slight smile.

"About time you awoke, layabout," Albin teased.

"I would have risen with the sun had not my rest been disturbed," Talan shot back with a grin.

"I fear I am to blame for your lack of sleep, Sir Talan." Lecie raked her teeth along her lower lip. "For that I thank you, and apologize."

"See what you did?" Albin cuffed Talan's shoulder. "You made her feel bad."

"I was merely jesting." Talan scowled at Albin while responding to Lecie. "'Twas my pleasure to be of assist."

"Better," Albin said. "Now if you will both excuse me, I shall see how Edric is faring."

"Thank you." Lecie shook her head with a smile. "I feel as if I am constantly repeating myself this morn."

"Talan," Albin said, "would you mind heading up to the tower without me this morn?"

"Not at all, I do most of the work anyway," Talan teased. "In fact, I was going to suggest that I take on Fulke's duties whilst we are here. That way, you can remain here unless a problem arises at the tower."

Clearly distraught by the idea, Lecie shook her head. "I could never ask either of you to do such a thing."

"You did not ask, we offered." Albin slipped from the room before Lecie could voice an objection.

After he was gone, Talan helped bundle the soiled linens. "I am sorry your father is so ill. He is a good man."

Close to tears, Lecie busied herself tidying the room. "That is very kind of you to say."

Sensing her discomfort, Talan switched topics. "I put up some barley to soak. Now that Albin is in residence, I have no doubt he shall drink through your current store of ale."

Glad for the change of subject, Lecie paused in her task. "I did not realize you brewed your own ale, Sir Talan."

"It was something I picked up in my youth."

"In your youth?" Taking in his boyish good looks, Lecie looked skeptical. "I take that to mean you believe you have reached your dotage?"

"At a score and four I sometimes feel much older than I am."

"There are times I feel much older than my years too," Lecie murmured. "I suppose everyone experiences that feeling at one time or another in their life."

"Certainly not you? I would wager you are no older than a score."

"How truly remarkable you should say that." Lecie's eyes flared slightly in surprise. "I have yet to reach a score."

"I know." Talan leaned forward as if to impart a secret. "Mylla let your age slip to me in London."

They laughed in unison.

Finished with her task, Lecie perched on the edge of the bed. "How old is Sir Albin, if you do not mind my asking?"

"Albin is the eldest of our band of knights at a score and nine."

"Why do you think it is he never married?"

"I believe it took him years to find the woman he would take to wife."

"So he has an accord with a lady?" Her heart sinking, Lecie studied her hands. "I should have guessed it."

"The problem is, he acts quite odd whenever he is around her," Talan hinted. "One wonders if he will ever work up the courage to proclaim his feelings for her."

"I hope she realizes how fortunate she is."

"In time I think she will be," Talan said before changing the subject. "Have you seen Mylla recently?"

At the mention of her closest friend, Lecie brightened. "I have been far too busy to call and she is not permitted in the tavern. Do you plan to see her whilst you are here? I heard you two became acquainted in London."

"I hope to see her this very day after I send a messenger to Maen pertaining to the progress on the tower."

"It pleases me to hear the baron is so well settled," Lecie said. "Since he is content to remain at home, I will begin letting his chamber. Tis the best we have to offer and we could use the additional income."

"If you like, I shall send along your good tidings," Talan said. "I would also like to lend you assist with the brewing when the barley I put to soak matures."

"Truth be told, I had barley set to soak in the shed ready to germinate, along with a batch ready to brew. The village festival is in a few days. Apart from the after crowd expected here, we set up a booth in the square during the day."

"Then it sounds like we arrived at the right time." Talan smiled. "If you have the malt dry and ground, I shall heat the water and drain the wort when I return. You are on your own when it comes to the herbs and yeast. If I meddle with your recipe, Albin will never forgive me for it."

"Are all knights so accommodating?"

"The Knights of Maen are a band unlike any other."

"I see that," Lecie said with a fond smile. Hearing Albin coming up the hall, she rushed to pull the covers down when he strode in with her father in his arms.

Plumping up the down pillows, she stood back so Albin could ease Edric onto the bed.

Gasping weakly, her father closed his eyes with a contented sigh and promptly fell into a doze.

Albin glanced at her when he followed Talan out of the room. Covering her father with a thin wool blanket, she heard them speaking in low tones in the passage.

Brushing the damp hair from her father's forehead, she looked up to find Albin staring at her from the doorway. "I believe he will rest easier now."

"Aye," Albin said with an inscrutable look. "Might I have a word with you in private?"

"Of course." Closing the shutters to darken the room, Lecie stepped past him into the passage. "Is something amiss?"

"Edric is in a great deal of pain… more than he lets on," Albin said. "Her ladyship Reina is skilled in the healing arts and may have medicine to make him rest easier. If you would allow it, I will send a messenger to Castell Maen."

"Would you really do that for me, Sir Albin?" Lecie's eyes lit with hope. "I shall be forever grateful to you."

"Aye," Albin admitted softly. "I would ride there myself if need be."

Searching his eyes, Lecie felt a flutter low in her stomach.

Clearing his throat, Albin broke eye contact. "Right, well. I was wondering if you would do something for me in return."

"Anything," Lecie whispered. "What is it you would like?"

"Will you show me how to make ale?"

"I fear if I instruct you on how to make ale, I shall never see you again."

"You have nothing to fear on that account, lass."

"Why is that?" Lecie asked breathlessly.

"I shall still need a place to stay when I come here."

"Oh." To hide her disappointment, Lecie turned on her heel toward the steps. "In that case, we best get started."

"Lecie?"

Turning back, she waited with a slanted brow.

"Never mind," Albin said shaking his head. "Let the instruction begin."

Chapter Three

Forget Father Godfrey's vision of hell, Albin believed he was in his own personal version of it. Perched on a stool set close beside Lecie's in the hot brewing shed, Albin watched her go about the task of making ale.

"Sir Albin?" Lecie repeated for the second time.

"What was that you said?" Yanking on the sweat-soaked collar of his tunic he longed for some fresh air to slake his lustful thoughts.

"Would you please pass me the long handled ladle behind you, and the straining cloths?"

Passing the items to her, his gaze settled on a solitary bead of perspiration that had formed on Lecie's temple to track down her face and along her neck before soaking into her thin linen apron.

"Tis a tedious task in the warmer months," she said wiping her brow with the back of her hand. "This part will take some time if you would like to get some fresh air."

"I would never abandon you," Albin said softly.

Lecie's hands slowed and she met his intense regard. "You sound so solemn of a sudden."

"Do I?" Running a hand along the back of his neck, Albin chuckled. "I suppose ale is more important to me than I thought."

"Oh." Disappointed, Lecie returned to her task.

Mentally cursing, Albin regretted not paying close attention when Gervase and Guy wooed women.

He watched in torment when Lecie leaned forward to stir, her breasts straining against the fabric of her brown kirtle. Shifting uncomfortably on the stool he perched on, he wondered how long he could withstand being so close to her without making a complete fool of himself.

"Are you certain that you do not require some fresh air, Sir Albin? Your face is quite flushed."

"Tis nothing I cannot handle. I rather hoped, however, that there would be something more I could do. I feel quite helpless just sitting here."

"Brewing is a more time consuming task than a strenuous one. After soaking the barley for several days I drain the water to germinate the barley. Once that is done the malt is dried and ground, hot water added, and the wort drained off." With a sly smile she added, "Only then is yeast added with my secret recipe of herbs."

"I never realized the effort that went into it brewing." Albin moistened his lips when he followed the track of another bead of sweat along Lecie's neck. "Still I can vouch to you having the best ale I have ever tasted."

"It pleases me that you enjoy it so much though I cannot lay claim to the recipe," Lecie said continuing her task. "It has been in my family for generations and I have already shared it with Osana and Sabina. One day, it will again be passed on."

"That is a heritage to be proud of."

"I do not know about that," Lecie said with a laugh, "tis only ale after all. There is nothing noble about it."

"On that we are not in accord for I cannot agree with such a blasphemous statement."

"Pray, do not let Father Bartholomeo hear you say such a thing. He will have you on your knees doing penance for a fortnight."

"Has he ever had a taste of your ale?" Albin countered.

"Father Bartholomeo does nothing that would give him the slightest amount of pleasure," Lecie said. "Still, I have always known your fondness for the brew. In the past, I put barley to soak whenever you walked through the door."

"Forgive me." Albin grew serious. "I feel guilty for adding to your burdens."

"Do not be. Your patronage alone has kept the family well fed," Lecie teased with a smile.

"Do you ever grow weary of it?"

"It reminds me of the times I spent alongside my mother."

"You did not answer my question," Albin said taking the ladle from her so he could continue the stirring.

"To be completely honest, it has been a chore of late with all else going on around here."

"You should no longer have to do it at all," Albin said. "Surely there is someone else who can take over the task?"

"Betta is too old, Gunilda and Harsent are useless, the girls are far too young to handle the vats, and the inn cannot afford to hire more hands. So you see there is no one else."

"How can you not afford to take on more workers when the tavern is more often than not filled to capacity?" Albin appeared perplexed. "It seems to me you should be turning a decent profit."

"I am a woman, Sir Albin. Accounting is a man's work."

"Who did Edric put in charge of it, surely not Hamon?"

"He has been in charge of the till for quite some time now."

"How old is the lad again?"

"This winter Clayton will be passing into his sixth year."

"Twill be several years afore the lad can take charge," Albin said. "You will make yourself ill working at your current pace."

"You speak as if I have a choice."

"If Edric trusts Hamon with the till then the churl should do more about the place."

"You do not like him very much, do you?"

"I do not like him at all."

"Nor do I," Lecie admitted. "There are times I am forced to put Joseph to work behind the bar because Hamon has gone missing."

"I never realized how difficult running an inn could be."

"You are a knight of the realm, Sir Albin. I would say what you do is considerably harder."

"In case you have not heard, I am more of a retired knight of the realm now," Albin said. "Our good King Henry is no longer all that fond of Fulke's ragtag band of knights."

"I oft hear rumors from passing travelers." Lecie picked up a ladle to stir with him. "Surely the tales of his lordship have been exaggerated?"

"That all depends on who said it." Albin looked over at her. "What rumors have you heard?"

"Not long ago a band of knights wearing Lord Fortescue's arms stayed the night here," Lecie said. "They were traveling home from court and spoke of little else. One of the more fanciful tales they shared involved Baron Reynault—"

"Baron Savaric of Reynold," Albin corrected.

"He and Baron Erlegh," Lecie said. "Did they really come to blows in the palace?"

"Twas more of a one-sided match after Fulke heard Reynold had assaulted Reina," Albin said. "I blame myself for the attack on her ladyship. Twas I who should have been escorting her back to her rooms that night."

"Good lord," Lecie whispered. "Did he…"

"Aside from several bumps and bruises, thankfully she was otherwise unharmed," Albin said. "Had he gone further, nobility be damned, I would have slayed him on the spot."

"You stopped him?"

"Aye."

Sensing the incident still troubled him, Lecie moved on. "Is it also true that his lordship challenged King Henry in open court in defense of her ladyship?"

"I do not know how much of a challenge there was, yet tis true he drew his sword," Albin said. "It was definitely implied that my liege would do whatever it took to keep his beloved safe."

Lecie stopped stirring altogether. "Are you jesting with me?"

"I wish I were. Seeing my liege and lady surrounded by the king's guards with their swords drawn is a vision I shall carry with me to the end of my days."

"Is it also true that you came to his lordship's defense?"

"It did not come to that, lass," Albin confided. "Still had we not been ordered to stand down by Fulke, to a man our swords would have been drawn."

"Surely it would have meant death for you all."

"Fulke is not only my liege, he is my oldest friend. He would have done the same for me."

"You are so brave," Lecie said softly. "All of you are."

"A man will do anything for the woman he loves." Albin broke her intense gaze by focusing on his stirring. "As to being brave, I am no braver than you."

"Me? What would make you say such a thing?"

"What you do is as brave and noble a calling as what I do."

"Sir Albin. If I knew to what extent you enjoyed my ale, I would have gifted you with a barrel long afore now," Lecie said with a laugh.

"No, I meant all that you do. Few men could handle the burdens you have undertaken."

Sobering, Lecie began stirring again. "There are times that I wish I was never born into such a life as this."

Cursing himself for bringing up something unpleasant, Albin reached out to touch her hand. "There is nothing wrong in wishing for something better, lass."

"You are kind to say so." Studying his hand resting lightly on hers, she straightened to catch her breath.

"You think too highly of me. I am not always kind."

"I have never seen you be anything less than kind."

Focused on her parted lips, Albin began to close the distance between them. "If you knew where my thoughts lay, you would think otherwise."

"Then tell me what you are thinking right this moment," Lecie whispered tilting her face to meet him halfway.

They abruptly broke apart when the door swung open.

Sticking her head in, Betta said, "Hamon has been found and is looking for you, Lecie. I told him I did not know where you were."

"Thank you, Betta," Lecie said in a shaking voice. "I shall speak to him as soon as we are finished here."

Watching the door swing shut, Albin said, "Why does Edric trust Hamon so much when he is so lax in his duties?"

Lecie hesitantly returned to stirring. "Likely because Hamon has been tapster here for so long and believes he can be trusted. Besides, when he fell ill he had no other option."

"I see," Albin murmured.

Stirring a large portion of measured herbs and yeast into the vat, Lecie leaned back. "It needs a few days to sour but if you would like a taste you are welcome to it."

"I never turn down ale."

Ladling some of the brew into a cup, she passed it to him and stood. "Best let it cool a spell. There is not much to boast about hot ale."

"Thank you."

"Thank you for keeping me company"

"It has been my pleasure," Albin replied softly. "I think it best I make use of the bathing room."

"Let me speak to Hamon afore I heat the water for you," Lecie offered. "It shall not take me but a trice."

"You will do no such thing." Following her out of the shed, they enjoyed the cool breeze on their overheated skin.

Albin stared at her profile when she turned her smiling face toward the sun. Inhaling deeply, she stood with her eyes closed. "I do so love the autumn."

"I love it more than you will ever know," Albin responded softly.

Her lips quirking, she glanced sideways at him. "I have never heard a man say such a thing."

Clearing his throat, Albin kicked a stone beneath his black boot. "The end of harvest is something to celebrate."

"Aye, it is," Lecie agreed with a sigh. "I fear I have tarried long enough." With a parting smile, she left him staring after her as she entered the kitchen.

Lost in thought, Albin was about to enter the common room when the irritation he heard in Lecie's voice drew his full attention.

"What business is it of yours where I have been keeping myself? I needed your assistance earlier and you were once again nowhere to be found."

"When are you going to realize you are going to need me after Edric passes, love? I can take care of you and the children."

Anger surged through Albin as he towered over Hamon. "Is there a problem here, Lecie?"

"No, Sir Albin," Lecie assured him. "On occasion I find it necessary to remind Hamon of his duties."

"I know my duties," Hamon griped.

"Then I suggest you go about them." Albin moved forward forcing Hamon to stumble several steps back.

"What business is it of yours?" Hamon sneered at Albin. "I have dealings of a private nature to discuss with Lecie."

"Then I suggest you stop wasting time and conclude your dealings so Lecie can be on her way."

"I said they were private." Hamon gave Albin the once over. "The inn is no business of yours."

"Nor is it any of yours," Lecie snapped. "When you see fit, you work here and naught else."

Staring Hamon down, Albin quirked a brow.

"The booth is set in the square for the festival," Hamon seethed. "Gunilda said she would work it for a week's lodging."

"Tell her that will be fine," Lecie said. "I suggest you get yourself behind the bar. With it being so close to the end of harvest, villagers will have coin to spend."

Hamon waited until he was out of Albin's reach to sneer at him. "Just how long are you planning on staying in Rochester?"

"For as long as I feel like it," Albin said before following Lecie up the steps.

Watching the gentle sway of her hips, he averted his eyes when she paused outside Edric's door. "Are you sure you do not need assist with your bath, Sir Albin?"

Forbidden images of Lecie's naked flesh pressed against him flashed through his mind as he focused on her inviting smile. His throat suddenly dry, he shook his head. "I can manage, lass."

"Very well," she said with a parting smile. "I shall see you later."

Staring at the closed door she had slipped through, Albin came to his senses and wondered how long he had been standing there.

Once he was soaking in the cool water of a full tub, he eavesdropped on Lecie and Betta's mundane conversation as they cleaned the nearest chambers. Discerning the raised voices of children in the passage, he rinsed in a rush. Opening the door, he spotted Lecie speaking with them in a room just off the access ladder leading to the garret.

"I will hear no more about it, Clayton," Lecie scolded. "You are going to take a bath after Osana and Sabina."

Her face flushed with color when she spotted Albin watching her.

"You cannot blame him, lass." Albin defended Clayton. "No lad that age cares much for washing."

"True as that may be, he is beginning to stink like spoilt milk."

"I may have a solution," Albin said approaching. "If Master Clayton agrees to take a bath, would you permit me to take the children to the festival in the square? If you could spare them for a time after their chores, I am sure tis something they would enjoy. They often have minstrels, jesters and the like to entertain the crowds."

"They do indeed. The villagers speak of little else for a sennight afterwards."

"Of course you would already know that." Albin shook his head with chuckle. "It was a rarity for me at their age to enjoy such frivolity."

Impatient to see if Lecie would approve, the children began pleading.

"I shall bathe every day for a sennight," Clayton swore, "and I shall even wash behind my ears if you let us go."

"You have done so much for us already." Lecie's gaze moved to her father's door when he started another bout of rattling coughs. "Are you sure you do not mind?"

"I would not have offered if I did," Albin said. "They are only children for a short time. Let them enjoy a day away from the constant toil. Better yet, come with us."

"Please say yes," Sabina pleaded. "Clayton will take a bath and we promise to get all of our chores done aforehand."

Lost to his gaze, it took another round of coughs for Lecie to respond. "I gratefully accept your offer to take the children." She lightly brushed against him when she moved past. "Please, excuse me."

♥

Joining Talan for supper at sundown, Albin kept a watchful eye on Hamon at his post behind the bar. As the common room filled with jovial villagers anticipating the festival, he found what he had long suspected to be true. For every coin Hamon collected for the till, he pocketed one for himself.

Anger surged through him as he leaned close to Talan. "Keep an eye on Hamon when he collects the next charge."

Talan lifted a cup to his mouth while his eyes followed Hamon. After collecting several coins off the bar, he watched Hamon slip something into a pouch beneath his soiled tunic. "It stops now."

"Easy." Albin gripped Talan's forearm to keep him from standing. "We cannot stop anything until we can prove what he has been doing."

"I knew something was amiss when Lecie mentioned needing additional income." Still in a temper, Talan's voice carried to the tables around them. "How long have you known about this?"

"Lower your voice," Albin said. "I suspected when Lecie told me the inn was not profitable enough to hire new hands. Boasting a dozen chambers and more often than not filled with patrons there is no way they should be struggling to make ends meet."

"Then tis likely Hamon has been filching coin for quite some time now. There is no telling how much coin he has pilfered."

"I would wager it has been going on since Edric fell ill," Albin said, "only we need to prove it."

Easing back into his seat, Talan kept his gaze fixed on Hamon. "Then let us go about proving it."

"The way I see it, all we have to do is measure how many cups of ale a barrel holds. That way we can keep track of how many cups are sold on average each day by counting the amount of coin in the till at closing."

"That is a sound idea, although it will take some time for the measuring. We shall also need access to the till. Do you know if Lecie has control of it?"

"Tis highly unlikely so I will keep watch at closing to see who takes charge of it." Albin's eyes flashed to the steps. "I would wager tis Hamon. He must leave just enough in the til to avoid bringing suspicion upon himself."

"Can I get you more ale, my handsome knights?" Gunilda ran a fingertip along Talan's neck as he leaned away from her with a look of revulsion.

"No," he responded curtly. "I shall summon you if I do."

"I shall have another." Albin slid his cup so Gunilda could refill it.

After refreshing Albin's cup, Gunilda frowned at Talan before blending back into the crowd surrounding them.

"I have not seen Lecie since I returned from the tower." Talan glanced toward the kitchen. "She is usually about in the evening is she not?"

"Not of late," Albin said taking a long swallow of ale. "It appears her day never ends."

"Where is she now, caring for Edric?"

"Aye." Albin leaned back in his seat to stare at his cup. "The poor man seems to struggle more with his malady at night. I have sent a messenger to her ladyship. I am hoping she has something to ease his pain."

"I fear before long he shall feel pain no longer," Talan replied low. "Atween you and me, it surprises me he has lasted this long."

"I fear you are right. He weighs no more than a feather and cannot keep anything down for long."

"You are good friend to them. Lecie is fortunate to have you to lean upon."

"I am no friend to Edric," Albin scoffed, "and if I were as honorable as you, I would stay far away from Lecie."

"What do you mean?" Talan's brow creased in confusion. "I know for a fact that they are both grateful for your assist of late. Lecie herself has said as much."

"I am going for a walk." Shoving his chair back, Albin stood. "Keep an eye on Hamon but do not let on that we are on to him."

"What is troubling you? You have not been yourself since we arrived in Rochester."

"I fear I shall never be the same again."

"Then tell me what is wrong so I can help you," Talan coaxed. "God knows you have heard enough of my troubles of late."

Ignoring the offer, Albin averted his eyes. "Have you ever coveted something you could not have, Talan?" His knuckles whitened when he gripped the back of the rail-back chair. "Desired it so much you felt you would go mad without it?"

"Only if Mylla is lost to me will I know how that feels," Talan responded softly. "What does that have to do with you?"

"Everything." Tossing a few coins on the table, Albin added, "I appreciate your offer but no one can help me anymore than I can help you."

Talan watched Albin go and took a long swallow of ale. He had no idea how to help his friend.

By the light of the moon, Albin made his way to the river. Beneath the shadow of the rising tower, he stood staring blindly at the glistening water.

♥

The hour was late by the time Lecie finished with the next day's preparations. Intent to check on the children and her father one last time, she instructed Hamon to lock up and turn in after the last few remaining patrons departed.

Bolting the bathing chamber's door to take a long soak, she relaxed in the tepid water after washing her hair. She woke with a start to the sound of Tugger whining behind the door. "I am coming," she called. Tempted to return to her garret in her cream chemise, she pulled on and laced her confining kirtle in the event she ran into someone.

Absently running a comb through her drying tresses, she unbolted the door to admit the anxious dog. With tail wagging furiously, Tugger nudged her with his muzzle nearly knocking her over.

"Leave off, you giant beasty." She gave him an affectionate pat on the head before he bounded down the steps ahead of her.

Frowning to see Harsent had once again been lax in clearing the tables, she made her way through the kitchen to the back door. Likely sleeping off another heavy bout of drinking, Lecie resolved to have words with the tavern wench in the morning about keeping up her end of the board agreement.

Whining, Tugger jumped at the door.

"Be about your business and come right back." Lecie yawned as she let him out. "I mean it," she called when the dog bolted into the darkness. "I am far too weary and cold to wait long on you."

Chafing her arms in the brisk air of the back garden, she waited for her eyes to adjust to the darkness. Tugger barked several times in the distance and she soon spotted the outline of a man returning with the dog trotting by his side.

Only Sir Albin's broad muscular form could dwarf Tugger's immense size. A slight smiled played about her lips while she listened to Sir Albin speak companionably to the dog.

He drew to an abrupt halt when he spotted her.

"Good eventide, lass," he greeted softly.

"Hello, Sir Albin."

Tugger looked from one to the other for instruction before darting back into the darkness.

Oblivious to the dog's absence, Albin gestured to the ground beside him. "I did not think you meant for the dog to be out all night."

"No I did not," Lecie replied breathlessly. "I would dread if something were to happen to him. He more than earns his keep by hunting rabbits for the inn."

"Not to mention the lad seems quite fond of him."

"Yes, not to mention that," Lecie said. "We are all quite fond of Tugger, drool and all."

"Your hair is wet, lass." Albin reached out a hand only to snatch it back at the thought of touching her. "You are bound to catch a chill."

Clasping his hand, Lecie brought it to her cheek. "Thank you for caring about my wellbeing."

"Lecie," Albin said in a strained voice, "you need to go back inside now."

Emboldened by the darkness, she turned her face to kiss his hand. "And if my choice is to stay here with you instead? What then?" Turning her gaze up to him, her eyes sparkled in the moonlight. "Would you send me away?"

With a low groan of defeat, Albin pulled her into his embrace. Seizing her parted lips, his arms snaked around her back to draw her closer.

Slipping her arms around his lean waist, Lecie stood on tiptoe when he deepened the kiss.

With a curse, Albin tore himself away to stare down at her in anguish. "I will not bring dishonor to a dying man." Abruptly releasing her, he moved past her. "Come inside and warm yourself."

Still reeling from their kiss, Lecie stared after him in confusion. Hearing the crack of a twig, she scanned the darkness by the stables. Calling loudly for Tugger, she held the door open for the dog as he came bounding out of the darkness.

Concealed in the shadows she failed to see Hamon watching them with his thin lips curled into a spiteful sneer.

Chapter Four

Lecie woke before dawn with the memory of Albin's lips pressed against her own. Lost in thought, she stared at the roof timbers above her head replaying his curious words to her. Wondering if her father would approve of Sir Albin, she decided to speak to him after waking the children.

Excited about the festival, the children were up and dressed by the time Lecie tucked her hair into a snood and dressed in a white linen chemise and garnet kirtle. Entering her father's room, she found him curled on his side resting fitfully.

"Lecie," he croaked in a hoarse whisper when she touched his shoulder.

Rushing to fill a cup of water from the pitcher on the stand beside him, she slid her arm beneath his shoulders to prop him up. "Here, Da."

Taking a few swallows of the cool liquid, he dipped his head in thanks.

"Did you rest at all?" Easing him back onto the pillows, she noted his ashen color with alarm.

"A tad," he whispered, searching her face. "You look different this morn."

"I do not know why you would say such a thing." Lecie forced a smile. "I am the same as I was yesterday."

"No," her father rasped. "There is a sparkle in your eye...you seem...happier this day."

"You know me so well." Perching on the edge of the bed, Lecie reached for his hand. "Da, what do you think of Sir Albin?"

"He is an honorable man. You could do no better." Her father gently squeezed her fingers. "Why do you ask this of me?"

"I just wondered," Lecie hedged. "I believe him to be honorable as well."

"I see," her father replied knowingly. "Mayhap you find him to be a handsome man as well?"

"Da," Lecie scolded. "I was just wondering what you thought of him that is all." Rising, she headed for the door. "I shall bring you some broth as soon as I see to the children."

"Has Sir Albin made advances toward you?"

Her father's soft words drew Lecie up short. Turning back, she met his pain-filled gaze with a calm she did not feel. "No, Da. He has not."

"I thought not." Nodding slightly, Edric closed his eyes. "He is far too honorable a man to shirk his duties to his lordship."

"What would his duties have to do with it?"

"He is not in Rochester to woo a lass, he is here on a mission for his liege. Knights take their oaths seriously."

"Cannot they have a life outside of their duties?" Albin's odd behavior began to make sense to Lecie and she suddenly felt guilty for pressing her attentions on him.

"I know not many who do." Rolling on his side, Edric put an abrupt end to the conversation.

Lost in thought on the way to the kitchen, Lecie came to the realization that Baron Erlegh's knights were all unattached. The baron himself had even acted displeased when she would ask after Sir Albin. An embarrassed flush suffused her face as she swept into the kitchen to prepare the morning meal. Being a commoner, she would never understand the rules that governed the upper classes.

Carefully turning the pan of yeast rolls browning above the fire, she inhaled sharply as her fingers touched hot metal when Hamon's raspy voice startled her. "Must you always sneak up on people?"

"Aside from that bit, you seem to be in high spirits this morn, my love." Leaning back against the table, Hamon crossed his arms over his chest. "Now what would the reason for that be, when your father is above gasping out his last?"

Favoring her burned fingers Lecie whirled around to glare at the loathsome man. "How dare you speak so about my father?"

"I am merely stating a fact is all." Running his tongue along his thin upper lip Hamon fixed his gaze on her bosom. "We both know soon enough you shall need the protection of a man." Straightening he leaned his ruddy face close beside Lecie's ear to whisper. "And we both know a knight of the realm is beyond your reach."

"How dare you." Leaning away from Hamon's foul breath, Lecie slapped him hard across the face. "Pack your belongings and be gone from here."

"Do you think you are giving me the sack?" Hamon's lip quirked as he lightly touched the outline of the handprint left on his cheek. "You know as well as I you cannot."

"If you insist on having a man sack you, I shall ask my father to do it," Lecie snapped. "Either way, by day's end I will see the last of you."

"Your father would never agree to it. He knows you cannot run the inn alone." Unperturbed, Hamon glanced briefly over Lecie's shoulder. "He also knows since women cannot own property, the lad will need a man to oversee things until he comes of age."

"Twill never be you," Lecie replied in defiance. "I would rather see the inn sold than have the likes of you run it."

"We shall soon enough see about that." Hamon reached out to cup her chin with rough calloused fingers. "I suggest you learn to curb that sharp tongue of yours and accustom yourself to the idea of my being your lord and master."

Jerking her face away from his touch, Lecie's hands itched to slap him again. "Be gone from my sight or I shall set Tugger upon you."

"That worthless beasty cowers at the sound of thunder." Pausing on his way out, Hamon turned back to her. "By the way, your rolls are scorched."

♥

Albin was nervously pacing in his chamber, dreading the thought of facing Lecie.

Dressed in his standard attire of black breeches and tunic bearing the Erlegh coat of arms, his boot heels kept up a repetitive tattoo on the planked flooring.

Raking his hands roughly through his tangled curls, he tormented himself with thoughts of what she must think of him.

"Zounds," he swore upon hearing a soft knock on the door. Half fearing it would be Lecie he drew the bed curtains to conceal the unkempt bed. With a deep calming breath, he cursed again to see his hand shake when he twisted the latch.

"Did you say something, Sir Albin? I could not make it out."

Albin's eyes dropped to Clayton standing in the passageway sporting a big dimpled grin. "Good morningtide to you, lad, twas nothing worth repeating."

"My father sent me to say he would like a word with you this morn if you can accommodate him."

"Your father wishes to speak with me?" His mind reeling at the implications, Albin scanned the passageway half expecting to see Edric approaching to call him out.

"Aye, I memorized every word." Throwing up a hand in parting, Clayton took off at a run. "I shall see you later. I need to finish the last of my chores afore the festival."

Angry at himself for betraying a friend, Albin assumed Lecie had confessed his inappropriate behavior of the evening past.

The one thing he swore he would never do had come to pass. He had brought shame and dishonor to a dying man.

Prepared to accept the consequences, he straightened to his full height and boldly headed down the hall. It was only staring at Edric's door that his hand briefly hesitated when he raised it to knock.

Hearing the raspy summons to enter, he opened the door with a repentant expression. "You wished to see me, Edric?" Closing the door behind him, Albin moved to the bed.

"Aye, I did." Edric struggled to prop himself up so Albin rushed to lend him assist. "Thank you, Sir Albin." Gesturing to the stool beside the bed, he continued, "Please make yourself comfortable."

Albin perched uncomfortably on the stool until it collapsed beneath his weight. "I will stand," he said picking himself up off the floor. "I want you to know that I am prepared to make amends in any way you deem fitting."

"Tis only a stool. A series of wracking coughs shook Edric's emaciated frame. Accepting a cup of water from Albin, he took a long drink before handing it back. "Thank you."

"Have your say," Albin said solemnly meeting the elder man's gaze.

"As you know, I am not long for this world." Edric weakly waved a hand when Albin would protest. "If not for the precarious state in which I leave my children, I would even now seek my eternal rest."

"And Lecie?" Albin questioned softly.

"Aye, my Lecie," Edric said. "I fear she shall soon have the weight of the world on her slight shoulders." Struggling for breath, he shifted his gaze to Albin. "Would you grant a favor to a dying man, Sir Albin? I know I have no right to ask it of you but my pride died some time ago."

"Name it," Albin replied with conviction. "Whatever it is, it shall be so."

"If his lordship gives his consent, would you take Lecie for your wife?" Edric reached out to grip Albin's hand. "There is no one else I would entrust her to and if she is not soon wed my children will be destitute."

The last thing he expected Albin's chiseled brows drew together as words escaped him.

"I know what I ask is not just." Edric broke the uneasy silence. "We are far beneath your status, yet fear of the unknown emboldens me. I have a dowaire set aside for my girls hidden in the floorboards beneath this bed. You would also have the profits of the inn until Clayton—"

"I do not want coinage from you, Edric." Hamon's visage flashed through Albin's mind as he calmly met Edric's gaze. "You have my word I will make Lecie my lady on the condition that she willingly accepts me."

Edric's entire body relaxed and tears filled his eyes. Blinking away the moisture, he could only nod in thanks.

"Rest at ease, my friend." Albin lightly clasped Edric's forearm. "Even if she turns me down, I shall see that Lecie and the children want for nothing so long as I shall live."

Pulling a thin leather cord necklace from around his neck, Edric held it out to him. "Tis the finest thing I have to my name. Please accept it as something to remember me by."

Albin palmed the gold crucifix dangling from the cord. "This rightly belongs to your son."

"Soon enough you will be my son."

Leaving Edric to rest, Albin stepped into the hall. Expecting the worst, Edric had given him what he wanted most.

Glad no one was about he headed to his chamber to sort through the latest turn of events.

♥

By late morning, the common room was empty and the children were fidgeting anxiously waiting for Albin to escort them to the festival.

Once the barrels of ale, casks of wine, and earthenware cups were on the way to the stand set up in the village square, Lecie busied herself with preparations for the evening meal. The inn boasted a large crowd on festival days since the end of harvest celebration often carried into the wee hours of the morning.

Her hair tied back in a snood she absently brushed a hand along her brow leaving a light dusting of flour behind. With the trenchers prepared to hold the meat roasting on spits in the common room, she slid another tray of rolls above the hearth fire in the kitchen.

"Hello, lass."

Albin's deep voice had her self-consciously reaching for her hair as she looked up. "Hello, Sir Albin."

"Could you spare me a moment? I would like to have a private word with you in the garden."

"Is anything wrong?" Wiping her hands on the apron around her waist, Lecie hurriedly untied it.

"That all depends on how you look at it."

Lecie's brow furrowed at his odd response.

"Sir Albin!" Clayton came running into the kitchen followed by Osana and Sabina. "Are you ready for the festival?"

Albin hid his frustration behind a smile. "I am indeed, lad."

"Clayton," Lecie said, "Sir Albin and I were talking."

"What about?" Osana piped in.

"I do not think tis any of our business," Sabina chided her twin softly.

"Seeing as how you three are prepared to set off, it can wait until later this eve." Albin turned his attention back to Lecie. "Are you sure you cannot join us?"

"I am needed here." Lecie returned his smile. "Still, I hope you all enjoy the day."

The children were rushing outside when Lecie called them back. From a shelf built into the stone above the hearth, she retrieved an earthenware jar. Tipping out the contents into her palm, she distributed the few coins inside to the children. "Have a care to the amount of sweets you eat or you shall all have bellyaches afore nightfall."

Clayton wrapped his arms around her waist in a brief hug of gratitude. With an ear-splitting whoop of joy, he darted out the door.

More demure, the twins shared a pleased smile and began to discuss what they would purchase with their newfound wealth.

Albin watched the trio exit with a fond smile before facing Lecie. "It was to be my treat today, lass."

"We are beholden to you enough as it is, Sir Albin."

"Lecie," he hesitated, capturing her gaze. "I do not have a way with words and could never spout a sonnet like Sir Guy."

When he fell silent, she stepped closer to him. "Do you think it is pretty words I seek?"

"No." He shook his head with a slight smile. "I know you to have more substance than that. I cannot imagine your head being turned by mere words however pretty sounding they may be."

"And are you trying to turn my head?" Lecie searched the depths of his warm brown gaze. "I warrant it would not take much."

"Lecie—"

"Sir Albin, where are you?" Clayton called loudly from the yard. "If we tarry overlong we shall miss the puppet show."

"You best be going." Backing away, Lecie retrieved her apron. "I vow the children shall be dragging you out by your ears should you delay further."

"Aye, no doubt they would," Albin said with a fond smile. "We shall speak later?"

"We shall," Lecie responded, "and I shall look forward to it."

With his hand on the latch, Albin turned back to her. "Are you sure you cannot join us?"

"I would like nothing better yet I fear the supper offerings shall be scant if I do."

"Then I shall bring you a sampling of everything you missed."

"Thank you." Lecie stood staring after him before reluctantly turning back to her task.

Deep in thought, she did not hear Sir Talan address her until he spoke again. "I hope I am not interrupting."

"Sir Talan, please forgive me." Lecie looked up with a start. "I did not hear you come in."

Dressed in charcoal breeches, a black tunic bearing the Erlegh coat of arms and black leather boots, Sir Talan's soulful blue eyes lit up when he smiled. "My apologies if I startled you. I was merely wondering if Sir Albin has departed."

"Aye," Lecie said returning his smile. "He left not long ago with the children."

"Then after I pay a call upon the sheriff, I shall meet up with him in the village," Talan said. "I have not seen Hamon about this morn. Do you know where I can find him?"

"He left early this morn with Gunilda to set up the ale stand. Is there something I can help you with?"

"I was going to offer my assistance is all. Shall he be remaining at the stand for the duration of the festival?"

"It is expected of him." Lecie then changed the subject. "I hope you do not find this too bold but may I ask if your business with the sheriff has something to do with Mylla?"

"You are welcome to ask me anything, and to answer your question, I have the honor of escorting Mylla to the festival midday."

"I am beyond pleased to hear it." Lecie instantly brightened at the news. "Mylla is extremely dear to me."

"She speaks highly of you as well."

"You are kind to share that with me," Lecie said. "In return, I should warn you that you will likely not be her only escort."

"Undoubtedly we shall be properly chaperoned," Talan said with a chuckle. "Shall we look for you later at the festival?"

"Alas, I cannot. Hamon shall send Joseph should there be a need to replenish the ale." Scooping vegetables into the cook pot, Lecie added, "Please extend my warmest greetings to Mylla."

"I shall," Talan said on his way out. "I am sure she will be as disappointed as the rest of us that you will not be able to join us."

"Perhaps next year I will be able to sneak away for a bit." Swinging the cook pot over the fire, she called, "Enjoy the day with your lady fair."

Happy for her childhood friend, Lecie smiled when she heard Sir Talan whistle a merry tune as he passed through the garden.

Her thoughts on Albin, she lost herself to the task of cooking and did not hear the back door open.

Adding more wood to the hearth, she yelped in fear when a muscular male arm reached past her to swing the cook pot away from the spitting fire. Straightening, she whirled to find Albin grinning at her.

"Sir Albin, what are you about?"

"After giving it much thought I have come to the conclusion that I would not be much of a knight if I failed to rescue you."

"Is that right?" Half believing he was jesting with her, Lecie's voice faltered. "And what exactly is it that you are rescuing me from?"

"From yourself, lass. In case you have not heard, there is a festival in the square this day."

"That does have a ring of familiarity about it," Lecie managed in a breathless whisper. "What is it you propose?"

"Is not it obvious? I have come to escort you and will accept no excuses."

"I cannot leave my—"

"Betta will see to Edric," Albin said with a smug smile.

"There will be no supper prepared—"

"Have you not been to a festival? There is an array of tantalizing dishes to entice the crowd. I have no doubt your guests will return with full bellies and well into their cups. And in the unlikelihood that someone requests food, I shall scorch rolls for them myself."

"It appears you have well thought this through," Lecie said with a begrudging smile. "May I ask how you managed to escape the children in order to come back for me?"

"I ran into Leofrick who offered to keep an eye on them until I returned with you. He, along with Mylla, and Talan are to meet us by the stand after the puppet show. You would not make a liar out of me, would you, lass?"

"There is so much yet to do." Lecie absently wiped her hands on a rag. "I have never before shirked my duty to the inn."

"Shall I ask Edric if he will allow it?"

"You already know what he will say."

"That I do." Reaching his arms around her waist, he untied the apron at her back. Balling it up he threw it over his shoulder where it landed on the table. "Shall we go?"

A tingle surged through Lecie when Albin's arms grazed her hips when he stepped back. "Would you give me some time to refresh myself?"

"Gladly." Albin smiled victoriously. "Take all the time you need but be quick about it. Time's a wasting."

Rushing up the steps, Lecie nearly knocked Betta off her feet at the top.

"Lord of mercy," Betta exclaimed. "What devil is at your heels?"

"Forgive me." Out of breath, Lecie scooped up the sheets Betta dropped. "Sir Albin has asked to escort me to the festival. Would you mind overmuch keeping an eye on my father?"

"Dear me that is something, is it not? You go on ahead and I shall look after your da."

"Could you also heat the cookpot when you finish up here? The trenchers and rolls have already been seen to."

"I shall see to everything." Betta reached out to pat Lecie on the arm. "Tis good to see you so animated again. Go and enjoy yourself."

"You shall have a day of leisure all to yourself for this," Lecie called from the ladder leading to her garret.

Slipping into a fresh kirtle of deep green, she ran a comb through her dark silken tresses and decided to leave it unbound for once. Pinching her cheeks for a spot of color, she hastened down the steps only slowing to take a few deep breaths near the bottom.

Albin stood from his perch on a stool before the bar when she approached. "You look beautiful, lass."

"Thank you." Blushing to the roots of her hair, Lecie gestured toward the door. "Shall we go?"

Falling into pace with the crowd heading toward the center of the village, Lecie's heart raced each time Albin would lightly clasp her arm to assist her around horse dung and deep ruts in the hard-packed dirt road.

With his hand resting at the small of her back, he guided her through the milling crowds packing the square.

"Mylla," Lecie called excitedly when she spotted her friend standing beside Sir Talan.

"Lecie." Mylla rushed over to hug her. "Sir Talan said you would not be coming today but then Sir Albin said you would. I am so pleased that he managed to convince you. It has been far too long since we have seen one another."

"It has been far too long," Lecie said with a smile. "I am so happy I allowed Sir Albin to talk me into coming with him."

"As am I," Albin spoke softly from behind her as he passed the pair to speak to Talan.

Lecie blushed and Mylla giggled.

"That was quick," Talan said when Albin joined him.

"It appears Lecie is not the kind of woman who makes a man wait. Have you been watching Hamon long?"

"Long enough," Talan replied cryptically with a nod toward the stand.

"Is something amiss, Sir Albin?" Confused by their somber manner, Lecie broke off her conversation with Mylla.

"Nothing that you need to concern yourself with," Albin said. "You are to enjoy yourself whilst Talan and I briefly discuss more mundane topics."

"If you wish." Lecie's brow furrowed in thought when she watched the pair walk a short distance away. "Mylla, did Sir Talan happen to mention anything untoward prior to our arrival?"

"Nothing I would construe as odd," Mylla said. "All he said was that he needed to speak to Albin. Since we were to meet you both here, he told Edmund and Caine to go ahead and get their swords sharpened in the armourer's tent."

"I wondered where your escorts had gone." Lecie smiled despite a niggling feeling in the pit of her stomach. "Tis not like your da to send you off without at least one of your brothers by your side."

"Tell me about it. It really is quite tiresome. I have been unable to convince him to allow me to visit you. He said tis unseemly for gently bred women to be seen in a tavern." Mylla reached out to take Lecie's hand. "Not that he thinks less of you for it. He cares about you very much."

"I know," Lecie said. "He comes often to visit with my father. I do so enjoy when they talk of better times."

"How is your father? All mine will say is that he is on the mend." Mylla shook her head with a disgusted look. "I swear he treats me like a child."

"I am sure he is only trying to protect you from the unpleasant truth."

"Is it as bad as all that then?"

"I fear my father is growing weaker by the day." Tears filled Lecie's eyes and she blinked them away. "Atween us, I do not expect him to see the first snowfall."

"I am so very sorry," Mylla said passing Lecie a lace kerchief. "Our fathers were childhood friends just like you and I. We shall always look out for you. You know that, do you not?"

"Thank you." Dabbing at her eyes, Lecie passed the kerchief back. "So tell me about Sir Talan. I can see you are smitten with him."

Blushing, Mylla glanced over her shoulder at Talan. "I am more than smitten. I am in love."

"Mylla, that is wonderful. Does your father approve?"

"The decision may not be his to make."

"What do you mean?"

Close to tears, Mylla struggled to compose herself. "I tried so hard not to think about it today. I even promised Talan."

"What is it?"

"Do you recall me telling you about meeting the king's itinerant justice when I was in London?"

"I do. You said he was repugnant and overly bold in his attentions toward you. After your experience, I paid more attention in the tavern when I heard his name being bandied about. He is the most horrid of men and cruelly punishes people for the slightest of offenses." Lecie glanced between Talan and Mylla when the situation became clear to her. "Wait, are you saying Justice de Glanville seeks an accord with you? Mylla, tell me tis not so."

"Tis what I fear most," Mylla admitted. "The justice and his clerk have made many unexpected calls upon my father of late, and the justice always insists upon my being present."

"Oh, Mylla." Lecie's heart sank for her friend at the implications. "He is a member of the king's domas. He will not take kindly to being denied your hand."

"You tell me nothing I do not already know. He has the influence to strip my father of his position."

"So why does not Sir Talan marry you to thwart Justice de Glanville's plans? If he has not yet declared himself, you could claim ignorance if he were to take offense."

"My father will not entertain the idea," Mylla said. "He believes the justice has all but stated his intentions toward me and would not risk offending him. The only reason he allowed me to come today was so that I can spend a little more time with Talan afore we are forced to forever part."

"Surely your father would not force you to marry someone so vile?"

"What choice does he have? One negative word to the king and my father loses the only livelihood he has ever known. The position belonged to my grandfather, and after my father, it will pass to Edmund."

"So your happiness is to be sacrificed," Lecie said. "Tis not fair."

"Talan said not to fear since he will not let me go so easily." Mylla forced a bright smile. "I am placing my trust in him."

"Then I shall pray every day that all goes well for you both."

Squeezing Lecie's hand, Mylla said, "Enough about my troubles. Tell me about you and Sir Albin. I have never seen a man so in love."

"What do you mean?" Daring to hope, Lecie darted a glance toward Albin and caught him looking at her. "Why would you think Sir Albin is in love with me?"

"Do not you think it obvious also?"

"No, I do not." Lecie slightly shook her head.

"After briefly speaking with him earlier I knew straightaway," Mylla said. "He drove Talan to distraction talking about how hard you work. In fact, he would not stop until Talan suggested that he go and fetch you. It was ever so sweet to hear Sir Albin say he had every intention of doing so and would not take no for an answer. Twas then I knew how much you meant to him."

"I had no idea," Lecie murmured. "Sir Talan mentioned that Sir Albin was interested in a woman so I assumed everything he did for me was out of kindness."

"I would wager my ribbon coin that Talan was speaking about you," Mylla said. "If you like, I can confirm it with him."

"Oh, you cannot do that. Then they will know we were talking about them."

"Can you not at all discern Sir Albin's interest in you?"

"There are times when I think he cares for me as much as I for him, yet he always manages to leave me wondering if tis something I imagined."

"Well there is nothing imaginary about it," Mylla said. "He looks at you with such a yearning my heart almost breaks for him."

"Are you absolutely certain?"

"With four older brothers, I can most assuredly tell when one of them is besotted. Well, except for Edmund that is. His only love seems to be following in Da's footsteps."

"I so want to believe you." Sneaking a peek at Albin, Lecie found him staring at her. She stood mesmerized by the look of longing on his face until he abruptly broke eye contact.

Clasping Talan's shoulder, Albin guided his friend into the stream of people moving in the opposite direction.

"See what I mean? Tis almost as if he is afraid of me." Turning back to Mylla, Lecie froze at the look of dismay on her friend's face. "What is it?'

"Ah, fortune has indeed favored me this day."

Lecie's gaze shifted to the elder heavyset man garbed all in black with the king's crest emblazoned on his tunic. Doffing his black velvet cap, his full lower lip jutted out as he appraised Mylla with dark shifty eyes.

"Lord Justice, what an unexpected visit." Lowering her eyes, Mylla shifted uneasily.

Passing his cap to his harried young clerk, Justice de Glanville searched the crowd around them. "You are in public without escort?"

"I am with my brothers, Leofrick, Edmund, and Caine, Your Lordship." Mylla's voice was barely above a whisper forcing Justice de Glanville to step closer. "They are all nearby as is Sir Talan."

"Sir Talan?" Justice de Glanville's graying brows drew together in a frown. "He is a knight who serves the disgraced Baron of Erlegh, is he not?"

"He is, Your Lordship."

"What business does he have escorting you here?"

The look of panic in Mylla's eyes had Lecie scanning the crowd for some sight of Albin or Talan to rescue them from the man's vile presence.

"Sir Talan is a friend of my brother Leofrick's, Your Lordship."

"I see." With narrowed eyes, he finally acknowledged Lecie's presence. "And who might you be?"

Calmly meeting the arrogant man's gaze, Lecie's mouth felt dry. "I am Lecie, Your Lordship. My father owns The Wounded Stag."

"You have very unusual eyes, almost golden." Without breaking his intense stare, he called his clerk forward. "What say you about this woman's eyes, Roger?"

Lecie shared a startled glance with Mylla before meeting the clerk's appraising gaze.

"The witch drowned by your command last winter boasted eyes like this woman's, Your Lordship."

"I thought as much myself." Justice de Glanville's smile was chilling when he reached out to grip Lecie's chin with soft pudgy fingers. "What was your mother's given name?"

"Elena, Your Lordship," Lecie managed in a trembling voice. "We lost her in childbirth several years past."

"In that case, perhaps the witch was a distant kin of yours." Dropping his hand, he refocused his attention on Mylla. "I am passing through on orders from the king and cannot tarry overlong. Tis fortuitous that I ran into you since I only stopped to pass a message onto your father."

"What would that message be, Your Lordship?"

Seeing Mylla close to tears, Lecie wrapped an arm around her waist to lend her support.

Justice de Glanville took note of it with narrowed eyes. "Inform your father that once I conclude my business to the west of here, I plan on calling upon him. Twould please me much if you refrain from venturing out in public with any non-relation until then."

"Shall I tell him your request has to do with the king's business, Your Lordship?"

"You may tell him it has to do with you, dear Mylla." Reaching out, he lifted Mylla's slender hand to his thick lips. "I shall make all haste so as not to keep you waiting overlong for my return."

Chapter Five

Believing Talan would rescue her, Mylla used his approach as an excuse to pull her hand away from Justice de Glanville. Lowering her eyes, she stood meekly to the side.

Blocking Talan's view of the justice, Albin addressed the elder man. "Your visit is unexpected, Lord Justice. Are you in Rochester to survey the tower's progress?"

The justice glared up at Albin who stood a full head above him. "I am no lowly builder, and why I am here is no concern of yours."

"Right you are," Albin said. "However, if you would like to take a tour whilst you are here, I am the man to take you."

"Should you not be there now?" Craning his head around Albin's broad chest, Justice de Glanville pinned Talan with his cold gaze. "I doubt our good king would approve of your dallying in the square when there is work to be done."

"There is only so much progress that can be done each day, Lord Justice. I am more than willing to give you a detailed accounting of the work that has been done to date so you can judge for yourself."

"If I wanted a detailed accounting, I would ask for it. Now step aside, I would speak to your counterpart."

"Lord Justice." Refusing to lower his eyes, Talan maintained eye contact while he waited for the justice to speak.

"Our king has told me of your obstinate nature, tis a wonder he let you live."

"I am grateful to be the object of our good king's benevolence," Talan said. "Now if you will excuse—"

"No, I will not excuse you." Flicking his eyes at Mylla, the justice frowned to see her standing so close to Talan. "What business do you have in Rochester?"

"Did you not hear Sir Albin?" Talan raised his voice intimating that the lord justice was hard of hearing. "We are here at our liege's behest to assess the progress of the tower."

Talan's disrespectful tone had Lecie turning frightened eyes on Albin.

Blocking Talan completely, Albin bowed to the justice. "Lord Justice, twas a pleasure to see you again. If you will excuse us, we must return the ladies to their chaperones so they can enjoy the mimes together."

"Mimes?"

"I do so wish to see them," Lecie squeaked in a nervous trill. "What say you, Mylla?"

"The mimes are my favorite," Mylla said catching on.

"Then let us be off." Extending his arm, Albin presented it to Lecie.

Offering his arm to Mylla, Talan jerked his head in the justice's direction.

His face a mottled red, the justice was about to speak when Mylla captured his attention by dipping into a quick curtsy. "I shall pass your message along to my father, Lord Justice."

"See that you do." Glaring at Talan the lord justice watched them go.

"Easy, lass," Albin whispered when Lecie attempted to quicken their pace. "Give me a smile and stroll with me."

"What if he stops us?" Lecie plastered on a fake smile. "He could do anything to us and we would be powerless to stop him."

"We are safe for now."

"How do you know?"

"Ranulf de Glanville has a close acquaintanceship with a baron well known to me. Men of their ilk prefer aiming at the backs of their enemies, not facing them head on."

"He is as vile as I thought him to be." Lecie hazarded a glance at Mylla. "You could not have come at a more opportune time."

"Had I known he was in town, we would not have come here."

Once they were out of sight of the justice, Talan turned back to them with a grim look. "I think it best if I were to return Mylla home."

"Unfortunately, I agree," Albin said. "I shall escort Lecie back to the inn and meet back up with you at the ale stand."

"What of the children?" Lecie looked over at the stage where the show was about to begin. "Should we not fetch them as well?"

"Let us not spoil their fun. Leofrick will keep an eye on them until I return."

Hugging Mylla, Lecie whispered, "Have faith in him."

"I do," Mylla whispered back.

Setting off in opposite directions, Lecie led the way through the milling throngs with Albin close behind her.

A pair of jesters briefly blocked their way to dance around them while tossing flower petals above their heads. Bowing low before her, one of the jesters presented Lecie with a scrap of blue silk.

Accepting a coin from Albin, his glowering gaze had the troop moving off.

Albin slowed when they were passing the last of the stalls. Spotting a table set with an array of hair ornaments, he guided her forward. "Take your pick to remember the day."

"That is not necessary, Sir Albin. I shall always remember this day."

Gesturing to the table with a sweep of his hand, he smiled. "Humor me."

Her stomach fluttering by the look in his eyes, Lecie perused the hair combs. Her eye resting on a delicate silver comb fashioned into a butterfly she picked it up. "This one is beautiful."

Settling on a price with the vendor, Albin passed the man a few coins.

"Thank you ever so much," Lecie said admiring the trinket.

"You are most welcome. May I?" Taking the comb from Lecie's hand, he smoothed the hair behind her ear to fasten it. "It becomes you."

Once they were clear of crowd, Albin once again extended his arm to her. "Tis not how I envisioned the day would go."

"I found it quite enjoyable until the end."

"You are only being kind," Albin said. "We were not there long enough to enjoy anything."

"Not true. I enjoyed seeing Mylla again, and your company."

Cupping her hand where it rested lightly on his arm, Albin smiled. "Edric is a blessed man."

Hurt that he kept mentioning her father whenever she attempted to get close to him, Lecie changed the subject. "Do you think Sir Talan should have insulted the lord justice like that?"

"The lad is in love with the justice's object of affection so there is no telling what he is capable of."

"I would not exactly call Mylla an object but I know what you mean." Drawing to a halt, Lecie looked up at him. "Is their love completely hopeless?"

Albin cupped her cheek with a sad smile. "I believe where there is love there is always a way."

"I shall pray tis so."

They walked the rest of the way in silence each lost to their own thoughts.

Entering through the back door of the inn Lecie opened her mouth to speak and felt foolish when she could think of nothing to say.

Albin reached out a hand only to pull it back again. "You have a flower petal tangled in your tresses."

"Oh." Lecie ran a hand through her hair. "It must have come from the jesters."

"You missed it." Plucking the petal free Albin tucked it into the belt of his tunic.

Willing him to kiss her, she stepped closer.

"Lecie…" Abruptly clearing his throat, Albin stepped back. "I really need to speak with you."

"Is not that what we are doing right now?"

"It is," Albin said, "only I had a more serious talk in mind."

"Oh?" Lecie smiled in anticipation. "I thought you had to return to the ale stand?"

"I do, Talan and the children will be waiting for me. Will you make time for me when I return?"

"Gladly," she whispered tilting her face up for a kiss. Her breath caught in her throat when his hands slid through her tresses to cradle the back of her head.

"Lecie," he spoke low as if in torment.

Closing her eyes, she leaned into him.

Gently kissing her forehead, Albin stood as if undecided. After a long tense moment, he released her to step back. "I must go."

♥

Once again perplexed by his manner, Lecie remained in the kitchen after Albin left to check on the meal preparations.

Betta had the stew finished, and trenchers and rolls waiting. Making note to make it up to her, she passed into the empty common room to survey its cleanliness with a critical eye.

She looked up with a frown when Harsent came sauntering down the steps. Dressed in a soiled brown woolen kirtle and stained cream kirtle, her graying black hair appeared oily and unkempt.

"You assured me last eve the floors would be seen to by this morn, Harsent."

"Leave off," Harsent said with a feigned pout. "You know I have been ill."

"Only from the amount of drink you imbibe in the evenings," Lecie scolded. "In that alone you do not hold up your end of the board agreement."

"Your father was much more understanding and pleasant," Harsent whined. "I do not see you treating Gunilda and Betta the way you do me."

"Gunilda and Betta see to their tasks without having to constantly be reminded of them," Lecie replied sharply. "Come dark the inn shall be fair to bursting so I suggest you see to the floor right away."

"I see no point in cleaning something that is only going to get soiled again." Harsent huffed as she passed Lecie on her way to the kitchen for a wash bucket.

Lecie headed up the steps for one last check on her father before the inn began to fill. A shadow crossed her eyes to see him resting uneasily. Feeling guilty for neglecting him, she dabbed at his brow with a cool cloth until the late afternoon sun began to slant across the floor.

"I love you, Da," she whispered when she leaned to kiss his damp brow. Straightening she screamed when someone seized her arms roughly from behind.

"Keep your trap shut or you will wake him."

Breaking free, she whirled around to face an agitated Hamon. "Take your hands from me," she seethed. "Why are you even here? You very well know Joseph cannot attend the stand alone."

Out of breath, Hamon's eyes darted over his shoulder as he once again seized Lecie's upper arm. "Your man is on his way back here and afore he arrives, you and I need to settle a few things."

"Unhand me." Lecie winced in pain as Hamon half-dragged her out of the room and down the passageway.

Jerking her around the steps leading to the garret, Hamon forced her into the children's chamber.

Suddenly frightened of his intentions, Lecie began to struggle in earnest when he turned to bolt the door. "I demand that you unhand me or I shall scream the rafters down."

In response, Hamon slapped her hard across the face. Shoving her down on the edge of Clayton's pallet, he moved to stand above her. "I do not have time to play nice so I suggest you listen well."

"How dare you," Lecie breathed, raising a hand to her stinging cheek. "If my father had any intention of keeping you on, I vow he will not after I inform him of this."

"Shut your hole," Hamon snarled, slapping her again. "I have had enough of trying to woo you with kindness."

"Woo me?" Lecie leapt from the bed. "I would rather starve and be destitute than accept one such as you."

"After seeing you whore yourself out to Sir Albin, I know that now." Shoving her back down on the bed he leaned so close to her, she recoiled. "I also know that you would do anything for the young ones."

"What are you talking about?" Lecie's heart began to race as she stared up at him.

"Your lover and his friend caught me filching from the till. They now intend to bring the sheriff back with them to have me arrested."

"You stole from my father? How dare you do such a thing after all he has done for you?"

Grabbing her by the throat with rough calloused hands, Hamon pressed his thumbs into her windpipe and began to squeeze.

Chapter Six

"You will hold your tongue and listen to me," Hamon ground out with a sneer twisting his thin lips. "Do you understand?"

Clawing at his hands, Lecie managed a slight nod.

"That is better." Shoving her away Hamon watched with satisfaction as Lecie gasped for air. "I would rather not have to beat you into submission. "Twouldn't do if the sheriff were to find marks upon your pretty face."

"What is it you want?" Lecie began to back toward the door. "You have already helped yourself to everything we have."

"True enough," Hamon said. "Thanks to your dear da, I would be considered a wealthy man."

"Then why do you not flee with your ill-gotten gains afore the law catches up to you?"

"Because I want more," Hamon snarled, "and you are going to give it to me after vowing to the sheriff that the charges laid against me are false."

"Why would I do such a thing? You deserve whatever happens to you for betraying my father."

"That is where you are wrong." Hamon's eyes glittered as he observed her actions with a smirk. "I have no intention of swinging for taking my just due."

"Your just due?" Angry now, Lecie straightened to her full height. "My father has treated you fairly and you know it."

"Aye, he treated me fair enough for a spell." Hamon licked his lips while he ogled her heaving bosom. "That is, until I approached him to make an offer for you. Twas then I realized I was naught but a lowly servant in his eyes."

"You are a lowly servant, and a mad one to think I would ever accept you."

"Regardless, we shall come to an accord."

"Think what you will." Lecie prepared to make a run for it. "I shall speak the truth when the sheriff arrives."

"Not if you value the lad's life."

"You can do nothing to him dangling from a gibbet."

"Mayhap I cannot," Hamon replied casually, "yet I know a few men who would be willing to do anything for a few coins." With a laugh he added, "By the look on your face I reckon you are regretting barring them from the tavern a few months back. They did not like being ordered about by a woman when all they did was beat on some whores. The way I figure it, they have been looking for some payback ever since. Hell, they might even do the deed for me gratis."

"Animals are more civilized than your friends," Lecie snapped. "Harsent and Betta wore their bruises for a full month."

"That should tell you all you need to know about me," Hamon smirked. "Make no mistake, the future of this family hinges on the boy's survival. Go against me on this, and he will not live to see the first snowfall."

"How could you even threaten such a vile thing?" Lecie spoke in a fearful whisper. "Clayton has always been fond of you."

"He often journeys to the river's edge with the mutt, does he not?" Hamon went on as if he had not heard her. "How easy it would be for him to fall in and drown."

"I will slay you myself afore you lay a hand on him," Lecie vowed.

"The boy's fondness for me shall be of benefit should it come to that," Hamon said with a slight smile. "Thank you for the reminder."

Tears of frustration filled Lecie's eyes as she mentally searched for a way out of her predicament.

"What do you think would become of the lasses were they no longer to have a roof over their pretty little heads? I would hate for them to be forced into pleasuring men for room and board at so early an age." Leaning forward, Hamon's foul breath caressed Lecie's face. "However, I would gladly volunteer to break them in should that time come."

"You are a fiend."

Hamon seized Lecie's upper arms eliciting a cry of pain from her. "I suggest you do exactly as I say, lest I prove to you what a fiend I can be."

"Unhand me," Lecie said lowering her gaze. "Give me your word that no harm shall come to the children and I will do whatever you say."

Instead of releasing her, Hamon dug his fingers into her soft flesh. "Know you this, should you warn your lover in any way the boy will die." Hamon laughed bitterly as he nodded. "Aye, I know where your mind ventured, love. You think me daft to have not thought my plan through? If I am seized this day or another, there is nowhere you can hide the children that my friends cannot find."

"Do I have your word no harm shall befall the children after I lie for you?"

"Whatever makes you feel better, love." Hamon yanked Lecie against his bony chest to run his tongue along her cheek. "After you banish your lover and his fellow knight, I will get me a taste afore we discuss our future arrangement."

Repulsed by his touch, Lecie swallowed the bile burning the back of her throat. "How can I possibly ban Albin and Talan? His lordship is a powerful man and is sure to take offense if his knights are barred from staying here."

"I have no doubt you shall think of something." Pushing her back onto the bed, Hamon's eyes slid to her exposed legs.

Scrambling to her feet, Lecie turned her head when Hamon attempted to kiss her.

"You will come around in time," Hamon said caressing her cheek. "Treat me kindly and I shall be a generous lover."

♥

Shortly after, Gunilda found Lecie sobbing softly in her father's room. "Sheriff Richard is below asking for you, Lecie."

Turning red swollen eyes to the smug woman, Lecie fought the urge to slap her. "How could you go along with Hamon after all my family has done for you? My parents took you in when you were selling yourself in the open gutters."

"Your father is not long for this world." Gunilda shrugged. "Grateful as I may be, I need to secure my future."

"And you think Hamon is going to take care of you?" Lecie shook her head with a bitter laugh. "He thinks only of himself."

"You tell me nothing I do not know. At least when he is running the inn, I shall no longer have to toil for my keep."

"He will never run the inn," Lecie swore.

"Oh?" Gunilda seemed genuinely surprised. "When he told me that he spoke to you, I thought he told you everything."

"Which is?"

"Why, he intends to marry you of course." Gunilda smiled, exposing several missing teeth. "How else could he gain guardianship over the boy?"

"You are as mad as he if you think that day will ever come." Lecie lowered her voice when her father shifted in his fitful sleep. "I gave him my word I shall cover his thievery and send the knights from the inn." Sweeping past Gunilda into the passageway, she added, "And that is all he shall ever get from me."

Gunilda followed her out to call softly, "I would not be so sure of that. In the end, Hamon always gets what he wants."

Lecie felt sick to her stomach as she numbly made her way down the steps.

She heard raised voices above the usual din of the crowd prior to entering the common room. Pausing only long enough to take a steadying breath, she ignored the feel of her heart breaking and stepped into the midst of the turmoil.

Spotting her, Sheriff Richard broke away from his sons, Edmund and Leofrick, who were keeping an eye on Hamon. "I fear I have brought more trouble to your door this day, Lecie."

"Shall we move to a quieter place, Sheriff?"

Extending his hand in the direction of the kitchen, the sheriff allowed her to precede him. She ignored the curious gazes cast her way by the villagers as she led the group to the narrow hallway in the back.

Noticeably quieter, she waited for the men to file into the passageway around her. Avoiding Albin's concerned gaze from where he stood alongside Talan, she clasped her hands to exude a calm she did not feel. "After these days past, I can scarce believe more trouble to be possible. What seems to be amiss?"

"First, I would ask after my old friend as I have been lax on my visits to him. How is Edric faring?"

"I fear he does not have much time left," Lecie replied softly. "He is in so much pain that I sometimes feel his passing will be a blessing."

"It saddens me to hear it," Richard said. "If you permit, I would pay my respects afore departing."

"I know he will be most pleased to see you."

"Now then, let us address the matter at hand." Clearing his throat, the sheriff gestured to Hamon where he stood confidently between Leofrick and Edmund. "Our visit here today has to do with your tapster."

"Hamon?" Lecie's eyes briefly settled on the loathsome man before returning to the sheriff. "Whatever could he have done to warrant such an imposing show of force?"

"He is a thief," Albin spoke up from his place beside Talan. "We caught him stealing from the till numerous times. There is no telling how far back his thieving goes."

Lecie calmly faced Albin and forced herself to feel nothing. "You say that you witnessed Hamon stealing from the till, Sir Albin?"

"I did." Confused by her manner, Albin continued, "Talan and I both saw him pocket a coin for every one he collected at the bar so we set a trap for him today in the square."

"What Sir Albin states is true," Edmund said. "I witnessed it for myself earlier this day. Afore we could arrest him, he fled. Unfortunately, he threw us by heading into the woods or we would have arrived here sooner."

"No matter," Albin said, "he did not have enough time to remove the evidence from the premises. A thorough search should uncover proof of his thievery."

Lecie refused to meet Albin's penetrating gaze by focusing on the bridge of his nose. "Let me get this straight, you set a trap for Hamon without first approaching me?"

"Tis a serious allegation and we needed proof." Albin stepped closer to her. "Why are you behaving this way, Lecie?"

"I have no idea what you mean."

Albin noted Hamon's smug look and came to the correct conclusion. "He may not have had enough time to move the coin but he certainly had enough to threaten you. What did the wretch say to you?"

"My, Sir Albin, you really do have a fanciful imagination." Lecie then lowered her eyes to speak the lie to the sheriff. "I am sorry you wasted your time but this is all a misunderstanding. Twas I who asked Hamon to pocket the coins."

"The hell you did." Albin stepped closer to Lecie causing her to step back. "Tell me what he said and I shall drag him to the scaffold myself."

"Sir Albin," Sheriff Richard said. "I must ask you to calm yourself."

"Sheriff," Lecie said, "I asked Hamon some time ago to pocket half of each charge in the event we are raided. That way, we would not lose all of our profit."

"That was very wise of you," Richard said. "Inns bring in strangers and one cannot be too careful nowadays."

"Now that we have cleared that up, we are quite busy as you can see." Turning her attention to Hamon, she added, "Serve the sheriff and his sons whatever they would like for going to such trouble on our behalf."

"Your pleasure is mine, Mistress Lecie." Hamon intentionally bumped into Albin on his way to the bar. "

"You low lump of a turd," Albin seethed. "If you think—"

"As for you, Sir Albin," Lecie interrupted before he could say more. "You have accused a loyal worker of a grievous wrong which very well could have cost him a hand, if not his life. The only way I can see to make amends to him is to ask you and Sir Talan to withdraw from these premises at once. You are no longer welcome here."

"That seems a bit much, do not you think?" Leofrick spoke from behind his father. "After all they were seeing to your welfare."

"'Tis not our decision," Richard chastised his son.

Silently communicating with Talan with a jerk of the head, Albin waited until Hamon was out of earshot.

Obviously pleased by the outcome, Hamon filled cups of ale to overflowing with a self-satisfied smirk.

"Now that he is gone, will you speak the truth, lass?"

"Are you calling me a liar, Sir Albin?"

"I will take that as a no." Shaking his head, he shouted, "Hamon should have known better than to threaten the children."

Lecie gasped and her eyes darted toward Hamon.

Glancing over his shoulder, Hamon's panicked expression told Albin all he needed to know.

Regaining her composure, Lecie raised her voice to be heard over the descending silence. "Once again, I am afraid I do not know what you are talking about, Sir Albin."

"Do you not?" He questioned her softly, his gaze never leaving hers. "I have come to know you so well that I think otherwise."

"Sheriff," Lecie said turning her back on Albin. "You said twas my decision. Is it not my right to refuse these men room and board?"

"Since Edric is unable to make such decisions, you currently have the right to act on his behalf," Richard said. "Yet are you sure tis something he would do? These men are not only knights of the realm here at the behest of King Henry, they are friends."

"I have made my decision and since as you say, tis my right to do so, I would like them to depart posthaste."

"Perhaps we should bring the matter to Edric's attention."

"Would you burden a dying man with such as this? Regardless of their rank, duty, and familiarity, I will not have them falsely accuse a member of my staff." When the sheriff was about to argue, Lecie added, "Can I, or can I not have them arrested for trespass if they refuse to leave?"

"Lecie." Sheriff Richard appeared scandalized. "I know you have been overly taxed of late, yet you must think of what you are saying."

"Are you refusing to do your duty as sworn to the king, Sheriff?"

The sheriff seemed unsure of what to do when Tugger bounded into the passageway with Clayton hard on his heels.

Jumping up on Albin the dog whined for attention. "I did my best to stay in the kitchen like you instructed, Sir Albin. Tugger had other ideas."

"No harm done, lad." Albin's eyes narrowed on Lecie. "Besides, it looks to me like we are finished here."

"Clayton," Lecie said rushing to his side, "tis past time for your bath. Go on up and I shall join you momentarily."

"Do I really have to?" Clayton turned an imploring gaze upon her.

"Take Tugger above this instant," Lecie snapped.

Stung by her harsh tone, Clayton turned sad eyes on Albin. "Thank you for taking me to the festival today."

"Twas my pleasure, lad." Albin ruffled Clayton's hair with a fond smile. "Best do as you are told now."

"Thank you too, Leofrick," Clayton called as he led Tugger away. "The puppet show was ever so much fun."

Lecie observed the twins hovering within earshot through the archway leading to the kitchen. "Osana and Sabina," she snapped, "see to Clayton and go to bed."

Sharing a perplexed look at Lecie's unusual display of temper, the twins hastened up the steps.

Emboldened by Lecie's defense, Hamon came to pass out cups of ale to the sheriff and his sons. Passing close behind her in the narrow space, he lightly caressed her shoulder.

"Lecie, I understand—" The sheriff stopped mid-sentence when Albin made a lunge for Hamon.

"You lying, thieving churl," Albin snarled seizing the startled tapster. "What did you say to her?"

Talan put Albin in a chokehold to pull him off Hamon. "This is not the way to go about it," he whispered in his friend's ear.

Shoving Hamon away from him, Albin fumed in silence.

"We shall do as Lecie has requested and make camp at the tower for the duration of our stay in Rochester." Talan informed the astonished sheriff.

"Under the circumstances I believe that would be best."

"As do I," Talan said before turning to Lecie. "Would you permit us to gather our belongings?"

"By all means," Lecie said breaking eye contact.

"Albin," Talan prodded softly, "come, my friend."

His fists still clenched, Albin stepped in front of Lecie. Only when she reluctantly met his gaze did he nod curtly in dismissal. "Goodbye, Lecie."

"Fare thee well, Sir Albin," Lecie whispered.

She wiped a stray tear from her cheek when she moved to watch Albin ascend the steps. Noting Hamon's regard, she turned her back on him. "Sheriff, we have a stew this eve if you and your sons would care for some."

"I believe we have already overstayed our welcome." Gesturing to his sons, Richard's gaze touched on Hamon. "If you will permit it, I would like to pay my respects to your father now."

Glancing over her shoulder at Hamon, Lecie struggled to keep her tone neutral. "Hamon, I shall return to lend assist after Sheriff Richard pays his respects to my father."

"Do hurry," Hamon said with narrowed eyes, "tis more than I can handle by myself."

Sheriff Richard quietly observed the exchange before extending his arm toward the steps, "Shall we, Lecie?"

Her heart breaking, Lecie was oblivious to the curious stares directed her way as they made their way through the tables.

Sheriff Richard on the other hand was keenly aware that the topic of conversation had changed. "Go about your business," he called. "Nothing worth gossiping about has occurred here."

On the way up the steps, Lecie prayed for one more glimpse of Albin before he walked out of her life forever.

The sheriff clasped her arm when she was about to enter her father's chamber. "Is it true, Lecie? Did Hamon threaten you?"

An image of Clayton strolling alone along the riverbank had her shaking her head. "No," she replied truthfully, "he has not threatened to harm me."

The sheriff searched her eyes for the truth until he seemed to accept her response. "I realize the strain you are under of late. You do know you can come to me with anything, do you not?"

Her gaze involuntarily moving to Albin's door, Lecie came close to blurting out the truth. "Thank you, Sheriff. I do know that."

♥

Shoving his belongings into his saddle-pack, Albin mumbled an expletive.

Talan was standing in the doorway waiting for Albin to finish when he caught sight of Lecie entering her father's chamber. "Are you sure about this?"

"Aye." Albin angrily snatched up his pack. "She was scared and I would wager my sword arm he threatened harm to the children."

"Then we shall get to the bottom of it," Talan said. "Only do try and keep your head about you until after we leave. The last thing we need is for Richard to arrest you for... well... for being you."

Ignoring Talan's advice, Albin shoved past him. "If that shite Hamon so much as looks in my direction I shall wring his scrawny neck."

"Bloody hell," Talan hissed, "do not make threats within earshot of the sheriff."

"Hang the sheriff," Albin grumbled. "If he were worth his salt he would have already wrung a confession out of the sod."

Passing the master chamber the anger drained from Albin's face when he spotted Lecie kneeling beside the bed holding Edric's hand. His first thought to comfort her he stood undecided in the doorway.

She briefly looked up at him with anguished eyes.

"We must go," Talan said softly from behind him.

Tearing his gaze away from Lecie, Albin bounded down the steps.

Since dark had fallen the common room had filled to standing room only.

Weaving their way through the boisterous crowd, Talan waved Leofrick back into his seat when he shifted to stand. "We came to take our leave, my friend."

"And to ask that you keep a wary eye on Hamon," Albin added glancing toward the bar. "He is blackmailing Lecie sure as I am standing here."

"Cool your ire." Leofrick spoke above the din of drunken revelers. "My father is not fooled by Hamon. I could tell by his manner."

"Then why has he not arrested the fiend?" Albin shot back.

"Easy." Talan leaned close to say. "You risk causing offense to the few who are willing to lend us assist."

"Forgive me," Albin grumbled to Leofrick, "I am unused to feeling helpless."

"Not necessary." Leofrick brushed it off. "We are as fond of Lecie as you appear to be, only in a more familial way."

"My concern is for the children as well."

"Of course it is," Leofrick said with a telling grin. "Now that Edric is incapable of handling the situation, my family will look after them."

"That is good enough for me," Albin said with a nod.

"Talan." Leofrick changed the subject. "Why do you not come for a visit on the morrow? After the misfortunate turn of events at the festival, I know Mylla would be pleased to spend more time with you."

"Thank you, I shall." Nodding to the remaining men, Talan nudged Albin toward the exit. "We will make camp on the south side of the tower should you have need of us."

Reluctant to leave, Albin took his time mounting his horse. With a pensive look, he spurred his horse into an easy trot beside Talan's.

The two friends rode east on the path winding alongside the River Medway. Passing flickering lights of several small campfires, Albin dismounted in the shadow of the scaffolding rising high above them. Securing his horse for the night, he ignored the curious gazes directed at them by the itinerant workers.

"Hamon knows we are onto him," Talan said unbuckling his saddle. "He will not do anything foolish so soon after speaking to the sheriff."

Resting against his saddle on the damp ground, Albin responded with a non-committal grunt.

Talan settled down beside him preparing to wait out Albin's foul mood.

Gazing at the star-filled night sky, Albin eventually broke the silence. "Lecie loves Edric."

The last thing he expected to hear, Talan studied Albin's silhouetted profile. "Did you have some doubt?"

"I just never realized how much is all."

"Edric is all she and the children have." Talan propped himself on an elbow. "Once he is gone, Lecie will be left without a man's protection. If Hamon is any indication, you can see for yourself what is in store for her."

"Edric made me promise that I would look after her," Albin admitted. "More than look after her, he asked me to marry her."

"Is that not something you have wanted for some time?"

Albin jerked his head in Talan's direction. "Leofrick alluded to it and now you call me on it. Was I so obvious?"

"Even Gervase discerned your feelings for Lecie."

"Zounds," Albin swore, "I have tried so hard to conceal my feelings for her."

"Why would you do that? Tis obvious Lecie shares your attraction even our liege has made mention of it."

"I cannot believe I have to explain this to you," Albin said. "Edric is my friend. I would never dishonor him in such a way, and I cannot believe you of all people would even consider it."

"You think me callous?" When Albin refused to respond, Talan continued, "Edric would rest easier knowing Lecie's future is secured. If you were in his place, would not you?"

"I wish to discuss it no further." Albin changed the subject. "What do you suggest we do to expose Hamon?"

"Since we have been banned there is very little we can do," Talan said. "On the morrow I was going to ask Leofrick, Frederick, and Caine to keep a close watch on Hamon and the children. They will be more apt to help us than Edmund. He is a self-serving sod if I have ever met one."

"Keeping watch over them will not expose Hamon for what he is."

"Then what do you propose?"

"I have to get Lecie alone," Albin said without elaborating.

"Do you honestly think she will confide in you?" Talan settled back against his saddle. "By her reaction in the common room, tis obvious she fears Hamon."

"I do not plan on giving her a choice," Albin ground out. "I will not rest until she tells me what hold Hamon has upon her."

Pulling his cloak tight around him, Talan closed his eyes. "When exactly do you plan on approaching her? She rarely leaves the inn."

"When I am assured the festival revelers have returned to their cottages."

His eyes flying open, Talan sat up. "You mean to return to the inn this night? Do you think it wise?"

"Aye," Albin said, "I do. I shall not have Lecie live another moment in fear of Hamon."

"Of course you are right. Hamon's chamber is off the common room. Do you think we can enter without his knowledge?"

"We? You are courting the sheriff's daughter," Albin said. "Do you think it wise to risk a charge of trespass?"

"Lecie would never follow through with pressing charges against us." Talan brushed off the threat with an air of confidence. "How could you even think she would?"

"To protect the ones she loves, I believe her to be capable of much more than that."

"Either way, I am going with you." Talan resettled himself. "Your temper cannot be trusted in the vicinity of Hamon."

"You keep mentioning my temper. What of your display this afternoon with de Glanville?"

"I suppose we both shall just have to work on it," Talan said. "One thing is for sure, if de Glanville thinks I will meekly step aside so he can wed Mylla, he is in for a rude awakening."

"Is he? What do you plan to do about it?"

"Let us deal with your situation first." Talan closed his eyes. "Wake me when tis time to go."

His thoughts turning to what he would say to Lecie, Albin once again resumed his stargazing vigil.

♥

Apart from a few drunken stragglers at the bar, the common room stood empty when Lecie wearily made her way up the steps to the sleeping chambers. Checking on her father one last time before turning in, she found herself entering Albin's vacated chamber.

Setting the lit tallow on the dresser, she opened the shutters to let in the cool evening breeze. Moonlight streamed across the polished wood flooring as she gazed down at the gardens lost in thought.

Tears burned the back of her eyes and she eventually blew out the tallow to curl up in her chemise on the unmade bed. Giving into her heartbreak, she inhaled Albin's musky clean scent on the sheets and sobbed brokenly until exhaustion finally claimed her.

In the middle of a disturbing dream, Lecie woke to the sound of the floor creaking outside her door. Fearing it could be Hamon, she climbed from the bed to put her ear to the door.

Her protective instinct had her flinging the door wide when the tread of booted feet made their way past. Startling the silhouetted figure far too tall and muscular to be Hamon, she stood her ground. "Who are you and what do you want?" The fear in her voice palpable, her heart hammered against her ribcage.

"Have no fear, lass, tis me."

"Albin." Lecie came close to collapsing against him in relief. "What are you doing here?"

"I need to speak with you."

Recalling the danger he placed Clayton in by returning, she motioned him into the chamber so she could close the door. "I thought I made it perfectly clear that you and Sir Talan are no longer welcome here."

"Aye, you did that well enough." Closing the distance between them in two strides, he gazed into her upturned face. "What has Hamon threatened you with?"

"I do not know what you are talking about." Unsettled by his nearness, Lecie averted her eyes. "You accused an innocent man of a heinous crime and I merely held you accountable for doing so."

"Bullocks," Albin swore softly. "You cannot even look me in the eye when you spew that shite."

Accustomed to hearing vulgar language in the tavern, Lecie did not even flinch. "Men like you deem themselves above commoners like me and Hamon." Calmly meeting his gaze, Lecie struggled with her roiling emotions. "Is that the reason you took such offense to being banned from the inn?"

"There is nothing common about you." Seizing her shoulders, Albin pulled her against him. "What has he threatened you with, lass? Tell me so I can help you."

Torn between her fear of Hamon and her instinct to trust Albin, she remained speechless. Her golden-brown eyes glittered when she stared up at him in mute appeal.

"Lecie," he whispered brokenly.

In response, her full lips parted in the only invitation he was waiting for. Seizing her lips, Albin dragged her against the hardness of his chest. Gently coaxing her lips apart with the tip of his tongue, he slipped it inside to join with hers in a dance as old as time.

Crushed against his chest, Lecie's hands slid around his waist to draw him even closer as she moaned with the pleasure his touch elicited.

Lifting her off the ground, Albin crossed to the bed to follow her down upon it without breaking their kiss.

He broke away for a breath, cradling her face in his hands. "God forgive me, I am not strong enough to resist you."

"I am not asking you to," Lecie said breathlessly.

"Edric." Albin spoke the name standing between them.

"What about him?" Lecie searched Albin's troubled gaze.

"Are you certain you want to do this to him?"

"He would not approve so I have no intention of telling him," Lecie said reaching up to caress his rugged jawline.

Albin remained undecided until her fingers gliding through his hair snatched any thought of refusal from him. "I have waited for this moment for what seems to be the whole of my life," he said giving into temptation.

"Then let us not waste it," she breathed. "Kiss me, Albin."

Capturing her lips, Albin slid his calloused sword hand up her slim waist to cup a full breast beneath the thin linen chemise. A low groan escaped him when Lecie arched her back into his caress seeking more.

His mouth trailing along her face and neck, Albin pulled the chemise down to expose Lecie's breasts to the cold night air. The peak of one hardened as he lightly thumbed it before drawing it into his mouth.

Lecie's small gasp encouraged him as she twined her fingers in his hair to hold him close against her.

Lifting his gaze to hers, Albin's lids were heavy with desire as he rent the chemise from collar to hem in one fluid motion. "I must see all of you."

Lost to the first stirrings of desire, Lecie watched him as he drank in the sight of her naked body.

"I will gladly pay penance for the rest of my life for this one night with you." With the look of a starved man, Albin nudged her knees apart before capturing her lips in a bruising kiss.

Lecie moaned in ecstasy when the feel of his body against her bare flesh had her seeking something she could not name.

Reaching between their bodies, Albin untied his breeches to shove them down. "Forgive me I can wait no longer to claim you."

In one fluid motion, he entered her only to gasp in astonishment when he broke through her maidenhead.

Lecie's shocked cry of pain had Albin leaping backward off the bed. Frozen in shock, he stood staring down at her. "Impossible," he breathed. "How can this be?"

Alarmed by his reaction, Lecie scrambled to cover her nakedness with the coverlet. "Did I do something wrong?"

"You are a maiden," Albin accused.

Stung by his tone, Lecie sat up. "Of course I am…was. Why would you believe otherwise?"

Roughly dragging his hands through his hair, Albin frowned when he spotted a smear of blood on the sheets. "It cannot be."

"Oh, I see." Anger suffused Lecie's cheeks with color when she stood on the bed to meet his confused gaze. "You think because I run a tavern that I am naught but a whore."

"I think no such thing," Albin retorted, belatedly adjusting his clothing. "That is the last title I would lay at your feet."

"I do not believe you." Lecie backed out of his reach when he held a hand out to her. "By virtue of breeding, all titled men believe themselves superior to those they deem beneath them."

"You are being nonsensical." Albin attempted to sooth her. "I do not put myself above anyone nor do any of Fulke's knights for that matter. We have all earned by toil and blood what we have in this life."

"Then why did you believe me to be unchaste, if not for the fact that I am a lowly alewife?"

"I will not have you talk about yourself in such a manner," Albin said failing to make sense of the situation.

"Then answer my question," Lecie shot back. "Why did you doubt my chastity?"

"How can you possibly be chaste?" Albin came close to shouting. "You are a married woman with three children!"

Stunned into silence, Lecie stood looking at him with a blank expression until his words slowly sank in. Her eyes narrowed to angry slits the instant she realized the misconception he had assumed for so long. "You believe Edric to be my husband?"

"Is he not?" Confused, Albin reached for her shoulders.

"And if that were not bad enough." Lecie slapped his hand away to leap from the bed. "You believe me low enough to make a cuckold of a dying man. A man lying paces from this very room."

"Well," Albin mumbled once again reaching out to her, "I did not exactly look at things that way."

"Of course you did or you would never have made mention of him." Humiliated and embarrassed, Lecie attempted to cover every inch of her exposed skin. "How dare you, and how dare I for believing better of you."

"Please—"

"Get out." Lecie's voice was so low she cleared her throat to speak louder. "Get out and never come back."

"Lecie—"

"Leave before I scream," she snapped. "I do not ever want to see you again."

"Surely, you can see how I would mistake the situation?" Albin struggled in vain to make amends. "I had no idea. None of us did."

"You are an outright liar," Lecie shouted loud enough to be heard in the passageway.

"I speak the truth." Albin spoke in a soothing tone. "Fulke assumed as I. Although he did not approve, he accepted my feelings for you without condemnation."

Past conversations with his lordship asking after Albin played in Lecie's mind. Angry tears burned the back of her eyes when she said, "Then you are both fools."

Glancing nervously at the door when the sound of voices carried to them, Albin swore, "I know I have been a fool but I am not leaving here until we sort this out, lass."

"There is nothing to sort out," Lecie angrily responded. "Darken my door again and I shall have you arrested for trespass."

"Please do not do this," Albin implored, "twas a simple misunderstanding."

"Our entire acquaintanceship has been a misunderstanding," Lecie said backing him into the passageway. "Goodbye, Sir Albin." The instant he cleared the threshold, she slammed and bolted the door.

"But I love you," he whispered to the empty passageway.

Chapter Seven

Hearing stirrings in the adjacent chambers, Albin rushed down the steps and nearly ripped the inn's door from its iron hinges when he stormed outside.

Talan raced from the shadows with sword drawn, expecting trouble. "Albin, are you mad?" he hissed, sheathing his weapon when no one followed after his friend. "You are bound to awaken the entire village."

"I do not give a bloody—"

"What did Lecie say to get you so riled?"

"How do you know twas Lecie?" Untying his horse, Albin fought to gain control of his temper.

"Owing to the fact that I spied Gunilda slip into Hamon's chamber shortly after you went in." Talan glanced toward the dark windows of the inn. "We best be off since I would not be surprised if they were to awaken after your boisterous exit."

"Then let us be off afore he shows himself and I slay him." Vaulting into the saddle of his black destrier, Albin spurred the animal into a gallop.

Spotting light coming from the tavern, Talan quickly followed.

Ashamed and disgusted, Albin's pace had clumps of soil churning beneath the battle-trained horse's hooves. He did not slow until he reached the Tower.

Reining up, he dismounted to give the horse an affectionate slap on the hindquarters. "Do not wander far afield."

Talan slowed to a halt to dismount at a much more leisurely pace. "Care to enlighten me as to what happened back there?"

Dropping to the ground, Albin covered his face with his hands. "I am a bloody fool that is what happened."

Settling down beside his friend, Talan gave him time to settle down.

"We were wrong about Lecie," Albin said after a lengthy silence.

"How so?"

"She is not Edric's wife," Albin said. "She is his eldest daughter."

"How could you not know that?"

Swinging his head to look at Talan, Albin's dark brows drew up in surprise. "Are you telling me that you knew?"

"Mylla told me as much when we first met in London," Talan said. "By your interest in her I assumed you knew."

"Bloody hell," Albin swore nearly gaining his feet. "It should have been obvious to you that I did not."

"I thought you were unsure of your feelings for her." Talan lowered his eyes. "In hindsight, I can now see what you mean."

"You think? Even Fulke does not know the truth of their relationship," Albin hissed. "He all but assured me that he would have my back were I to make a cuckold of Edric."

"Well now that you know the truth, why are you not pleased?"

"I insulted her most grievously." Closing his eyes, Albin shook his head in frustration. "She will never forgive me and rightly so."

"What did you say to her?"

"I am so ashamed I cannot bring myself to tell you."

"Listen to me," Talan said. "Lecie is nothing if not compassionate. Tell her how you feel, and I am sure she will forgive you."

"No, she will not." Albin settled down on his side facing away from Talan.

"Albin…"

"Get some sleep," Albin muttered. "I still have to figure out what to do about Hamon."

"Would you like me to—"

"No, and I do not wish to discuss it further," Albin ground out hating himself.

Long after Talan fell asleep, Albin lay awake. Recalling the feel of Lecie in his arms, he memorized every detail of their brief time together knowing it would have to last him a lifetime.

♥

Lecie stood with her back against the chamber door after Albin left. She idly listened to lodgers moving about while they attempted to discover the noise that had awoken them.

One boarder's angry voice broke through her chaotic thoughts. "I shall have words with the innkeeper come first light."

"You certainly will not." Lecie recognized Betta's weary tone. "The poor man is knocking at death's door."

"That is no excuse," the gruff boarder complained. "I did not pay good coin to be so rudely awakened in the middle of the night."

"No doubt a lovers spat." Another voice faded off down the hall.

Lecie waited until the passageway grew quiet before collapsing to the floor in sobs.

Her cheek to the hardwood flooring, she wept until sheer exhaustion swept her into a fitful sleep filled with disturbing dreams.

She woke in the dawn's early light stiff and disoriented. Sitting up she took in the state of the disheveled bed while scenes from the night before flashed through her mind.

Slowly gaining her feet, her eyes focused on the proof of her maidenhood staining the sheets. Angry tears filled her eyes as she crossed to the bed to tear the soiled linen from it.

Bundling the sheet into a ball, she retrieved clean clothing from the garret and made her way to the bathing chamber.

Albin's musky scent wafted up to her when she disrobed causing angry tears to slip down her cheeks. Tossing the chemise on top of the bed linens, she began to scrub herself hoping to erase the memory of his touch.

Tender and sore, she now had a newfound respect for the women who serviced the tavern. No wonder they needed to fortify themselves with drink first. Determined to be more understanding of their plight, she quickly dried off to dress.

Donning a brown chemise, she struggled with the side laces on the cream wool kirtle she pulled over top of it. Her hands shook when she recalled Albin's hands caressing her.

With an unladylike curse, she finished in a rush. Intent to dispose of the evidence of her shame, she snatched up the bundle and hastened to the kitchens to stoke the fire.

Betta strolled in when she was tossing the sheet into the flaming hearth. Watching the linen smolder and turn brown to black, Lecie buried her feelings behind a mask of calm.

"Whyever are you burning costly linen, lassie? Your father shall not take kindly to you doing such a thing."

"As you well know, my father is beyond taking me to task for such things."

"You seem out of sorts this morning," Betta said with a look of concern.

"I am tired." Lecie eased her tone. "Would you mind waking the children for me?"

"Worry not, I shall see to them." Gently squeezing Lecie's shoulder on her way out, Betta added, "We cannot afford to have you fall ill."

Brushing a tear from her cheek, Lecie busied herself preparing the morning meal.

♥

Later in the day Albin stood at the tower half-listening to the master builder drone on about construction costs when the messenger he sent to Castell Maen rode into view. Excusing himself, he met the rider in the courtyard.

"I have medicine from her ladyship, Sir Albin." Digging into his worn leather pack, the messenger passed him a velvet pouch. "Lady Reina instructed that a fair measure be added to broth or warmed cider thrice a day."

"Do you carry any other news from Castell Maen?"

"Aye, Sir." The messenger lowered his voice. "Her ladyship wishes you and Sir Talan good health. Baron Erlegh asked me to convey that he is in high hopes that all is going well with you on the battle front."

"The battle front?"

"That is what he said, Sir. He further instructed me to say that he looks forward to the day that you return with a lady in tow to bend the knee."

"Battle front indeed," Albin scoffed under his breath when he recalled the wager he made with Fulke. Digging a few silver coins from his pouch, he handed them to the messenger. "Thank you for your haste."

"I shall again draw near to Castell Maen on my way south," the messenger said mounting his horse. "Do you have a response for his lordship?"

"I do," Albin said with a glum look. "Tell him I am a hopeless case and whilst here will dedicate my time to the tower. Sir Talan's predicament appears to be no better than mine."

"Aye, Sir."

Talan approached from the back of the tower as the messenger rode off. "Did her ladyship send medicine for Edric?"

"That she did." Albin tossed Talan the pouch. "And it looks like you will have to be the one to deliver it."

"What would you have me say to Lecie when I do?"

"Instruct her that a fair measure needs to be added to broth or warmed cider thrice a day." Albin said. "I shall pray it eases Edric's pain."

"Surely there is something on a more personal note you would like me to pass along?"

"Tell her..." Running a hand along his whiskered jaw, Albin exhaled heavily. "Nothing."

"Albin."

"Edric suffers whilst you waste time on something that cannot be fixed," Albin said gazing off toward the village. "Let it be."

Briefly gripping Albin's shoulder, Talan shook his head. "You give up far too easily, my friend."

"It appears we must follow through with your plan," Albin said. "After you deliver the medicine, explain all to Mylla's brothers, will you?"

"Why do you not come with? If we discuss it altogether we may come up with something better."

"Of late I have been neglectful of my duty to Fulke," Albin said. "That is one thing I can fix."

"Tis a pity you will not at least deliver the medicine," Talan said heading toward his horse, "I know how grateful Lecie will be to receive it."

Albin mentally weighed his options. Even despising him as she did, he knew she would be grateful. Perhaps then she would be more willing to accept his apology. Running after Talan, he felt a glimmer of hope.

Already in the saddle, Talan passed the pouch to Albin with a pleased look.

"I have no intention of surrendering," Albin grumbled as he spurred his horse in the direction of the village.

"Twould surprise me if you did."

Reaching the inn, Albin slowed his horse to a walk. "I think it best that you go in alone and tell Lecie that I would like a word with her in private. I shall wait in the garden but do not be overly surprised if she refuses to see me."

"I shall just have to convince her," Talan said dismounting. "Whatever you said to offend her, this is your best chance to make amends. Do try not to louse it up."

"Thanks for your vote of confidence." Albin scowled. "If Hamon gives you any trouble, summon me at once."

"Think you I cannot handle him myself?" Talan's hand slid to the hilt of his sword. "He would not be fool enough to take me on so I may have to goad him a bit."

"What are you two doing here?"

The taunting voice from behind them had Albin reaching for his sword.

"Ah," Talan said, "speak of the devil and he appears."

"You have not answered my question." Keeping his distance, Hamon kept his gaze fixed on Albin.

"Tis not your concern," Albin sneered.

"Oh, but it is," Hamon said. "Lecie banned you from the place with the sheriff as witness, or have you forgotten so soon?"

"And who is going to stop us? You?" Talan laughed.

"I suggest you ask your mistress to attend us afore I take pleasure in removing you from our path," Albin said approaching Hamon. "The choice is yours but either way, we will speak to her."

Assessing the situation, Hamon's lip curled into a sneer. "Wait here."

"That went well," Talan said watching Hamon race through the back door.

"It took every ounce of my self-control not to run the..." Albin fell silent when the door to the inn swung outward.

Followed closely by Hamon, Lecie stepped into the yard with an impassive look. Ignoring Albin altogether, she focused solely on Talan. "You wished to see me, Sir Talan?"

"Aye Lecie, we did. In response to Sir Albin's message, her ladyship has sent medicine for your father."

"He is desperately in need of something to ease his pain." Her eyes flying to Albin's, Lecie struggled with her composure when he handed her the pouch. "I do not know how to thank you."

"Lecie," Hamon spoke from behind her. "Have you seen Clayton about? I need his assist with something."

"You thieving piece of shite," Albin snarled, making a lunge for Hamon. "I know you used the boy to threaten her."

"No," Lecie shrieked when Talan tackled Albin driving him face first into the ground. "Do not hurt him."

"Get off me," Albin ground out when he could not toss Talan off his back.

"Give me your word you will make no move against Hamon," Talan hissed in his ear. When Albin refused to speak, Talan adjusted his knees in the center of his back. "I can remain like this all day if need be."

Albin bucked until with a loud curse he stilled. "I give you my word not to hurt the sod."

Rising, Talan offered Albin a hand up.

With narrowed eyes, Albin knocked Talan's hand aside to stand. "We shall speak of this later."

"If I were you," Talan said to Hamon, "I would wipe that smug look off your face afore Albin breaks his word and I let him."

Wisely holding his tongue Hamon kept a close watch on Albin.

"Lecie," Talan said as if nothing out of the ordinary had occurred, "Lady Reina instructed that a fair measure of the medicine be added to broth or warmed cider with each meal."

"Thank you. If you will excuse me, I shall see that my father gets some right away."

"Lecie," Albin said when she turned to go, "I make no apology for my attack on Hamon, yet I regret it distressed you."

"Twas not he I was concerned about," Lecie replied softly. "After your kindness, I could not bear to see you hurt."

"Then admit he threatened the lad and I vow he will pay for it."

"You mistake my momentary concern for forgiveness, Sir Albin." Avoiding his gaze, Lecie studied the curve of his full lower lip. "I assure you there is no change in my intent of yesterday."

Turning her back, Lecie entered the inn.

"Seems like she is shut of you once and for all," Hamon taunted over his shoulder as he followed Lecie inside.

Talan gripped Albin's shoulder to keep him from going after Hamon. "Well that meeting could have gone better."

His mouth dropping open, Albin turned an incredulous look on his friend. "Do you think? Why did you stop me from giving Hamon the beating he so rightly deserves?"

"I may not be savvy like Gervase and Guy when it comes to romance but I would wager pommeling Hamon is not the best way to get back into Lecie's good graces," Talan said. "Tis obvious she is afraid of him and I agree with you, it likely has something to do with Clayton."   "Then all we have to do now is find out what Hamon's planning so we can put an end to him once and for all," Albin said with a determined look.

"Right you are," Talan agreed. "By the way, did it escape your notice that's Lecie's concern lay with you?"

"You heard her, it changes nothing."

"I do not know about you, my friend, but I rarely concern myself with people I do not care about." Slapping Albin on the shoulder, Talan said in parting, "Something for you to think about."

Watching Talan ride off, Albin's gaze shifted to Edric's open window.

♥

"Get out of my way, Hamon." Intent to give her father the medicine, Lecie attempted to leave the kitchen with a cup of cider in her hand.

"You did well out there," Hamon said. "I must say, it stung me a bit to hear twas Sir Albin's welfare and not mine that you were concerned about."

"Twould never be yours." Lecie moved to slip by him when he roughly seized her upper arm.

"I suggest you sweeten your words to me," he hissed in her ear, "lest I forget myself and treat you no better than you deserve."

"Go to the devil." Pulling free of his grasp, Lecie passed into the common room. "I must ease my father's suffering."

Several local patrons looked up in surprise at her unusual show of anger.

Pausing to collect her tumultuous thoughts at the top of the steps, Lecie willed her racing heart to slow. Despite all that had occurred between them and against her own wishes, she knew that she was in love with Albin. If not for Hamon's subtle threat against Clayton, she never would have been able to ignore the longing she saw in his eyes.

With a steadying breath, she pasted a smile on her face and entered her father's chamber.

Moaning weakly in his sleep the dark shadows beneath his eyes stood out in stark contrast to his ashen face.

Lecie's smile faltered when she knelt beside the bed. "Da," she spoke softly to wake him, "I have medicine from Lady Reina that will help you rest easier."

His pain-filled eyes fluttered open to focus on her face. "Elena," he wheezed, "you have come for me at last."

"No, Da." Tears filled Lecie's eyes at the mention of her mother. "Tis, Lecie."

"Lass, I had hoped—"

"I know," she interrupted before he could finish. "I brought medicine to make you more comfortable."

"Dr. Rayburn?" he managed.

"He shall never darken our door again." Propping him up, Lecie held the cup to his lips. "Sir Albin was kind enough to send a messenger to Baroness Erlegh on our behalf."

Drinking as much of the cider as he could manage, he lay back. "He is a good man."

"Aye, he is." Lecie averted her eyes by placing the cup on the nightstand. "Do you need anything else?"

Closing his eyes, her father shook his head. "Naught that you can help me with."

"Then get some rest." Lecie stood to place a kiss on his forehead. "I shall check on you in a short while."

"Lecie?" he called when she reached the doorway. "I could not be a prouder father."

"I love you too." Lecie smiled tenderly.

"Such a touching scene atween father and daughter," Hamon said with a sneer after Lecie entered the passageway.

Startled by his presence, her smile melted. "Do you not have the bar to tend?"

"The men can wait a spell." Lifting a shining tress of her hair Hamon brought it to his nose to inhale its scent. "You and I need to talk."

"I fulfilled my end of the bargain," Lecie spat, yanking her hair free. "We have nothing further to discuss."

Turning her back on him, she descended the steps.

"We shall soon see about that," Hamon murmured when he opened the door to her father's chamber.

Chapter Eight

Lecie found Osana alone in the brewing shed when she entered to check the supply of ale. "Where have Sabina and Clayton gotten off to?"

Glancing up from her task of measuring barley, Osana straightened. "Sabina had to make use of the privy. We finished our chores early and thought to assist you in here."

"That is very kind of you both." Lecie smoothed a wayward lock of blonde hair behind Osana's ear. "Where is Clayton?"

"I know not." Osana shrugged. "Last I saw of him he was running toward the river after Tugger."

"I told you not to let him out of your sight." Lecie spoke more harshly than she intended. "How long ago did he leave?"

"Soon after he finished pulling turnips in the garden." Osana's eyes filled with tears. "Forgive me, Lecie. I forgot I was to watch him."

"There is nothing to forgive," Lecie said, wrapping an arm around her sister's slender shoulders. "I am the one who should be apologizing for my temper."

"Lecie, you ruined the surprise," Sabina whined from the doorway.

"I was surprised, dearest." Lecie forced a smile. "Mother would be as proud as I am to see you both carrying on the family tradition."

"We still need your assist with the portioning," Sabina said. "We have not got it quite down yet."

"There is something I must do but I shall return long afore that to help you." Pulling the door closed, Lecie hiked up her skirts and took off at a run toward the river.

Out of breath with her side cramping, she slowed to a walk when she spotted Clayton strolling along the sloped bank beside Sir Talan.

With Tugger chasing rabbits in the brush a few paces ahead of the pair it was an idyllic scene that had her recalling better days.

Dipping her head to acknowledge Sir Talan, she turned her temper loose on Clayton. "Did I, or did I not tell you to stay close to the inn?"

"I am close to the inn." Clayton pointed to a spot behind her. "I can see the slates on the roof from the top of that rise."

"And I can see that I am going to have to be more specific in the future," Lecie said ruffling his blond hair.

"No harm would have come to him this day," Talan interjected softly. "I was fortunate enough to spot him on my way to the sheriff's."

"Once again I am beholden to you, Sir Talan." Lecie reluctantly met his knowing gaze.

"Master Clayton," Talan said, "why do you not see what Tugger has cornered in the brush?"

Without asking for Lecie's permission, Clayton took off running.

"He minds you," Lecie said, following her brother's progress. "If you distracted him to speak about Sir Albin, I have nothing to say."

"Will you not at least hear me out?"

Crossing her arms, Lecie remained silent.

"Albin did not confide what transpired atween you but I do know he is deeply troubled by it," Talan began. "He is not the most eloquent of men when it comes to the fairer sex, he never has been."

"You came here to tell me about his past failures with women?"

"No, of course not," Talan said, "not that he does not have a past with women, only that he has never sought a relationship with one afore now."

"What exactly are you trying to say, Sir Talan?"

"Can we sit? I mean, would you mind?"

Sitting on the grass with her legs tucked beneath her, Lecie waited for him to continue.

Taking a seat beside her, Talan's tracked the progress of a barge moving slowly up river. "I realize I am fumbling things but please bear with me. The last thing I want is to make things worse."

"Sir Albin is fortunate to have a friend like you," Lecie said taking pity on him. "Say what you have to say, I will withhold judgement until the end."

"You really are too kind," Talan said. "I thought if you knew a little bit more about Albin's past you might understand whatever it is he said that vexed you, was likely misconstrued. Mayhap you will even find it in your heart to forgive him."

"Whilst I doubt it, please go on."

"I met Albin the day I met Fulke," Talan began. "I was living with my Uncle Hewett after the death of my mother. He fostered, you see. That is why Fulke came to live with us after the death of his parents and siblings in a fire."

"I had no idea," Lecie murmured.

"Tis not common knowledge," Talan said. "Anyway, wherever Fulke went Albin was quick to follow. I shadowed the pair everywhere and mimicked their training. When it came time for them to depart, I pleaded with Fulke to take me with him. Not wanting to take responsibility for me, he initially refused. My liege was different then, you see. He was still grieving the loss, and angry at the world. If not for Albin's intercession, my life would have taken a much different course."

"So you feel indebted to Sir Albin?"

"Not at all," Talan said with a chuckle. "I have more than made up for my gratitude and we have butted heads on countless occasions since then. Despite the fact that I have always been envious of their close bond, Fulke and Albin's friendship was forged by fire when they were mere lads."

"I already know how loyal Albin is to his lordship," Lecie said. "What does that have to do with me?"

"I wanted to give you an example of Albin's character. Whilst he has many friends, there is only a handful of people that he completely trusts, and only a few he opens his heart to." Talan made sure Clayton was out of earshot before saying, "Lecie, what I tell you now must be kept in the strictest of confidence. Albin would never forgive me if he knew I spoke of it, especially to you."

"You have my word."

"Albin's father physically abused him," Talan said with a solemn look, "and I am not talking about the occasional cuff to correct his behavior. Joffrey would brutally beat him with anything close to hand. Often times he would not stop until Albin fell unconscious. Had Albin been a slighter man, he would not have survived adolescence."

"Why?" Openly weeping, Lecie's heart ached to hear such things.

"Albin was extremely close to his mother. His father found that unmanly so attempted to toughen him up," Talan said. "After Liane passed on, Albin practically lived with Fulke's family. Since he was not the eldest son, Joffrey allowed it. When Fulke became an orphan, the village elders decided to send him to train for the knighthood. He refused to go without Albin so the elders shamed Joffrey into letting his son go."

"How did they shame him?"

"I believe it had something to do with Albin's older brother but what, I have no idea. If I had to guess, twould have to do with Glenbard turning traitor against our king."

"Albin told you all this?"

"No, nor would he," Talan said. "Fulke confided all this to me after Albin and I had a violent disagreement not long after we left my uncle's. I took offense at something he made light of and my liege wanted me to understand why Albin so often conceals his true feelings behind jest. That is why I am telling you all this now."

"I appreciate your doing so but Albin did not say anything inappropriate to me," Lecie hesitantly admitted. "He...we..." Lowering her head, she blurted, "He discovered I was a maiden... after wrongly assuming that Edric was my husband. I took offense."

Not at all what he was expecting, Talan straightened. Suddenly everything made sense to him. "I see," he said after a lengthy silence.

"Do you?" Lecie faced him. "Albin assumed the worst of me afore martyring himself to his desires. What kind of honorable man does that?"

"Men in love are apt to do and say things they would not normally do," Talan said. "Is it not the same for women?"

"You are saying that Albin is in love with me?"

"Do you recall our conversation in your father's room about Albin having formed an attachment to someone?"

"Aye," Lecie acknowledged.

"The person I spoke of was you, Lecie. It took me some time to realize it but when I did, Albin's odd behavior whenever we arrived in Rochester suddenly made sense. He is in love with you and was conflicted by the misconception he had about your marital status. I believe what happened atween you is proof of what I say. Especially since he only went inside that night to speak to you."

"I do not understand. How is that proof?"

"Honor means everything to a knight," Talan said. "Believing you wed, Albin struggled to keep things chaste atween you. Obviously, he failed. And knowing him like I do," Talan went on, "I am sure he bungled whatever followed your... encounter."

"That is putting it lightly," Lecie said with a reluctant smile. "Thank you for telling me these things."

"I hope I helped."

"Only time will tell. Can I ask what happened to his father?"

"He died alone," Talan said. "His body was not found for some time so no one knows how it happened. We received word of it shortly after the peace accord was signed atween King Henry and King Louis. He died not knowing his youngest son who he believed to be worthless had been knighted for valorous actions in battle."

"How did Albin react to his father's death?"

"He made a morbid jest and then went for a long walk so I honestly do not know."

"You have given me much to think about," Lecie said with tears in her eyes.

"Aside from your disagreement with Albin, there is something else that I wanted to speak to you about."

"What would that be?"

"I wanted you to know that we are very fond of Clayton and the girls. If Hamon is any way using them against you, we can help you."

"You could put an end to Hamon, not his threats."

When she refused to elaborate, Talan did not push her. "Just know we will always be here for you should you have need of us."

"That is very kind."

"How is your father faring if you do not mind my asking?"

"I gave him the medicine her ladyship sent afore I left." Relieved he had changed the subject, Lecie relaxed slightly. "I pray it eases his pain."

"Tugger caught two rabbits," Clayton called running over to them. "Can we have them in a stew for supper tonight?"

"We shall not be having anything if I do not return soon," Lecie said rising. "Bid your farewell to Sir Talan as we have detained him long enough."

"I wish I did not have to." Clayton turned sad eyes on Talan. "How come you and Sir Albin are no longer staying at the inn? Sir Albin promised he would show me how to play chess afore he returned to Castell Maen."

"Then he shall, lad," Talan said keeping his gaze on Lecie. "Sir Albin always keeps his promises."

Averting her eyes, Lecie whistled for Tugger.

The dog came bounding out of the brush with another wild hare clamped between its teeth.

"Enjoy your visit with the sheriff's family," Lecie bid him in parting. "Please extend my fondest greetings to Mylla."

"I shall." Talan leaned down to Clayton's eye level. "Next time you see fit to wander off by the river, twould please me greatly to accompany you. Mayhap we can even go fishing for your supper."

"I would like that very much." Clayton beamed. "Do tell Sir Albin to come for a visit soon. I miss him"

"He will be very happy to hear it." With a last long look at Lecie, Talan strode off to retrieve his horse.

"Are you ready to return to the inn, little man?" Lecie turned her attention to Clayton. "I am sure I can search out a sweet or two for you."

"Lecie, is Da going to die soon?"

Unprepared for the question, Lecie searched for the right words to prepare him for the inevitable. Dropping onto the dry riverbank, she patted the spot beside her. After Clayton complied, she said, "I fear he does not have much time left with us."

Clayton's eyes filled with tears while gazing at the untouched forest across the river. "I will miss him terribly but I know our mother will be glad to see him."

Absently brushing away her own tears, Lecie's love for him nearly overwhelmed her. "You are as wise as an elder."

"I have to be," Clayton sniffled, "I shall be the man of the family soon."

"This is not the childhood I wanted for you." Her voice breaking, Lecie turned away to keep him from seeing her tears.

"Worry not," Clayton soothed, "I shall make certain everything is alright."

"I know you will." Lecie smiled as she gained her feet. "Will you promise me something?"

"Anything," he swore when he scrambled to his feet beside her.

"Promise me you will never again wander off alone or go anywhere with Hamon, regardless of what he tells you."

"Hamon?" Clayton's smooth brow creased in confusion. "Am I not to trust him?"

"No, you are not." Lecie fisted her hand before extending her pinky finger. "Swear to me you will stay clear of him as much as possible."

Hooking his pinky finger with hers, Clayton nodded solemnly. "I swear it."

Slightly relieved, Lecie strolled alongside him in companionable silence while Tugger ran ahead.

Passing the stable, Lecie froze when she recognized Dr. Rayburn's horse tied up outside. "Da," she whispered.

Clayton slipped his hand in hers when she led the way through the garden.

Entering the kitchen, she lightly squeezed his hand for support when they spotted Betta hunched over the cook table weeping.

Her arms crossed before her sagging bosom, Gunilda eyed Clayton from her post beside the door. "Your father is dead. You are now master here."

"Lackwit," Lecie swore, releasing Clayton's hand. "How dare you inform him in such a way?"

Shrugging her shoulders, Gunilda kept her gaze on Clayton's stricken face. "Dead is dead. What difference does it make how he finds out?"

"You drasty wench," Lecie raged. "Address him again and you shall be scraping out a living in the gutter."

Gunilda's eyes flared in anger yet she kept her silence.

Betta's harsh sobbing was the only sound heard in the kitchen as the two women stared each other down.

Eventually, Gunilda backed down afraid of what she found in the infuriated golden gaze boring into her.

"The village leech is awaiting payment." Gunilda jerked her head toward the common room.

Still seething, Lecie tone was sharp. "Where are the girls?"

"Harsent is consoling them in their chamber."

"Come with me, Clayton." Sweeping past Gunilda, she snapped, "Clear out the patrons and close the tavern. We are in mourning until further notice."

Lagging behind up the steps, Clayton stopped short of entering their father's chamber. "Lecie, do I have to see him like that?"

The pleading in his voice had her dropping to her knees before him. "You do not have to go in if you do not want to."

"I suppose I will one day regret not bidding Da a final goodbye." Tears slipped down Clayton's smooth cheeks as he straightened to his full height. "Besides, I am now man of the family, and tis my duty."

"Your duty is to see to the family," Lecie corrected. "Osana and Sabina need you now more than Da does. Besides, he would rather have you remember him the way he was not as he lays now."

"Are you just saying that to make me feel better?"

"No." Lecie smiled though her tears. "I think tis what Da would want."

Throwing his arms around her, Clayton held tight. Once he released her, he scrubbed the tears from his face with the hem of his tunic. "In that case, I shall see to our sisters."

"There is a brave lad." Lecie watched him go struggling to maintain her composure.

Dr. Rayburn stood from the edge of the bed when she entered. "I was told you would see to the charge."

"Who summoned you here?"

"The stable lad was sent for me." Dr. Rayburn collected his leather satchel. "I know not who found the body."

"I had given him medicine earlier." Tears fell unchecked down Lecie's cheeks when she eyed her father's still form on the bed. "I had so hoped twould help."

"Obviously, you were wrong." Blocking her view of the bed, Dr. Rayburn held out his hand. "There are others in need of my services. I cannot tarry here all day."

"See Hamon for your payment."

"His death is a stain upon your soul," Dr. Rayburn said on his way out. "I could have healed him had you let me."

Lecie sank down on her knees beside the bed. Clasping her father's cold hand, she broke down sobbing.

♥

Returning to the tower after an abbreviated visit with Mylla, Talan noticed a group of solemn villagers streaming from the inn. He slowed his horse to a walk on his way past.

A portly man in a stained brown tunic jerked his thumb toward the inn on his approach. "I would not bother stopping. Tavern's closed until further notice."

Talan glanced at the upper floor with a heavy heart. "Why is that?"

"The innkeep died and his daughter ordered everyone out," the man complained. "She even sent the lodgers packing. Waste of good coin if you ask me."

"Has the village physician been summoned?"

"He already came and went."

"Thank you." Spurring his horse, Talan rode hard for the tower.

For something to do, Albin was toiling alongside the workers high on the scaffolding when Talan hailed him from the courtyard.

Climbing down the wood framework, Albin met him at the bottom. "Is Edric at peace?"

"How did you guess?"

"Your expressions have always given you away," Albin said raking a filthy hand through his disheveled hair. "We should have been there when it happened. Lecie should not have to endure such a thing alone."

"Do you still intend to go through with the original plan?"

"Sooner than we discussed," Albin said. "With Edric gone I expect Hamon will be forcing his will upon her afore long if he has not already."

"I agree." Talan hesitated. "Only…"

"Only what?" Shielding his eyes from the mid-afternoon sun, Albin scowled. "What are you not telling me? Has he—"

"Not that I am aware of," Talan rushed to assure him. "My only concern is that what we are accusing Hamon of planning is no less than what you yourself are about to do. Despite her feelings for you, Lecie may not take kindly to being coerced."

"I gave Edric my oath to take care of Lecie and that is what I intend to do," Albin said. "In time, I am sure she will understand the reasons behind my actions."

"You only mentioned one reason."

"So what if I did?" Albin grew impatient. "What is it you are hinting at?"

"I know you are in love with her. I just do not know why you refuse to admit it." Talan allowed the shadow of a smile. "Is it because you will have to bend the knee to our liege?"

"You dare jest at a time like this?"

"Soon enough I do not think there will be much to jest about," Talan admitted. "Besides, Mylla and I have a wager of our own."

"What kind of wager?"

"Mylla believes you are too loyal to choose love over duty. She does not believe you would ever leave the service of our liege to settle for the life of an innkeep."

"And you?" Albin's eyes narrowed suspiciously. "What is your wager?"

"Since I am of the belief that your heart has been well and truly spoken for by the fair Lecie, I wagered by harvest next you shall be brewing your own ale."

"Being enlightened of my plan, do not you think you have an unfair advantage over your intended lady?"

"Mayhap," Talan said, "but this is one wager I have no intention of losing."

"So you intend to use my unfortunate circumstance to further your own, is that it?"

"You could say that."

"Care to enlighten me?" Albin cocked a dark eyebrow.

"I would not be a knight of valour if I did."

"Mylla has definitely eased your righteous nature," Albin said with approval. "If you were not at present so annoying, I would be grateful to her."

Throwing his head back, Talan laughed. "She will be pleased to hear it."

"Cease your nonsense now." Albin led the way from the courtyard. "We have more important things to be dealt with."

"Surely you do not intend to arrive on Lecie's doorstep without the benefit of a bath?" Talan called from behind him.

"I am not a heathen," Albin said changing direction.

"What were you doing working on the tower anyway? We are not expected to toil."

"I was bored." Albin unbuckled his pack to pull out a laundered tunic and breeches. "Until the king's man arrives there has been naught else for me to do."

"You could have visited the sheriff's family with me," Talan said. "I know they would welcome you."

"And be a third in your party of two? No thank you." Stripping naked by the water trough, Albin scooped up a handful of soap and began to scrub his hair and body. Upending a bucket over his head, he shivered when the icy water coursed down his broad chest, tapered waist and muscled legs. Lecie was not the only thing he missed at the inn.

After toweling off with a linen cloth, Albin quickly dressed while Talan saddled his horse. Stowing his soiled garments, he took the reins to vault into the saddle in one fluid motion.

"Let us do this," he called to Talan spurring his horse toward the village.

♥

After she gained control of herself, Lecie retrieved her father's best tunic and breeches from the wardrobe. Laying it out on the bed beside his body, she began to straighten up the chamber.

Absently picking up her father's pillow from the floor, she tossed it on a chair and sank down on the edge of the bed. "Rest you well, Da."

Tears tracked down her cheeks as she mourned the man that had been her world since her mother had passed. His face relaxed in death, she once again held his limp hand to her cheek.

Faced with the ordeal of having him prepared for burial, she refused to ask Hamon for his assistance in dressing her father. After briefly checking on the children, she went in search of Joseph.

In the process of sending the boy to ask Leofrick for assistance, she looked up at the sound of approaching horses. Her heart began to pound when she spotted Sir Albin.

"Mistress?" Joseph inquired.

"Oh, Joseph, never you mind."

Torn between running to him for comfort and ordering him from her sight, Lecie stood motionless when Albin dismounted beside her.

"Lecie," he said, "I am so sorry, lass."

His tender words broke through her reserve and she found herself encircled by his gentle embrace when she broke down weeping.

"I am here now," Albin soothed.

Talan gave them privacy by leading the horses into the stable alongside Joseph.

"Well, well," Hamon's voice had Lecie scrambling out of Albin's arms. "What do we have here?"

Albin's eyes narrowed dangerously on Hamon when he spoke to Lecie. "Where are the children, lass?"

"Above with Harsent," she managed in a whisper.

"Let us go inside." Lightly clasping her arm, Albin led Lecie down the cobbled walk leading to the back door.

"Hold on." Hamon ran past to block the doorway. "Where do you think—"

"I shall finish with you later," Albin snarled pushing him roughly out of the way.

Knocked off balance, Hamon's arms pin-wheeled as he fell backward into the vegetable patch.

Seeing the exchange from the kitchen, Gunilda shrieked and came rushing out to render aid to her fallen lover.

Albin released Lecie when they passed into the common room. "Has your father been prepared for burial?"

The reminder of his mistaken assumption about her relationship status had Lecie bristling. "No," she said curtly. "I was just about to send Joseph for Leofrick when you rode up. What is it you want?"

"Only to help you."

"I shall make do on my own."

"Lecie, please…"

Without responding, Lecie turned her back on him to ascend the steps.

Tracking her progress with his eyes, Albin shook his head with a mumbled curse. "At this rate, she will never forgive me."

"Stay here should Hamon return to stir up trouble," Talan said. "I shall lend assist to Lecie."

"You heard what she said. She does not want our help."

"She said she does not need help. There is a distinct difference. Besides, "Talan added with a shrug, "she said nothing about me."

"Is that supposed to make me feel better?" Feeling helpless, Albin turned his anger on Talan. "I was not the only one banished from the inn."

"And yet here we are in the very place we are not supposed to be," Talan quipped.

"You took the words right out of my mouth." The sheriff spoke sternly from behind Talan. "I could arrest you both for trespass."

"Yet he will not." Leofrick squeezed by his father to address Talan. "Again we meet this day. Were it only under happier circumstances."

"I believe we all mourn the end of such a good man."

"We came as soon as we heard." Edmund made his presence known. "Is she above?"

"Aye," Albin said, "she refused our assistance."

"Well she did banish the pair of you so tis to be expected," Edmund said. "We will attend to what needs to be done."

Taking an instant dislike to the sheriff's eldest son, Albin scowled. "You know as well as we do that Hamon is behind Lecie's actions."

"Now is not the time to be discussing the matter." Talan spoke low. "Lecie is grieving a great loss."

"You are right." Albin lowered his head in contrition. "At the moment she and the children are my only concern."

"Has Father Bartholomeo arrived to shrive the body?" Leofrick joined the conversation.

"Not that I know of," Albin said. "I shall fetch him myself."

"I will tend to my oldest friend," Sheriff Richard said. "Leofrick lend me assist."

With an air of self-importance, Edmund moved to the front of the small group. "What would you have me do, Father?"

"Stay here and send the priest up when he arrives." Disregarding his son's look of disappointment, Sheriff Richard moved past him.

His mind on more important things, Albin did not see Hamon watching him from the stand of trees beside the inn when he rode off toward the church.

Adjusting his clothing, the tapster left Gunilda lying in a tangle of skirts without so much as an offer to assist her up.

♥

Edric's body had been washed and prepared for burial by the time Albin returned with the village priest. Wearing his finest garb and sewn into a linen burial shroud, he lay on a planked table in the common room for the final farewell.

The solemn group waited for the priest to administer the last rites so they could make the sad journey to the churchyard.

His heart aching for Lecie and the children, Albin stood quietly off to the side keeping watch on Hamon.

Their eyes swollen and red from crying the twins clung to each other for comfort.

Clayton stood bravely beside his sisters with a quivering chin. On the occasions his gaze would fall upon the shrouded figure of his father, Lecie would give his hand a reassuring squeeze.

"Shall we begin?" the priest intoned in a grave voice. Portly and balding, the elder looked down his hooked nose at Lecie. "It grows late and if the body is to be buried this day, we have no time to tarry."

Being strong for the sake of the children, Lecie cleared her throat to speak. "Please do so, Father."

Displeased by the family's lack of regular church attendance, Father Bartholomeo kept the farewell sermon short and to the point.

After the priest concluded with a prayer for the soul of her father, Lecie dried her tears. With a small smile of encouragement directed at the children, she prepared them for the short walk to the cemetery.

"If you please, Father," Hamon loudly announced from where he stood behind Clayton. "Afore we go, I would ask that you perform a wedding ceremony."

The room erupted into various reactions to the unorthodox request. Talan and Leofrick leapt forward to restrain Albin when he lunged to attack Hamon.

"Take it easy," Talan said losing his grip when Albin jerked his shoulder free. "You need to keep your head about you."

Yanking down the hem of his crumpled tunic, Albin dipped his head without taking his eyes from Hamon.

The children stood huddled together looking at Lecie for guidance.

Lecie's gaze was riveted on Hamon's hands where they rested alongside Clayton's neck.

Gunilda began to sob brokenly as Betta and Harsent consoled her under the incorrect assumption that she grieved for Edric.

Edmund and Sheriff Richard stood quietly off to the side waiting for the priest to respond to Hamon's ill-timed request.

"This is a time of mourning and the man must be buried without further delay," Father Bartholomeo intoned when the room settled down.

"I beg to differ, Father." Hamon refused to let the matter drop. "Dear departed Edric would understand and agree with my need for haste." Digging into a pouch tied to his belt, he removed several silver deniers. "Please accept my humble tithing for your trouble."

Father Bartholomeo pocketed the coins before his cold gaze darted to the trio of tavern wenches standing in the back of the room. "Which of the fallen women do you wish to wed?"

"I would never demean myself in such a fashion." Hamon's eyes held a threat when he looked over at Lecie. "Mistress Lecie is my intended. Tis what her father wanted."

"The hell you say," Albin roared, fisting his hands. "I swore to Edric that I would wed her."

Lecie's gasp was the only sound heard in the ensuing silence. Searching Albin's face, hope strove to overcome her fear of Hamon.

"It appears," Father Bartholomeo droned in a bored voice as he looked around at the stunned group, "that we have a conundrum."

Chapter Nine

"Like hell we…" Albin's words faded upon seeing the look Father Bartholomeo leveled on him. "Forgive my turn of phrase, Father. What I meant to say is that there is no way in he—" He glanced at Talan in silent appeal.

"Father Bartholomeo," Talan said taking the hint, "I am Sir Talan. Sir Albin and I are in the service of Baron Erlegh."

"So I gathered by your arms," Father Bartholomeo remarked. "Baron Erlegh is well known to me as a benefactor of the church. What have you to say on this matter?"

"What Sir Albin attempted to convey." Talan shot an exasperated look at his frustrated friend. "Is that shortly afore Edric's death, he gave his word as a knight of the realm to take care of the family, Lecie in particular as her husband."

"Only if she would willingly accept me," Albin added.

"And what of this tapster's claim that Edric conveyed the same wishes to him? I cannot in good conscience disregard his claim merely because a knight outranks him," Father Bartholomeo said. "The woman herself is naught but a commoner."

"If the tapster's claim gives you pause." Talan pointedly stared at Hamon's hands until the latter removed them from around Clayton's neck. "I would have you judge the character of both men."

Albin followed Talan's gaze and said, "Clayton, why do you not escort Osana and Sabina elsewhere whilst we sort this matter out?"

"Lecie." Clayton turned a solemn look upon her. "You know who da would have chosen for you. I know you do."

"Go along with you now, little man."

"I shall see to them," Betta said ushering the children toward the steps.

Once the children were gone, Father Bartholomeo said, "Being the last wishes of the deceased, tis not my decision to make. However, if it were my decision, I would place the children with a pious knight over a lowborn."

"So where does that leave us?" Hamon demanded.

"Since tis impossible to clarify Edric's wishes," Talan said. "I would like to offer a possible solution."

"One that will benefit your friend no doubt," Hamon scoffed. "I have known Edric the longest, he trusted me."

"How dare you make such a claim after what you did?" Knocking Talan's restraining hand aside an enraged Albin faced Hamon. "I would see you dead afore laying a hand on Lecie."

"Do you see how he is?" Hamon turned his full attention on the priest. "There is no telling how the orphans will fare if they are forced to live beneath his roof."

"Your ignorance is testament to the fact that you do not attend mass," Father Bartholomeo said with disdain. "For Proverbs 13:24 tells us that those who withhold the rod hate their children, but the one who loves them applies discipline."

"I would beat them into submission regularly," Hamon vowed.

"Over my deceased corpse you will," Albin swore.

"Saints bones," Talan softly swore in Albin's ear. "You are your own worst enemy. Keep your bloody mouth shut, and let me handle it."

Stunned by Talan's unusual flash of temper, Albin acknowledged with a slight nod.

"Allow Lecie to decide who she would have for a husband," Hamon said. "She above all else here would know her father's wishes on the subject."

"Father," Talan said, "afore you agree to such a thing, you should know that Sir Albin and I believe that the tapster has made threats of harm to the children should Lecie refuse his advances."

"Regardless, given the present circumstances and the late hour, it appears to be the only reasonable solution. As to the threats you allude to, I doubt the tapster will be so foolish with so many witnesses here about. " Steepling his fingers, Father Bartholomeo bent a disapproving look on Albin. "What say you to letting the woman decide? Would you abide by her choice?"

"Aye, I shall accept her decision." Albin stared into Lecie's frightened eyes. "Let Lecie decide who will share her life and bed from this day forth."

"Sir Albin, your coarseness is better suited for the battlefield." Father Bartholomeo huffed. "You are in the presence of a man of God."

"My apologies to all present," Albin mumbled. "I have had little time of late to attend mass."

"There is always time for God."

"Aye, Father." Flushing red, Albin studied the cross beams above his head.

"Well?" Father Bartholomeo turned pale blue eyes upon Lecie. "What say you? Which man would your father have you choose as husband?"

The color drained from Lecie's face when all eyes turned upon her. Despite her anger toward him, all she had ever wished for would come true if she were to accept Albin's hand. If only she could be absolutely certain that Hamon would not follow through on his threats against the children. Even if she were to confide in Albin, she knew he would not always be there to protect them. He had a duty to his liege and would be required to return to Castell Maen. What would happen then? The Wounded Stag had been in her family for generations. It was Clayton's by the laws of inheritance. She had no right to take it from him should Albin decided to relocate the family. In the end, she knew she had no choice. She must sacrifice her own happiness to protect and secure her siblings future.

Tears slipped from her eyes when she found her voice. "I wish to wed Hamon, Father."

"And you firmly believe tis what your father would have wanted?"

"Aye." Averting her eyes, Lecie nodded. "At all cost he would want me to do what is best for the children."

Albin was uncommonly silent when Talan said, "Tis fear alone that has her speak so, Father. Surely, you can see that?"

"The woman has made her decision," Father Bartholomeo snapped. "You heard with thine own ears that Sir Albin would abide by her choice so I consider the matter closed."

"Sheriff," Talan implored, "you cannot let this stand."

"You have something to add?" Father Bartholomeo turned his attention to Richard.

"I do not believe Edric would have chosen the tapster over Sir Albin," Sheriff Richard said. "I also believe that Lecie has been coerced into accepting him."

"Did the woman confide this to you?"

"No." Richard shook his head. "She did not."

"Did Edric tell you of his preference for a husband for his daughter?"

"No, he did not."

"They besmirch my good name for their own gain," Hamon interrupted. "Lecie herself banished these two knights from the inn. They should be arrested for trespass just by being here." His face beet red, he pointed at the sheriff. "You know what I speak is true, tell him."

"The tapster speaks the truth," the sheriff said with a look of distaste directed at Hamon. "Though I believe it has to do with the threats made against her."

"Such an unusual occurrence is this." Father Bartholomeo faced Lecie. "Has Hamon in some way coerced you into this marriage?"

Left with no other choice, Lecie opened her mouth to lie when Albin spoke from beside her. "Regardless of the man's threats, there is another impediment to the marriage I would have you consider, Father."

"Yet another impediment?" Father Bartholomeo's look was incredulous. "Is anyone here aware that a man awaits burial afore dark?"

"I am certain Edric would want this matter to be settled aforehand." Albin turned to Lecie. "Would you do me the honor of becoming my wife, Lecie?" His eyes spoke volumes as he willed her to change her mind. "Or must I speak my piece?"

Lecie's lower lip trembled, yet she managed to remain silent.

"Very well," he whispered for her ears alone. "One day I pray you will forgive me for what I now do."

Lecie clutched his arm to stop him. "Please do not do this."

Briefly cupping her cheek, his eyes begged for her understanding. "You have given me no choice." Facing the priest he said, "The impediment I speak of is that at this very trice, Lecie may be carrying my child."

"How could you?" she whispered brokenly from beside him.

Unable to bear her stricken expression, Albin kept his gaze fixed on the stunned priest.

"I knew it," Gunilda sniped from the back of the room. "Always playing at being the grand lady of the inn when it turns out she is no better than the rest of us."

"Be gone," Albin came close to shouting as he leveled a cold gaze on Gunilda. "You are not fit to be in the same room with her."

Gunilda stood stiffly to toss her lank braid over her shoulder. With a last longing look at Hamon, she slipped into the kitchen.

Father Bartholomeo pulled out a chair beside Edric's body and took a seat. "I could use an ale, tapster."

"You do not believe him, do you?" Hamon snarled. "He would say anything to inherit the inn."

"The inn is not his to inherit," Father Bartholomeo corrected. "And I suggest you not take that tone with me."

"Forgive me, Father." Hamon immediately backed down. "I am merely trying to follow through with my dear departed employer's final wishes." Scrambling behind the bar, he returned with a cup of ale for the priest.

"Is it true?" Taking a sip of ale, the priest eyed Lecie. "Have you committed a mortal sin by fornicating with the knight out of wedlock?"

Desperate and about to lose what he coveted most, Hamon interjected, "The child could very well be mine."

"You lying bastard," Albin snarled leaping to wrap his hands around Hamon's scrawny neck. "Lecie was a maiden when I took her."

Lecie's look of shock was not lost on the priest when Leofrick, Edmund, and Talan struggled to separate the two men.

Edmund managed to pry Albin's fingers from Hamon's neck while Talan and Leofrick forcefully dragged him away.

"Ease up," Talan hissed in Albin's ear.

His face an unhealthy shade of blue, Hamon inhaled deeply while he kept a wary eye on his adversary. Gingerly touching his neck, he sought protection by moving to stand beside the sheriff. "Are not you going to do something?"

"We are doing something," Sheriff Richard bent a disgusted look on Hamon. "We are trying to discern the truth from bold face lies."

Swallowing painfully, Hamon averted his eyes.

Finished with his ale the priest waited patiently until he had everyone's attention. "Now then," he called. "If the outbursts are finished, we shall conclude this sordid business."

Albin forced himself to relax after Talan and Leofrick released him. His narrowed gaze on Hamon, he waited for the priest's next words.

"I would normally hear your confession in private," Father Bartholomeo said to Lecie, "however, the circumstances being what they are..."

"I understand, Father," Lecie's voice shook. "Ask of me what you would."

"Would you tell the truth?" Albin blurted unable to stop himself. "If you do I swear by the almighty that Hamon shall not harm what you hold dear."

Meeting his steady gaze, Lecie forced herself to feel nothing. "On top of everything else you have faultily laid at my feet, do you now accuse me of being a liar as well, Sir Albin?"

"If in so doing you are under the assumption that it would protect someone you love, aye," he responded softly. "I do so accuse you."

"My father was wrong about you. You are not an honorable man." Her lip trembling, Lecie returned her attention to Father Bartholomeo. "I understand that a woman's word is nothing compared to that of a man's, yet you have mine that I shall answer truthfully."

"Have you dishonored yourself with Sir Albin like he claims?" Father Bartholomeo asked abruptly.

"Yes I have," Lecie responded, boldly meeting Albin's gaze. "How I wish it were not so."

"And Hamon?" the priest pressed. "Have you also shared your pallet with him?"

"No," Lecie spat. "I have not, nor would I ever willingly do so."

"In that case, I suggest you excuse yourself to prepare for your wedding to Sir Albin." Father Bartholomeo slightly softened his words. "Regardless of what you now think, he has proven himself to be an honorable man in upholding your father's wishes. Given the situation, you could do much worse."

Dipping her head in acknowledgement, Lecie then faced Hamon. "Get your things and be gone by the time I return." Regardless of the sheriff standing only feet from her, she added, "And know you this, if any harm comes to the children there is nowhere on this isle you can hide that I will not find and kill you."

"You impertinent wench." Hamon raised a hand to strike her.

Finding his hand held in a viselike grip, Hamon shrieked in pain when the bones in his fingers threatened to break.

"You heard her," Albin sneered, "be gone with you."

Surrounded by towering men, Hamon nervously glanced around for an ally. Met with animosity at every turn, he turned a spiteful look upon Albin. "Release me and I shall."

Albin forcefully shoved him away and grinned when Hamon fell hard against a table.

"I offer my congratulations to you, Sir Albin." Hamon performed a mock bow when he straightened. "Your gluttony for ale has led you to covet Lecie's hand, whereas I only coveted her heart."

"Get out afore I give you the thrashing you rightly deserve," Albin snarled.

"Until we meet again." Hamon bowed mockingly.

"Do not think it has escaped my notice that you lied to a man of God," Father Bartholomeo called to Hamon on his way out. "I shall expect to see you in the confessional come Sunday."

Without responding, Hamon slammed his chamber door.

"Excuse me whilst I prepare myself," Lecie murmured to no one in particular. "It shall not take me long."

Avoiding Albin's remorseful gaze, she rushed up the steps.

She angrily brushed at the tears slipping from her eyes refusing to think about what was to come. Hamon's accusation replayed itself in her head as she entered the children's room to dismiss Betta. She knew Albin was not marrying her for the inn. He was doing it to honor his vow to her father.

"Now then," she began in a falsely bright voice when she perched on the edge of Clayton's bed. "I know you must be confused by what transpired below so I would like to have a word with the three of you."

"We think you should choose Sir Albin over Hamon," Osana said.

"Do you say that because you do not like Hamon?"

"No," Sabina spoke up, "tis because we are fond of Sir Albin."

"You are?" Lecie questioned softly.

"Oh yes, ever so much," Clayton exclaimed. "Even Tugger approves of him."

"Well in that case, I suppose twill be easier to explain things to you since I am to wed Sir Albin."

"There was no need to explain anyway," Osana said. "Betta told us everything."

"Everything?" Lecie's eyes flared. "What exactly did Betta say?"

"She said you had little choice in the matter because you are now a woman without a man's protection and we should support your decision, whatever it may be," Sabina recited verbatim.

"I see," Lecie responded with a grateful smile. "I suppose I shall have to thank her for being so considerate."

"Why do you look so sad?" Clayton passed her the kerchief he had balled in his fist. "Do you not wish to marry Sir Albin?"

Accepting the damp piece of linen, Lecie shrugged. "I fear tis hard for me to explain how I feel at the moment."

"You can try," Clayton coaxed. "We shall be quiet and listen."

Despite her circumstances, Lecie smiled. "Whilst I am grateful, I doubt I would make sense."

"Do you love him?" Osana spoke up.

"Yes," Lecie admitted. "I love him very much."

"Then what is so hard to explain?" Sabina looked puzzled. "You are marrying the man you love."

"Tis far more complicated than that." Lecie heaved a sigh as she took in their solemn faces. "I do not think Sir Albin wants to marry me."

"Why not?" Clayton appeared confused. "You are comely and the nicest girl I have ever met."

"I think perhaps you might be a tad biased on my account."

"Why would he marry you if he did not want to?" Osana asked. "He is a man and has a choice."

"He made a promise to Da," Lecie replied softly fighting back tears.

"Well, if he does not love you now, he will," Clayton responded matter-of-factly.

"Mayhap you are right," Lecie agreed to end the subject. "We best go below for the ceremony now so we can see Da put to rest."

"Lecie?" Clayton's face fell. "Must we go to the churchyard after dark?"

"Not if we hurry." Lecie stood with a resigned look. "We can bid our final farewell with the sun's last rays, twas father and mother's favorite time of day."

"How come?"

"Every day at sunset, our parents would take a stroll together by the river. Regardless of what kind of day they had, they would return after twilight to greet us with smiles."

"I love when you tell us stories like that," Sabina said wistfully. "They must have loved each other very much."

"They did indeed." Lecie reached for Clayton's hand. "And now they are reunited."

"I no longer remember what mother looks like." Osana brushed at her cheeks.

"Then I shall remind you often." Pulling Osana into a hug, Sabina and Clayton joined in.

"Now then." Lecie eased away. "If we are to catch the last of the sun, we must be on our way."

"Must the wedding be today?" Sabina asked on their way down the hall. "It seems like a bad omen so soon after Da's death."

Not what she had in mind for her wedding day, Lecie responded with a heavy heart. "Under the circumstances, today is as good as any other. Moreover, tis what da wanted so do not speak of bad omens."

"You are not even dressed in your best." Osana stopped abruptly to eye Lecie's charcoal gray kirtle with a skeptical eye. "How can you marry a knight dressed as you are?"

"I think Lecie is beautiful regardless of what she is wearing," Sabina put in softly.

"Thank you." Nudging Osana forward, Lecie said, "Were it a happier occasion, I would take the time to change. As it is, I am in mourning for our father. I would not disrespect him by celebrating the day."

"We shall have the ceremony now and celebrate another day then," Clayton said.

"I would be lost without the three of you," Lecie said feeling slightly better.

"Do not worry," Osana called over her shoulder. "We shall always be with you."

Recalling Hamon's threats, Lecie whispered, "I pray you are right."

Chapter Ten

Albin did a double-take when Lecie returned wearing the same drab clothing. Her silken tresses escaping her linen snood and her eyes red and swollen from crying, she was still the most beautiful woman he had ever beheld.

Resigned to her cold aloofness, he stepped forward to present his arm. "Shall we see the matter done, lass?"

"If we must," she murmured without meeting his gaze.

Father Bartholomeo gave her the once over, yet refrained from commenting. "Shall we begin?"

Talan, Sheriff Richard, Leofrick, Edmund, and the children stood behind Lecie and Albin when the couple solemnly faced the priest.

Betta slipping in from the kitchen to stand along the back wall caught Lecie's attention. Motioning her forward, she said, "You have every right to be here."

When Father Bartholomeo opened his mouth to protest Betta's presence, Lecie calmly met his disapproving gaze. "I am just as fallen as she in the eyes of God, Father. Betta has been like a mother to me, and I would have her stand witness."

"You are marrying a knight of the realm and should learn to act accordingly. This woman is not only a fallen she refuses to repent for her sins by attending mass. She is unworthy to be present at this solemn occasion."

"If God is everywhere, she can very well pray wherever she so chooses." Refusing to back down, Lecie stood motionless in a staring contest with Father Bartholomeo.

"Daylight is wasting, Father." Albin broke the uneasy silence.

"You do not object to the wench's presence, Sir Albin?"

Albin reached his hand to cover Lecie's where it rested lightly on his forearm, grateful she did not pull away. "I have no objection if my betrothed wishes Betta to be here." He exhaled a slow breath of relief when Lecie turned thankful eyes upon him. With a slight smile, he once again faced the priest.

"Very well then." Father Bartholomeo intoned the words that would bind them together as husband and wife for as long as they both lived.

In a clear sure voice, Albin recited his vows and managed to hide his disappointment behind a stoic mask when Lecie faltered when asked by the priest to repeat hers.

Expecting a chaste kiss to seal their vows, Lecie stiffened when Albin pulled her up against his chest to hold her close.

Slowly releasing her, he searched her eyes for some sign of warmth only to be disappointed when she again faced the priest.

"Shall we depart for the cemetery now?" Lecie's voice was impassive. "I promised the children we would see to the matter afore dark."

Father Bartholomeo glanced toward the bar. "I believe a toast of good fortune for the couple is customary."

"If we must," Lecie conceded, "let us do so quickly."

The assembled group extended subdued congratulations to the newly wedded couple while Betta passed around cups of wine for a celebratory toast.

Wishing Albin and Lecie a long life, prosperity, and an abundance of children, Talan's attempt to lighten the mood fell flat.

Albin acknowledged the well wishes by holding his cup high. "Though I regret sharing this day with the loss of a dear friend, I consider myself most blessed to call Lecie my wife."

Lecie swirled the red liquid in her cup lost in thought. Slowly bringing it to her lips, she took a deep swallow.

Accepting a tithing from Albin, Father Bartholomeo stood. "Shall we depart for the churchyard?"

Reminded the day was not yet over, everyone set their cups down and followed suit.

Lecie placed one last kiss on her father's brow through the linen shroud when Albin and Leofrick prepared to move his body to the horse drawn wagon waiting outside.

Putting on a brave face for the children, Lecie held hands with Clayton as they walked behind the wagon.

Villagers returning to their dwellings for the night stopped and bowed their heads as the small procession slowly passed.

His head held high, Father Bartholomeo regally acknowledged the show of respect.

The sun's last rays found the priest somberly intoning one last prayer for Edric's eternal rest. Once the service concluded, and the last shovelful of dirt had fallen, the sheriff and his sons solemnly took their leave.

Torches set in brackets spaced along high street lit their way back to the inn. Lecie walked alongside Clayton, Betta, and the twins while Albin and Talan brought up the rear of the somber group.

"You children have eaten very little this day," Lecie said to fill the silence. "How about I fix us all something to eat when we get home?"

"I am not hungry," Clayton responded tiredly.

"Me neither," Sabina replied softly.

"I for sure am not." Osana cast a furtive glance back at Albin and Talan. "I would think Sir Talan and Sir Albin are though."

"What would make you think that?" Lecie cast a furtive glance back. Finding Albin's gaze on her, she jerked her head forward.

"Knights are always hungry," Osana said. "Especially knights of their size."

"Do you think I will grow as tall as they, Lecie?" Clayton stifled a yawn. "I would be a fearsome knight to behold if I did."

"You will grow no taller than Da," Osana spoke up.

With a disapproving look directed at Osana, Lecie said, "Which is tall enough to be a fearsome knight."

"I think so too." Kicking a stone out of his path, Clayton fell silent.

Reaching the inn, Lecie noted the swatch of black linen marking the door. Lightly touching the sign of mourning, her thoughts turned to the only other time they had closed the inn after the death of her mother.

"Are you alright?" Albin spoke softly from behind her.

"Fine," she said entering behind the children.

Clayton was about to follow the twins up the steps when he instead hugged Lecie. "I love you."

"I love you too, little man." Stroking Clayton's blond hair, she bent to kiss the top of his head. "I shall be up in a trice to tuck you in."

"Do you think Sir Albin can tuck me in tonight?"

"I would be honored," Albin said, "if your sister agrees."

"That will be fine." Unsure of what to do, Lecie decided to straighten up the common room.

Without speaking, Talan joined her. Taking down the boards that held Edric's coffin, he returned them to the stables.

Talan was rinsing the last of the cups and Lecie was sweeping the floor when Albin returned.

"Lecie, I cannot tell you how sorry I am for... everything."

"Thank you, Sir Albin," Lecie murmured while Talan slipped from the room to give them privacy.

"I was left with little choice. Surely you can see that?"

"You still had more of a choice than was given me." Willing herself to feel nothing, she paused in her task to meet his warm brown gaze. "Who will protect the children once you depart for Castell Maen?"

"Once I depart? Why would I do that?"

"Why would you not? You are under obligation to Baron Erlegh, are you not?"

"No, lass." Albin smiled to allay her fears. "After what happened in the palace, King Henry officially discharged me from service. I am here as a favor and under no obligation to anyone."

"So you plan on staying in Rochester?" Lecie attempted to make sense of it all.

"You were present at our wedding, were you not?" Albin teased. "If tis your wish to stay here, I will as well."

"But your family..." She knew so little about the man she had recently wed. "Would you live so far from them?"

"You and the children are also my family. I had hoped you would have realized that."

"Actually, I had not given it much thought."

"I can understand that. Had the circumstances been different, I would have proposed to you properly."

"As to that I must apologize. Had my father been in his right mind, he never would have coerced such a promise from you."

"Your father did not coerce me into marrying you, Lecie."

"Oh? Then why did you do it?"

Gently cupping her face, Albin searched her eyes. "Cannot you think of another reason?"

"Aye, I could. If not for my father's request, you felt you had no choice."

Dropping his hands, Albin stepped back. "Explain yourself, please."

"Tis obvious, is it not? You are a man of honor and contrary to what you initially believed of me, I was a maid when we—"

"Say no more," Albin ground out. "I now know how you felt."

"I do not understand."

"You accused me of believing the worst of you. Is it any different than what you now accuse me of?"

"If not for honor then why did you marry me?"

"I have never known a woman like you. I lost my mother at an early age, and being a younger son, my father never took to me." Albin spoke without bitterness. "I have always considered Fulke and the men my family. Of late, I added her ladyship and the babe they share. However," he continued after a pause, "when the opportunity arose to make you my wife, I jumped at the chance. I count myself blessed this day to gain one such as you."

Seeing the truth in his eyes, Lecie composure slipped. "Excuse me," she managed brokenly. Bursting into tears, she hiked up her skirts and fled up the steps.

♥

Hearing silence, Talan returned to find Albin staring at the ceiling with a perplexed look. "What did you do now?"

"I have no idea." Albin shook his head.

"Well, what did you say?" Talan pressed.

"Is it an insult to tell the woman you wed that you consider yourself blessed for having done so?"

"I suppose it depends on how you said it," Talan said after giving it some thought. "Were you impatient when you said it?"

"Contrary to what you think, my temper does not always get the best of me."

"Well if that is not it, all I can do is venture a guess."

When Talan refused to elaborate, Albin motioned for him to go on. "Care to share it with me?"

"I am no expert when it comes to women yet would say that Lecie is emotionally overwhelmed of late." Talan clapped Albin on the shoulder. "Give her some time. I am sure she will come around."

"Right." Albin nodded thoughtfully. "I suppose I should have held my declaration of affection for a more opportune time."

"Mayhap," Talan agreed. "Only, since this is your wedding night one would think it an appropriate occasion."

"You are of no help." Raking a hand through his dark locks, Albin sighed.

"Come, my friend." Talan took pity on him. "Let me stand you a few ales in celebration of your blessed union."

"You know," Albin said as he led the way to the bar. "I liked you so much better when you were a surly lout."

♥

After checking on the sleeping children, Lecie thanked Betta and told her to get some sleep.

Harsent was no doubt sleeping off an afternoon of heavy drinking in her chamber and Gunilda had yet to return after Albin ordered her from the inn.

Worried about replacing Hamon, Lecie entered the master chamber. Lighting the tallows, she threw open the shutters to erase the sour sick smell still hanging heavy in the air. After stripping the bed, she noted the stains on the feather tick and decided to have it replaced the following day.

Tears slipped down her cheeks when she began to pull her father's worn and patched clothing from the wardrobe. Her kind and honorable father had gone without while a man he trusted stole from him. If not for Sir Albin, she would now be married to the thieving villain.

Her thoughts inevitably found their way back to Albin. As much as she wanted to be angry with him, his consoling words and kindness erased whatever animosity she still held against him. She wondered if she would feel the same if Talan had not confided what he had about Albin's troubled boyhood and immediately knew she would. Admitting the truth to herself, she has been infatuated with Albin from the start.

A slight smile briefly lit her features when Lecie recalled their near kiss on the steps during his last visit to the inn with Baron Erlegh. What a silly, foolish man she thought fondly.

Tossing the pillows into the passageway to be discarded she heard the sound of drunken laughter below and crept to the top of the steps.

In an attempt to lighten the gloomy mood of the day, Albin and Talan spoke of better times. Lecie stood there for a spell listening to stories of their many antics at court and Castell Maen. Hearing Albin's deep throated chuckle reminded her of why she fell in love with the carefree jovial knight.

Determined to be a good wife to him, she returned to her chore. Resigned to the fact she must submit to his carnal desires, she was resolved to do her wifely duty with dignity. She could only hope Albin would kiss and hold her beforehand as he had their first time together. To feel like that again, she would gladly submit to the pain sure to follow.

Finished in the chamber, Lecie left the shutters open to give it a good airing. After preparing his usual chamber for Albin until the morrow, she made her way up to her garret to retrieve her best chemise and dressing gown. A bit worn, the deep brown velvet of the gown enhanced the golden color of her eyes. After a leisurely bath she dressed wondering what was keeping her husband.

The sound of snores hit her when she placed her foot on the top step to descend. She found the two friends at a table reclined in their chairs with their heads thrown back. Relieved she would not have to submit to Albin after such a trying day, she added some wood to the hearth to chase the chill from the room. Bolting the door, she cast an affectionate glance back at her husband and headed to bed.

♥

Albin's head rolled causing him to wake with a start. Disoriented, it took him a moment for his thoughts to catch up with him.

Nudging Talan with his foot to wake him, he took a long swallow of ale. "I need to talk."

His eyes red, Talan blinked awake. "What could you possibly have to say at this ungodly hour?"

"There is more to the story than I initially told you."

Shifting into a sitting position, Talan poured himself a cup of ale from the earthenware pitcher on the table. "I am listening."

Expelling a weary breath, Albin avoided Talan's searching gaze. "Something happened atween me and Lecie the night you and I came back to the inn."

"You tell me nothing that I do not already know," Talan said. "You admitted as much to everyone within earshot."

"Mon Dieu," Albin said, "I did, did I not? Tis a wonder Lecie can stomach the sight of me." Hating himself, he raised tormented eyes to Talan. "I had no idea she was a maiden. When I realized it..." he could not go on.

"You broke off intimate contact."

"Aye," Albin said with downcast eyes. "I all but accused her of being an innocent like it was a bad thing."

"Wait a minute." Talan held his hand up. "Is that the full extent of your intimate relations with Lecie?"

"She is too innocent to realize there is no way she could be carrying my child when I coerced her into marriage."

"Lecie was given a choice."

"Zounds," Albin swore. "Is that the best you could do by way of advice? She had no choice and you know it."

"Mayhap you are right."

"Saints bones, I would get more sympathy out of Gervase, and he has the emotional range of a twig."

"Make up your mind," Talan said. "Do you want sympathy or advice?"

"What good is sympathy at a time like this?"

"You really are a surly lout when it comes to the fairer sex," Talan said. "What I was going to say is that once this slight misunderstanding is put behind you, I have no doubt you will find happiness as man and wife."

"Well," Albin grudgingly conceded, "that is at least something."

"You are welcome." Talan shoved his chair back to stand. "Now I suggest that you find your wife, and show her naught but gentleness. From the sounds of it, she will no doubt be dreading your next intimate encounter."

"He giveth comfort and he snatches it away," Albin muttered.

"If tis fanciful tall tales you want, seek out Guy." Stretching, Talan raised a hand to his temple. "Too much excitement for one day, my head is pounding."

Albin glanced toward the upper level. "I am sure Lecie is already abed."

"Probably for the best."

"Whatever do you mean?" Albin threw his hands up in exasperation. "Did you not only a moment ago advise me to seek her out and woo her?"

"Forgive me," Talan said. "I am not the best giver of advice when overtaxed and well into my cups."

"Obviously." Albin rolled his eyes.

"Listen." Talan gripped Albin's shoulder. "Do you really want Lecie to associate her wedding night with the day she had to bury her father?"

Albin appeared appalled by the thought.

"That is what I thought," Talan said. "Hold her close whilst she mourns her loss. There will be time enough to properly celebrate your union later."

"Let us pray Lecie is of a mind to celebrate when that time comes," Albin said pushing his chair back. "Thank you for being here. I do not know—"

"Do not go getting all mushy on me," Talan said in parting. "It has never been our way."

"Indeed." Despite the inner turmoil he felt Albin grinned.

Entering the empty master chamber, Albin assumed Lecie had gone to his room. With a nervous smile, he lifted the latch. He did not need the moonlight streaming in through the open shutters to tell him the room was also empty.

He squinted toward the children's door at the end of the darkened passageway. Prepared to plead his case, he raised his hand to knock when he heard Lecie's voice from above.

"Please do not wake the children. They have had a trying day and need their rest."

"Lass?" Albin looked up. "What are you doing up there?"

"Wait and I shall come down," she called softly.

Surprised by her amenable attitude, Albin whispered, "Are you being pleasant with me?"

"Would you have me be unpleasant?"

"You are a cheeky one." Albin clasped her waist to lift Lecie clear off the ladder. Distracted by the feel of her through the thin linen chemise she wore, he missed what she said. "Say again?"

"You were sound asleep when I checked on you so I did not think you would be making it to your chamber."

"Would you have preferred it that way?" Cursing himself for asking such a question, he held his breath waiting for her response.

"Is it customary in the village you are from for a wife to sleep apart from her husband?"

"No." He found himself grinning in the dark. "Tis most definitely not."

"Then I suppose therein lies your answer." Lecie hesitated. "If you would permit, however, I would ask a favor of you this night."

Albin's grin vanished as fast as it had come. "After all I have put you through of late you deserve a boon. Ask and you shall have it."

"Would you mind sharing your old chamber until after I have the feather tick in the master chamber replaced?"

"The feather tick?" Albin attempted to wrap his mind around what she was saying. "Is that the favor?"

"Aye, I would feel better if it were—"

"By all means have it replaced," Albin said. "I shall even fetch a new one myself on the morrow if you would like."

"I suppose you shall be doing such things now that you are in charge." Lecie began to weep. "Forgive me. I would not have you think me ungrateful."

"There, there, lass." Albin gently gathered her into his arms to hold her close. "I did not mean to sound so curt. Your humble request caught me off guard."

"What did you think I was going to ask?" Seeking his comfort, Lecie wrapped her arms around his waist.

"When I discovered you were not in my bed…"

"I see," Lecie said brokenly after a few moments.

"You have been brave for so long, my Lecie." Albin swept her up into his arms and marveled at how right it felt to hold her. "I shall no longer allow you to bear your burdens alone."

Albin carried her along the dark passage by memory to his chamber. After striking a flint to light the lone tallow, he opened the bed-curtains to pull the coverlet down. "I shall join you in a trice."

Pulling off his boots, tunic and linen chainse, he debated whether he should keep his breeches on.

He gave up on that idea when he heard the sounds of his tempting wife slipping beneath the coverlet. Untying his breeches, he figured she would know if he became aroused in either case.

Wearing only his braies, he felt Lecie tense when he slid into bed beside her. "Know that I shall never give you cause to fear me." Easing her back against his chest, he kissed the top of her head. "I am not good at expressing my feelings but I also grieve Edric's loss. He was a good man."

"Twas not a sudden passing," Lecie said relaxing against him. "I just never thought twould hurt so much."

"Let it out, lass," Albin coaxed softly. "Holding it in only makes things harder."

"You express yourself far better than you give yourself credit for." Giving into her grief, Lecie sobbed herself to sleep, safe in the loving arms of her husband.

Chapter Eleven

Lecie woke in the pre-dawn hours curled against Albin's side. Lightly trailing her finger along the length of his bearded jaw she wondered what kind of man she had married. She had always known him to be kind and humorous but the depth of compassion he had shown her came as a pleasant surprise.

She stilled her light caress when he stirred in his sleep, only to resume when he settled back into a soft snoring.

Easing away from him, she boldly studied his wide chest furred with raven hair. Boldly lifting the sheet, she studied his lean waist, and long muscular legs before sliding to his thick arms corded with muscle. While he had callouses on both hands from his use of the longsword, his right arm was slightly larger than the left. She noted every scar on the parts of his body exposed to her and wondered from what battle they came to be there.

"If you keep looking at me like that, I shall not be responsible for what happens."

Lecie's eyes flared before meeting Albin's drowsy gaze. "Is it wrong for me to say I find you remarkably beautiful?"

"Beautiful?" Albin chuckled. "I must admit it shall be the first time I have been called such. As for it being wrong, I should say not since it pleases me greatly to hear it."

"Would you prefer me to call you handsome?" Lecie's golden eyes darkened when she focused on his parted lips.

"Look at me like that when you say it, and you can call me anything you want." His voice gravely from sleep, he reached out to cup her cheek. "I have yet to see a woman who could compare to you when it comes to beauty."

"I have heard her ladyship Reina is beautiful," Lecie said without a trace of jealousy. "The rest of his lordship's knights say tis so."

"As do I," Albin agreed. "Yet I stand by my statement."

"That you find me beautiful?" Lecie's voice was a breathless whisper.

"Beautiful and the most desirable woman I have ever beheld." Rolling her gently beneath him, Albin captured her surprised exhale when he kissed her.

Tingles raced up and down Lecie's spine when he deepened the kiss. With a will of their own, her hands snaked around his back to draw him closer.

Lifting his head, he stared into her passion filled eyes as he lightly ran his fingertips along her face and down her neck. "Are you feeling better this morn?"

"Well enough to realize that I spoiled our wedding night. Can you ever forgive me?"

"There is nothing to forgive," Albin said caressing her waist. "Would you grant me a request?"

"Anything," she breathed.

"I would have you consider this our first time together." Albin pulled the neckline of her chemise down to expose a full rosy tipped breast. Thumbing the pert peak of her nipple, he kissed his way down her neck and throat to replace his thumb with his lips.

Lecie slid her hands through Albin's curls to hold his head against her as she squirmed in ecstasy beneath him.

Her eyes flying open, she stiffened when she felt his manhood pressing against her. Determined to suffer through what followed with dignity, she hoped his caresses would make the pain more bearable.

"Trust me, lass. I shall never hurt you again." Kissing her, he gently slipped his tongue into her mouth the instant she opened to him.

Lecie began to melt beneath his experienced touch. Working his fingers against her moist heat, she never wanted him to stop. "Albin," she gasped, "that feels…wonderful."

"I know what you are wanting, lass. This time I vow you shall have it and more." Shifting between her legs, he replaced his fingers with his tongue.

"What are you… oh…" On contact all thought escaped Lecie and she spread herself to give him complete access.

Her hands twisting the sheets, Albin felt her tremble when she neared climax. Slipping two fingers inside her, he kept up a steady rhythm until with a startled cry, Lecie's legs clamped down on his head.

Breathless, Lecie lay unmoving when Albin tenderly kissed her inner thigh. "Surely, not again?"

Rising above her with a self-satisfied look, Albin pressed his erect manhood against her. "There is no such thing as too much of a good thing, lass."

Once again fumbling with the hem of her chemise, he glanced at her with half-slitted eyes. "How much do you value this piece of cloth?"

Lecie attempted to make sense of his question when Albin rent the material from hem to neckline. "Never mind, I shall buy you a score more of them."

"Oh."

Albin smothered her soft exclamation beneath a searing kiss.

Trusting him completely, Lecie found herself wrapping her legs around his hips when he positioned himself above her.

Sweat broke out on Albin's temples with the strain of holding back. Closing his eyes, he turned his mind to less pleasant things before he humiliated himself.

Afraid to move, Lecie searched his tense face. "Am I doing something wrong?"

"Kissing her lightly on the lips, Albin shook his head. "I just want everything to be perfect this time."

"I am your wife." Lecie caressed his damp brow. "There is no longer a need for you to resist me."

"You are more than just my wife," Albin said easing into her. "You are now my lady."

Distracted by his words, Lecie forgot to brace for the pain that did not come. Stretched to the limit to accommodate his size, she instinctively began to move beneath him.

"Am I hurting you?"

Unable to speak, Lecie shook her head and gripped his muscular buttocks to pull him tighter against her.

Slowly flexing his hips the friction of Lecie's tight sheath nearly drove Albin over the edge.

"Why was not it like this the first time?" Arching her back into his chest, Lecie yearned for something more.

"There is always pain for the maiden the first time. If I had known that is what you were…" Albin slowly began to slide his shaft in and out of her silken sheath. "Things would have gone differently."

"So it does not—"

"Love, would you like to have a conver—"

Lecie pulled his face down for a kiss. Caressing him everywhere her hands could reach, she wanted him to feel what she was feeling. The tingle began low in her belly and she knew what to expect but it was the way Albin was looking at her that brought her to a second climax.

Albin moved against her until with a guttural rumble of pleasure, he joined her at the height of ecstasy. Still joined, he rolled onto his side as if seeing her for the first time.

Confused by his manner, Lecie reached up to smooth his furrowed brow. "Are you alright?"

"I have never been more content than I am at this moment." Albin drew her close against his heaving chest.

"All this time I felt compassion for the women forced to sell themselves," Lecie said peering up at him. "What a fool I have been."

"You are no fool and tis not always like what we shared."

"No," Lecie whispered caressing his cheek, "I suppose tis not."

♥

After taking a leisurely bath, Albin descended the step in fine spirits. The chaos that met his eyes drew him up short. Unaccustomed to the tavern being closed, it seemed as if every villager now crowded the place.

With Hamon gone, Talan had taken it upon himself to step in. He now stood behind the bar passing out ales as fast as he could pour them. Betta and Lecie kept a steady pace from the kitchen to the tables filling orders of what little victuals they had left to offer. Even the children were involved in clearing and wiping down the tables.

Failing to catch Lecie's eye, Albin strode outside with a determined step. His wife and family would not toil when he had it in his means to do something about it. Thanks in part to his frugal ways over the years he had amassed a fair sum to spend his dotage in leisure. Add to that the considerable piece of land Fulke had gifted him with and many would consider him a man of wealth.

Joseph was busy tending to the horses crowding the stables when Albin approached so he retrieved his destrier and headed toward the tower.

Bypassing the scaffolding, he rode toward the itinerant encampment. It took him several hours of interviewing but he finally managed to secure the services of three men and their wives to work at the inn. The childless couples were weary of their nomadic lifestyle and eagerly agreed to his proposal of settling down in Rochester.

With a sense of accomplishment, he returned late morning to find the crowd had not lessened. He handed Joseph a coin along with the reins when he dismounted. "Do your best to find a place for him, and give him a good rubdown when you are able, lad."

Betta, the twins, and Clayton were at the worktable cutting vegetables to add to the pot already set above the cook fire when Albin entered through the kitchen door. "Good morningtide to you all."

"More like good day," Betta huffed from beside the hearth. "Lecie gave up looking for you some time ago. Until the stew is ready, ale is all we have left to serve. Soon enough even that will be gone."

"All will be well and my lovely wife will forgive me when she discovers where I have been," Albin said turning his attention to the children. "We did not get a chance to speak yester-eve but I would like you all to know that I am grateful to be part of your family."

"Must we call you Sir Albin now that you are married to Lecie?" Osana asked.

"You can call me whatever you like," Albin said with a pleased smile.

"I like, Albi."

"Albi?" Albin immediately regretted his choice of words.

"You did give her permission," Clayton chimed in.

"I quite like the name," Sabina said. "It suits you."

Albin appeared uncertain, knowing the jesting to be had at his expense. "I suppose twill take some getting used to."

"I am glad Lecie chose you." Clayton beamed.

"We are too," Osana spoke on behalf of her sister. "You are far kinder than Hamon could ever be."

Uncertain how to respond to the double edged compliment, Albin dipped his head in acknowledgement.

"Are you going to be our father now?" Clayton wanted to know.

"Lad, you had a father, and he was a good man," Albin said to his rapt audience. "I can never fill his shoes but if you will allow it, I shall walk in his footsteps."

"I would like that." Throwing his arms around Albin's waist, Clayton held tight.

Sharing a look with her shy sister, Osana said, "We would too."

"Thank you." Clearing his throat, Albin ruffled Clayton's hair. "I best seek out your eldest sister now."

"Sir Talan's assisting Lecie behind the bar," Betta called to him on his way out. "We rousted Harsent from her stupor to wait tables. Gunilda has yet to show up from who knows where so I have no idea who is going to turnout the chambers for the returning lodgers."

"Worry not," Albin said, "our lots shall soon be made easier."

Pausing in the doorway to the packed common room, Albin admired his wife where she stood alongside Talan behind the bar. Her hair pulled back into its customary linen snood the constant activity added a becoming flush to her fair features.

In the process of pouring a cup of ale, Lecie looked up and froze when she spotted him watching her. With an exasperated look, she handed off the cup and waited for him to approach. "So nice of you to join us, husband."

Noting how at ease Lecie appeared with Talan a twinge of jealously caught Albin off guard. "I see cookery is not the only thing you are adept at."

"Seeing as how the new innkeep departed without so much as a word to anyone, I had little choice in the matter," Talan replied taking offense at Albin's gruff tone.

"Instead of being vexed with Sir Talan, you should be thanking him for seeing to your duties," Lecie said. "We would have lost much needed revenue if not for his kind offer of assistance."

"And just where do you think I have been all day?" Albin bristled at the set down.

"I know not." Lecie responded to a customer's summons with a dip of her head. "You did not think it necessary to inform me."

"I am unused to answering to a woman." Albin attempted to defend himself.

"And here I believed myself more than just a woman to you," Lecie huffed before storming off with a swish of her skirts.

"What in the bloody hell just happened?"

"Never mind that now," Talan said. "You have a family and responsibilities now. You cannot just up and leave whenever the whim takes you."

"I damn well know what my responsibilities are." Albin watched Lecie as she purposely stayed at the far end of the bar. "That is why I spent this morn hiring a proper staff to run this place."

"Then why did not you tell Lecie that?" Talan refilled another cup and collected the coin for it. "I know she will be as pleased as I am to hear the news."

"I was about to until whatever happened, happened," Albin said tearing his gaze away from Lecie.

"What happened is instead of greeting her with good news, you allowed jealousy to get the better of you," Talan said. "Misplaced jealousy at that, I might add."

"Am I as transparent as all that?"

"Love makes fools of us all." Talan sympathetically shook his head. "When things settle down, I suggest you take her into the garden to share the news. She is bound to be more forgiving away from this madness."

"I will do just that," Albin said. "Need I apologize to you as well?"

"Would you?" Talan looked askance at Albin.

"My wife stirs emotions in me that I never knew existed so if I truly offended you, I would."

"I took no offense," Talan assured him. "'Tis none of my business and normally I would not ask, but you appear to be more of a novice at relationships than—"

"What is it already?"

"Might you perhaps be feeling less than adequate where Lecie is concerned? After all, your first encounter was not much of an encounter at all, and last night held little in the way of romance."

"I would have you know that I more than made up for my earlier shortcomings this morn," Albin said smugly.

"You did?"

"Do you doubt my word?

"Never that," Talan said with an innocent expression. "I only mentioned it since Lecie does not appear to have the satisfied glow I often see from a well contented woman."

"You are intentionally attempting to make me wroth with you," Albin accused. "To what end?"

"Your sense of humor is what drew Lecie to you in the first place, my friend. Do not lose it now you are wed."

"I shall bear that in mind." Surveying the crowd, Albin changed the subject. "Has Hamon been about to stir trouble today?"

"No, and I do not expect him to." Talan gestured to one of the tables with a tip of his chin. "Leofrick and Edmund have been here for some time keeping an eye out for him and his band of troublemakers."

"What do you know of his acquaintances?"

"According to Leofrick, they are bad news," Talan said. "Lecie banished the lot from the inn some time ago."

"I would wager Hamon mentioned them when he threatened Lecie."

"Has she confided in you about it?"

"There has been little time to discuss it overly much," Albin said. "Despite her outward appearance, she is still grieving her father."

"Aye," Talan said, "tis obvious when she thinks no one is looking. Mayhap Mylla can cheer her up. Richard is escorting her here at dusk so she can pay her respects."

"How convenient for you," Albin observed.

"More like inconvenient if I am to be stuck behind the bar." Moving a little ways off to wipe up a spill, Talan returned. "When is the staff expected to arrive?"

"Well afore dusk," Albin said. "That should give you enough time to make yourself presentable for your lady fair."

"You should worry about your own. I have not seen Lecie take a break since we opened this morn."

"Tis not the first time I have seen her overlook herself for others." Albin frowned. "I shall put my foot down immediately."

"You really do have a lot to learn about women," Talan said with a look of exasperation. "You cannot command her to take better care of herself."

"Then what would you advise?" Frustrated, Albin threw his hands up. "Plead with her?"

"I doubt with Lecie it shall ever come to that." Talan leaned close. "I think you will find the sweeter the request the more amiable the response."

"I do not have Guy's ability to woo a woman with pretty words." Albin looked doubtful. "I am bound to louse it up."

"Even if you are true to form, I think Lecie would appreciate the effort." Heeding a summons, Talan moved further down the bar.

Catching Lecie looking at him, Albin deflated when she abruptly glanced away. "How I long for the days on the battlefield," he spoke to no one in particular.

♥

Doing her best to ignore her husband, Lecie graciously acknowledged condolences while serving and clearing tables. She paused at a recently vacated table when a large group of strangers entered.

Making her way through the crowd to ask if they needed rooms, she drew up in confusion when Albin rushed to greet them.

"If you will be showing us our duties, we shall get to work straightaway, Sir Albin." A stocky red-haired man wearing a threadbare tunic spoke for the solemn group.

"Thank you for arriving so swiftly, William." Albin drew Lecie forward. "This is my wife, Lady Lecie. She will assign you chambers and instruct you all on your duties."

Lecie's confusion switched to surprise when the reason for Albin's earlier absence became clear to her. Before she had a chance to voice her gratitude, the man called William doffed his cap.

"Lady Lecie?"

"You are William?" Lecie smiled upon hearing her title spoken for the first time.

"Yes, My Lady." William gestured to the two men beside him. "This here is Merek, and Simon." Gesturing to the three women standing quietly behind him, he added, "These are our wives, Anne, Winifred, and Mary."

Noting the tattered state of the women's kirtles, Lecie looked up at Albin. "The men shall be splitting their time atween tending bar, keeping stock of the ale, and replenishing supplies from the village. The first purchase is to be a new feather tick for the master chamber. Would you please give them the necessary coin from the till after showing them around?"

"Your wish is my command," Albin said with a grin.

"Thank you kindly." Lecie dipped her head with a warm smile before addressing the women. "Please follow me."

Leading the silent women up the steps, Lecie instructed them to wait while she climbed into the garret. Rooting through her trunk, she withdrew a trio of chemises with coordinated kirtles.

On the way down the ladder, their low conversation abruptly ceased. "There is no need for formality," she assured them handing each a chemise and kirtle. "I cannot vouch for the fit, yet I am sure they will suit better than the ones you have now."

The eldest gray-haired woman named Winifred held up the clothing. "You are gifting us with these fine kirtles, My Lady?"

"My name is Lecie. There is no need to stand on formality with me. And yes, I am gifting them to you."

"Thank you, My–Lady Lecie," the youngest of the three women said. "I am, Anne, and we are grateful for your kindness and the position you have given us."

"Me and my husband are indebted to you both, Lady Lecie," Mary, the shyest of the trio stepped forward. "I cannot remember the last time me and my Merek slept with a roof over our heads."

"I am just Lecie, and the position was my husband's doing. I am grateful to him for it as well. Do any of you happen to know how to cook?"

"I am quite skilled in the task," Winifred said with a strained look.

"What is it?" Lecie stilled. "If you would rather do something else I am sure it can be arranged."

"Tis not that," Winifred said. "Might we have your permission to call you, M'lady?"

"You suggest a compromise to my informal nature?"

"We just would like to show you the proper respect," Winifred said.

"Then M'lady it is," Lecie said. "And since you can cook, your service is most desperately needed in the kitchen." Glancing between Anne and Mary, she added, "I shall need one of you to assist Winifred in the kitchen and serve meals in the common room. Betta,

Harsent, and Gunilda see to the chambers so the other will lend them assist. I must warn you, of the three, only Betta is worth her salt."

"If I may, I will keep the chambers tidy, M'lady," Mary said. "I am also skilled with a needle so can sew and mend whenever needed."

"Betta will be most pleased to hear it," Lecie said, "and how wonderful you can sew. I have wanted to replace the bed-curtains for ever so long."

"If you purchase the material, I will start on them straightaway."

"I shall do so as soon as I can find the time to visit the draper's." Showing Mary where the clean linens were stored in a cupboard, Lecie pointed out the chambers currently occupied. "Dirty linens are to be placed in the basket by the back door. The servants' quarters are on the ground floor. I am afraid you will find the tapster's chamber none to clean, and the others are currently being used for storage. I cannot spare you at the moment to settle yourselves but please do so when you find the time."

"Please do not worry about us," Winifred said. "We shall make do."

"Aye," Mary and Anne murmured in agreement.

"Very well." Leading the ladies through the common room, Lecie spotted Albin talking to the men behind the bar and felt a wave of affection wash over her.

Determined to express her appreciation later, she continued the tour by waving a hand in the direction of the privy before pointing out three doors along the dark paneled passageway. "They will be the best of the five chambers. Make use of whatever supplies you can find and remove the rest. Should you require anything else, please let me know."

"Worry yourself not," Winifred said, "we have made do with far less."

"I would have you consider this your home now," Lecie continued. "Mary, please find Betta to assist with the chambers whilst I show Winifred and Anne the kitchen and brew house."

Bobbing her head, Mary was about to depart when Lecie said, "The three of you should be aware that Harsent, Gunilda, and on occasion, Betta, service some of the men who visit here. I am unaware of your views on such things, yet thought it prudent that I mention it."

"We take no offense," Winifred said. "We have grown accustomed to living amid camp followers."

"I am relieved to hear it. For the most part, they are kind women who have unfortunately been given a sad lot in life."

"We shall get along fine," Winifred assured her. "Fallen or not, I believe we are all children of God."

"There is one other thing." Lecie glanced between the women. "I would ask you to keep a watchful eye on the children. The tapster did not leave on the best of terms and threatened them with harm."

"He would have to go through me first," Mary vowed. "God in his goodness has yet to bless me and Merek with children. If permissible, I would treat your children like they were my own."

"They are my younger siblings and I consider them fortunate to have such a devoted guardian," Lecie said. "They were last in the kitchen if you would like to introduce yourself."

Bending a knee, Mary rushed off.

"Of the three of us, Mary is affected most by not having children," Anne confided.

"I am sorry to hear of your troubles," Lecie said preceding the pair down the passageway.

"Please do not misunderstand," Anne said, "tis not that we cannot conceive, God willing, only Simon and I felt it best not to until we are more settled."

"Forgive me for being so intrusive," Lecie said, "but you are both young. However do you manage to abstain?"

Anne blushed and looked to Winifred.

"Though I warrant tis unlikely owing to my advanced age," Winifred said, "our husbands do not plant their seeds within us, M'lady."

"I see," Lecie said not understanding at all. "Thank you for clearing that up for me."

A question that had often puzzled her over the years, at one time Lecie had asked Betta how she and the other women had no children to call their own. Clearly uneasy with the topic, Betta had sent her on her way with a promise to tell her when she was older.

Determined to ask Albin about it at the first available opportunity, she led the women into the kitchen.

Introducing Winifred and Anne to Betta, Lecie addressed the children surrounding Mary. "I see you have met, Mary." Directing her gaze at Osana, she added, "I expect nothing less than your best behavior whilst in her company."

"I am always on my best behavior." Osana giggled. "Can we show Mary the back garden?"

"Of course you can," Lecie said. "If you run into Clayton, be sure to tell him not to wander afar."

"He already knows that." Osana rolled her eyes before hiking up her skirts to run after Sabina.

"They are delightful children," Winifred remarked.

"Now that you have come," Lecie said, "I pray they can return to being just that."

After finishing the tour in the brewing shed, Winifred stepped up to take immediate charge of the kitchen. "Now you leave everything to us, M'lady. We shall have everything in order afore the sun sets."

With a look of relief, Lecie returned to the common room feeling better than she had in months.

Catching Albin's eye, she gestured toward the door in invitation.

Albin immediately excused himself from the conversation he was having with William and Merek.

Once they were alone outside, Lecie turned to him with a sheepish smile. "It seems I owe you an apology and a debt of gratitude."

"Oh?" Albin lips cracked into a slight smile. "And why is that, my wife?"

"You know very well why. I took you to task and laid blame at your feet when it turns out you were doing my family a kindness."

"Our family," he softly corrected.

"Our family," Lecie repeated with a fond look. "I do not always find it easy to have so much responsibility placed upon me. The inn has been our livelihood for generations and I often find myself another person when it comes to the running of it."

Capturing her hand, Albin began to lead her away from the inn. "From this day forth we shall share the burden as equal partners until Clayton can manage the inn on his own. Agreed?"

"Gladly." Casting a glance back, Lecie hesitated. "Where are we going?"

"You and I are going to enjoy a leisurely stroll." Urging her onward, Albin took in the colorful foliage around them. "This has always been my favorite time of year."

Falling into an easy step beside him, Lecie glanced up at the billowing clouds high in the crystal blue sky. "My favorite time has always been winter."

"But winter is so drab and dreadfully cold," Albin said taking the path that led to the river. "I imagined you would have preferred spring."

"Not a bit." Lecie shook her head with a soft laugh. "Too much work to be done. In the winter we always have more time for leisure."

"You have had a hard life for one so young." Clasping her hand tighter, Albin held back a tree branch that blocked their path.

"It has not been harder than any other alewife's," Lecie said, "and since my belly is kept full, I have it far better than most women."

"Speaking of a woman's lot in life, may I ask you something?"

"Of course, you are my husband."

"Hamon threatened you, did he not?" Glancing sideways at her, Albin slowed his pace. "I know he did, I would just like to hear it confirmed."

"The vile man threatened Clayton's life." Tears shimmered in Lecie's eyes. "What he threatened the girls with was a fate worse than death."

"Knowing him, I can venture a guess but you are to fear him no longer." Albin's eyes narrowed. "Hamon is now my problem and he shall soon be dealt with."

"Tis not just Hamon. He knows unsavory men willing to do anything for a bit of coin. I banned a group of them and fear they may be out for revenge."

"I come with my own band of men," Albin said with a determined look.

"They are not honorable men. Please promise me you will be careful."

Bringing Lecie's hand to his lips, Albin said, "You have my word that I shall be ever vigilant."

They walked the remainder of the way in silence until they reached the muddy river bank. Observing the vessels and barges dotting the churning water, Albin frowned. "Market day must be approaching, I had hoped for some privacy."

Intent to recapture their earlier lighthearted mood, Lecie said, "I know of a place, if you do not mind the walk."

"Do you indeed?" Albin cocked a mischievous brow.

"However, if you would rather return to the inn…"

"Tis such a fine day for a long walk, do not you think?"

"It most certainly is." Lecie guided him back into the line of trees running parallel to the river.

Picking their way through the brush, they began to ascend a steep incline. Hiking up her skirts, Lecie accepted Albin's assistance when the ground grew damp and slippery. "We are almost there, I hear the water."

"Glad to hear it." Albin chuckled. "At this rate we shall be fortunate to make it back to the inn by nightfall."

"Twill be well worth it. My family has been coming to this place for as long as I can remember." Stepping into a small clearing, Lecie smiled up at him. "What do you think?"

High above them a waterfall flowed down smooth weathered rock into a deep clear pool at its base before streaming further along to plunge into the river far below them.

"I think we shall have to come here often." Unclasping his cloak, Albin spread it on the damp earth before drawing Lecie down beside him.

Surveying the private copse, Lecie leaned into him. "Do not you think it beautiful?"

"Peaceful perhaps," Albin said inhaling the fresh scent of her hair, "yet beautiful can only be applied to you."

"On occasion, you do have such a way with words." A flutter in the pit of her stomach had Lecie nestling further against him.

"Bear with me, lass, practice makes perfect." Easing her further back Albin gently captured her lips.

Lecie sighed against his lips when a warm tingle weakened her limbs. Adjusting to wrap her arms around Albin, she completely gave herself to the kiss.

After a long breathless moment, he ended the intimate contact by placing a series of kisses on her cheek and brow. "If we do not stop now, I fear there will be no stopping."

Not wanting it to end, Lecie peered up at him with a mischievous smile. "Did I mention that few people wander here?"

"You would make love in the open so close to the village?"

In response, Lecie's hands slid down the length of his chest to the hem of his tunic. "What more invitation do you need?"

"You truly are the greatest gift I have ever received." Albin seized her lips while lifting her to straddle his legs.

Without breaking their kiss, Lecie began to stroke Albin's manhood through his breeches. Reveling in the feel of his hardness, her breath came in quick shallow pants.

Albin groaned his frustration against her lips when he fumbled with the ties on his breeches.

Rising on her knees, Lecie hiked up her skirts. "I want you inside of me, husband."

"Then I shall teach you to ride me." Grasping her hips, Albin entered her slick warmth in one smooth stroke. "I have never afore wanted anything as much as I want you."

His words were lost on Lecie the instant he filled her. Placing her hands on his shoulders she instinctively found her rhythm.

Untying the laces of her chemise, Albin freed her full breasts to capture a nipple between his teeth. He felt her begin to tremble on her way to climax and sought to prolong the moment by rolling her beneath him.

Wrapping her legs around him to grip his thrusting buttocks, Lecie moaned when he seized her lips. Their tongues kept a steady rhythm as the falls roared high above and the wind blew through the trees.

Oblivious to everything but the other, their simultaneous cries of ecstasy joined with the cacophony of sound surrounding them.

Chapter Twelve

Relaxing on his back with his hands tucked behind his head, it finally dawned on Albin why Reina had such a profound effect on Fulke.

"What are you thinking about?" Nestled against his side, Lecie traced the line of his jaw with her fingertip.

"How content I am."

"I am pleased to hear it."

Tilting his head to look at her, he smiled. "The proper response would be that you are as content as I."

"Is that what you wish to hear?" Lecie perched on an elbow to gaze at him.

"Men need to have their egos boosted on occasion by their woman, so aye it is."

"You dear husband, are not like most men and I am no mere woman." Gaining her feet, Lecie held her hand out to him.

"Where are we going?" Accepting her hand, Albin reluctantly stood. "I had other things in mind afore we were forced to return home."

"Who said we were returning home?" Slipping out of her chemise and kirtle, Lecie kicked off her slippers to gingerly make her way to the water's edge.

Wading into the glistening pool, she cast an inviting smile over her shoulder.

"Lass, there is something you should know about cold water and a man's private bits…"

"Never mind then, I shall swim alone." Dipping beneath the surface, Lecie popped up shivering.

The tempting picture she presented was too much for Albin to bear so he waded in after her. "However did you learn to swim?"

"My father taught me in this very spot," Lecie said splashing him. "I intended to teach the children only there was never time."

"Then you shall do so now." Capturing her in his arms, Albin discovered the cold did not affect him nearly as much as he thought it would.

♥

The sun had begun to slant toward the west by the time the couple started back to the inn. Her hair still damp, Lecie stopped along the way to pick wildflowers to brighten their chamber.

Content to watch her, Albin tucked a purple bloom behind her ear. "It does my heart good to see you smile."

"I have you to thank for it." Bringing the colorful bouquet to her nose, she inhaled its fragrant scent. "Could we get away like this again?"

"Would the morrow be too soon?"

"Not soon enough for me," Lecie said slipping her free hand into his. "I quite like having you all to myself."

"Just what a man likes to hear from his wife." Albin grinned, sticking out his broad chest.

"Are you boasting about your manly prowess?" Lecie teased with a smile.

"Are you lodging a complaint?" he countered with a cocky grin.

"Not as of yet."

Laughing, Albin swept her up into his arms when they reached the road leading to the inn.

"We shall be seen." Wrapping her arm around his neck, Lecie scanned the modest wood and stone buildings on the outskirts of the village for any sign of curious onlookers.

"So what if we are," Albin said. "We are properly wed, are we not?"

"Aye, we are indeed."

Nodding to the villagers they passed, Albin carried Lecie to the door of the inn. He kissed her tenderly before setting her on her feet. "I shall look forward to this evening when I shall have you all to myself again."

"Will you tell me more about your life at Castell Maen?" Pulling a leaf from his tangled dark locks, Lecie let it flutter to the ground. "There is so much more I would like to know about you."

"We have the rest of our lives for such talk." Reaching past her to open the door, he waited for her to precede him. "I would rather do other things this night."

A becoming blush stained Lecie's cheeks when she said, "In that case, we can chat over supper."

"Deal." Smacking her lightly on the behind, Albin headed for the bar.

Casually eyeing the half-filled tables on her way to the kitchen, Lecie caught Anne on her way out balancing a tray filled with bowls of rabbit stew. "Is all going well?"

Dressed in her new kirtle, Anne bobbed her head with a pleased smile. "Aye, it most certainly is, M'lady. This is the start of the supper crowd but we are prepared."

"I am glad to see you all have settled in so quickly." Lecie moved out of Anne's way. "Have you had time to select chambers for yourselves?"

"There will be time for that after we close, M'lady."

"If there is a lull, I would have you do it aforehand," Lecie said. "I know how tired you all must be."

"Worry you not about us, M'lady. Bobbing her head again, Anne went on her way.

Entering the kitchen, Lecie eyed the full prep table with approval. "Everything looks and smells delicious, Winifred."

"Thank you, M'lady." Winifred beamed while reaching for a pitcher. "The children have been fed and Mary took charge of them to see to their baths." Passing Lecie a cup of cider, she continued, "As you requested, the feather tick in the master's chamber has been replaced and your belongings have been moved in alongside Sir Albin's."

Unused to someone else taking charge, Lecie was slow to respond. "Thank you."

"Did we overstep our bounds, M'lady?" Her hand paused above the cook pot, Winifred's brow creased with worry. "You were not here to direct us so we took it upon ourselves to see to things."

"On the contrary, I am grateful," Lecie said. "It will take me some time to get used to having such an able staff."

Visibly relaxing, Winifred acknowledged with a slight curtsy. "Sir Talan mentioned that you did not have a proper wedding feast so when you are ready, I have prepared something special for you and Sir Albin. The garden is so nice this time of day."

Touched by her thoughtfulness, Lecie felt tears burn the back of her eyes. "That was very kind."

"Tis the least we can do, M'lady. You have no idea what these positions mean to us."

"If you will excuse me," Lecie managed, "I shall inform my husband of your thoughtfulness."

Despite the crowd and noise in the common room, she walked up to Albin, wrapped her arms around his waist, and began weeping.

Alarmed, Albin excused himself from the conversation he was having with William and Merek to guide her up the steps.

In the silence of the upper passageway, he gathered her in his arms. "What has upset you so, lass?"

"Tis nothing really," Lecie said brushing away the tears with the back of her hands. "I am just so very grateful for all you have done."

"I would do anything for you." Cupping her face, Albin lightly caressed her cheekbones with his thumbs. "Anything."

Covering his hands with her own, tears sparkled in Lecie's eyes. "Will you one day grow to love me?"

"Ah, Lass, I have loved you from the first moment I set eyes upon you." Albin tilted his head with a slight smile. "And though I lost the wager, I will gladly take a knee afore Fulke to thank him."

"You love me?" Disbelief had Lecie searching his eyes.

"Of course I love you. I would not have wed you otherwise."

Cupping his cheek, she shook her head in amazement. "I thought you married me out of a sense of duty to my father and because…well…you know."

"Most assuredly not, and had you believed for one trice that I would have stood aside whilst you saddled yourself to Hamon you are again clearly mistaken." Drawing her up against him they kissed until a guest returning to his chamber interrupted them.

Linking hands, they shared a smile as the man hurried past.

Once they were alone again, Lecie wrapped her arms around his waist. "What wager did you make with his lordship?"

"Never mind about that," Albin said, "tis an inside jest atween Fulke and me."

"Oh." Lecie's initial surprise quickly turned to passion when he captured her lips.

Mary departing the children's chamber had them abruptly breaking apart.

Clearing his throat, Albin said, "My wife is in need of a leisurely bath afore we sup together."

"I shall fetch clean linens for her at once." Changing direction, Mary hurried down the passageway.

"Which reminds me," Lecie said. "Winifred has prepared us a proper wedding feast to be served in the garden."

"Then I shall see you soon." Winking, Albin descended the steps whistling a merry tune.

Lecie looked wistfully at Mary when she returned holding a stack of clean linens. "Have you ever had your fondest wish granted?"

"Aye, M'lady, I have indeed," Mary replied softly. "I have always wished for a small place for me and Merek to call our own and you and Sir Albin have given that to us this very day."

Sobered by Mary's humble wish, Lecie clasped the older woman's forearm. "Now that it has been granted you must wish for something else."

"I suppose I shall," Mary replied thoughtfully. "If tis not too bold to ask, now that your wish has been granted, what else would you wish for, M'lady?"

"I wish that you and the others would call me Lecie yet I see that is never going to happen," Lecie teased. "I suppose we shall both have to think of something else."

♥

Dressed in a cream linen chemise, Lecie donned her finest dark green woolen kirtle kept for special occasions. Sliding in the silver comb Albin gifted her with near her temple she left the rest of her hair unbound to flow loose down her back. Pinching her cheeks for added color, she glanced in the water jug to discern her reflection.

"You look beautiful, lass." Albin's deep voice startled her from her vain observation.

Dressed in his finest charcoal tunic and black breeches, his knee-high boots gleamed in the meager light. His hair wet and slicked back from a recent bath, it had yet to curl into its usual disarray. Noting his smooth cheeks and recent beard trim, Lecie's heart began to pound. "As do you, my husband."

"There was a time when I would have taken offense to being called beautiful," he teased, stepping forward. "Yet coming from you, I accept it as the highest compliment."

Gesturing to the room, Lecie clasped her hands to keep them from shaking. "Is not the chamber beautiful? You could not have chosen a finer staff for the inn had you tried."

Skimming over the scrubbed and polished chamber with new garnet brocade coverlet and flower filled jugs, he returned his gaze to her. "Tis dull in comparison to you."

"I am sure Winifred is wondering what is keeping us." Lecie's smile faltered. "Shall we go below?"

Albin closed the short distance between them to take her into his arms. "After all I have put you through, you now boast the nerves of a chaste bride?"

Laughing softly, Lecie tipped her face up to his. "Silly, is it not? For the life of me I cannot explain it."

"Silly it may be but endearing none the less." Kissing her soundly on the lips, Albin drew back. "I shall ever regret the way we began."

"No, Albin, please do not regret a thing. I would have nothing mar the joy we have found together."

"You truly are an amazing woman." Lightly capturing her lips, Albin deepened the kiss when her arms snaked around his back. Lifting her up against his hardened manhood, he gazed down at her with desire filled eyes. "How hungry are you?"

"Famished... for you."

"Good answer." Kicking the door closed, he carried her to the bed.

Spread on the coverlet beneath him, Lecie's hands deftly untied the lacings to his breeches. Slipping her hand inside the linen, she slowly stroked the velvet length of him. "I love touching you," she breathed.

"Two can play at that game, lass," Albin said hiking up her skirts. Fingering her moist heat, he watched a becoming flush creep into Lecie's cheeks. "Is this what you want?"

"Yes...no." Pulling him against her, she said, "I want you inside me."

Urging her legs further apart, Albin slid into her. "Is this what you want?"

"Yes." Wrapping her legs around his back, Lecie caressed his flexing buttocks. "Oh, yes."

"What you do to me, lass," Albin panted struggling to hold back.

Beyond speaking, Lecie closed her eyes and threw her head back. Her body shivered when she climaxed with a breathy cry.

Driving into her a few more times, Albin bucked against her with a guttural moan before collapsing on the bed beside her.

"Winifred will wonder what is keeping us," Lecie said climbing from the bed to straighten her clothing.

Out of breath, Albin propped himself up on his elbows with a stunned expression. "Mon Dieu, wife, do you ever tire?"

"This is no time to be a layabout," Lecie said with a teasing smile. "There is celebrating to be done."

"At the very least you could at least behave like I moved the earth for you," Albin grumbled as he righted his attire. "It most certainly did for me."

Lecie reached up on tiptoe to run her fingers through Albin's damp curls. "How can I prove to you how pleased I am?"

"I can think of a few ways."

"Can they wait until we retire or are you up to it now?" Lecie teased.

"Saucy, insatiable wench." Albin captured her hand with a satisfied grin. "Come, I would not disappoint the new cook."

"Her name is Winifred and she is ever so nice," Lecie said on their way out of the room. "At first she was extremely withdrawn but I have already grown quite fond of Mary as well. I am sure Anne is just as pleasant, yet have not had dealings with her to the extent of the others." When Albin smirked, she tugged on his hand. "Why are you looking at me like that?"

"You are a veritable chatterbox when you are nervous." He chuckled. "I find I like that quite a bit."

"And you are truly exasperating at times." Preceding him down the steps, she glanced back at him. "Are you aware of that?"

Reaching the ground floor, he leaned close to whisper over the din of the crowd. "I like to keep you on your toes."

Pleased to see everything running so smoothly, Lecie led the way through the tables to the kitchen.

Winifred glanced up from her task when they entered. "I have everything ready for you in the garden." Sliding a tray of rolls above the fire to bake, she brushed the dried flour from her hands. "I shall be out to serve you both in a thrice."

"Thank you," Albin said escorting Lecie out. "After the noise and smoke of the common room I look forward to a peaceful supper with my bride."

"Twas Winifred's idea," Lecie said when they stepped into the cool evening air. "I wonder why I never thought of dining out."

Albin held out a chair for her at the table set in the center of the moonlit garden. "Knowing what I do of your dining habits, tis no wonder to me."

"I suppose I have always been too busy to enjoy dining." Admiring the flickering tallows and vase of wildflowers placed in the center of the table, Lecie lifted the cup beside it filled with honeyed mead. "It appears Winifred has thought of everything. She even managed to provide the wedding drink."

"Mead is considered the wedding drink?" Albin sipped the amber liquid. "Tis overly sweet, is that why?"

"The honey makes it so." Taking a sip, Lecie set her cup down. "Would you like to hear the tradition behind it?"

"I would." Entranced by the way Lecie was looking at him Albin gave her his full attention.

"Whilst I do not know the origin, tis customary for the newly-wed couple to drink mead each night for a full cycle of the moon. Some call it the honeymoon. Tis said to promote healing, fertility, and prosperity throughout the first year of marriage."

"Although I prefer your ale, I shall gladly follow the tradition for you."

"I believe a simple toast each day with mead would suffice in keeping with the tradition."

"Are you always so accommodating?"

"Marriage is a give and take, and you have already given me so much."

"You are far too easily pleased and I am thankful for it."

My parents worked together in all things," Lecie said watching him closely. "I would like the same to be said of us."

"You are and will always be my equal in all things." Reaching for her hand, Albin smiled. "Never doubt it."

"Thank you." Lecie studied their joined hands. "You are a gift I never thought to receive and I…"

"Here we are," Winifred called on her approach. "I hope you both enjoy fish." Setting wood planks before them, she stepped back with a smile. "William is quite adept at setting snares in the river."

Inhaling the appetizing aroma wafting from the flaky seasoned fish and vegetables, Lecie looked up with a grateful smile. "You have made this a most special day and we are ever so grateful."

Holding her hands out, Winifred bowed slightly. "Enjoy."

Once they were alone again, Lecie took a bite of the fish and marveled at Winifred's skill to create such appetizing dishes with so few ingredients. "You promised to tell me more about your family, Alby."

"Alby?"

"Sorry, I heard what the girls renamed you. We tend to give nicknames to those closest to us," Lecie said. "If you would rather me not—"

"Alby's fine," he assured her. "Only twould be best if you did not call me that in front of the Erlegh men, or tavern patrons, men in general so to speak."

Laughing, Lecie shook her head. "Men are so silly when it comes to showing affection of any kind."

"Not all men yet you do have a point." Taking a long swallow of mead, Albin set his cup down with a grimace. "Do you still want to know about my past?"

"More than anything." Afraid her mannerisms would give away the fact that she already knew so much about his boyhood, she continued to eat.

"There is nothing remarkable to tell about my birth family," Albin admitted. "Since I was not firstborn, I held little value in the eyes of my father. Not that I minded, he was cruel and often beat my mother for the slightest offense. If he did it in front of me, I would intercede only to have him beat me for defying him."

Once again compassion for his upbringing brought Lecie to tears. "I am so sorry. I cannot imagine how horrid it must have been for you."

"Do not be sad on my behalf, twas long ago and all but forgotten," Albin said pushing his supper aside. "Shortly after my eldest brother Glenbard sided with Clito against King Henry and fled the country, my mother fell ill and succumbed to her illness. I have no doubt she is finally at peace. At any rate she is finally free of the brute that sired me."

When he grew silent, Lecie reached to touch the back of his hand. "What happened after your mother passed on?"

Albin shrugged. "I kept myself scarce until Fulke lost his family in a tragedy. When he left to foster for the knighthood in a neighboring fiefdom, I went with him."

"In the end it sounds like your father did one good thing for you." Brushing a tear from her cheek with the back of her hand, Lecie hoped it went unnoticed.

"It might sound that way but tis far from the truth." Meeting her tender gaze, Albin smiled bitterly. "I told him he would never hear from me again if he allowed me to go."

"Albin," Lecie breathed, "I cannot bear to think of how much that must have hurt you."

"It ended well." Albin brushed off her concern. "Sir Hewett became more of a father to me than my own ever was, and I have always considered Fulke to be my one true brother."

"Then I am glad you found each other early on in life."

"As am I," Albin admitted. "Sometimes I think Fulke knows me better than I know myself."

"How so?"

Albin leaned back in his chair to admire her. "He knew of my feelings for you even as I struggled to conceal them."

"I would have to believe he knew of mine for you as well. Often enough I asked after you when you did not journey to Rochester with him." Averting her gaze, Lecie studied the dark beyond the garden. "He must think I am a horrible woman."

"Not for much longer," Albin said with a look of regret. "Talan has already sent a messenger to Castell Maen with news of our union."

"All that truly matters to me is that things worked out for us. Everything else will sort itself out in time."

"I cannot wait for you to meet her ladyship. She is going to love you."

"From what I heard spoken about her the feeling will be mutual," Lecie assured him. "'Tis no wonder his lordship is loath to leave home."

"'Twould take more than a mere tower's construction to force Fulke from Castell Maen these days," Albin said with a grin. "A happier man I have yet to meet."

"Excluding you of course," she teased.

"That goes without saying." Albin's dark eyes glittered in the moonlight. "No man alive is happier than I right now. I thank the good lord every day for blessing you with such a forgiving spirit."

"Truth be told, tis still a work in progress when I dwell on it, yet I am getting there." Lowering her eyes, Lecie kept the conversation on safer ground. "What is the babe's name?"

"Reina and Fulke named her, Catrain Malina, in memory of their mothers. Young Warin called her Raine one day, and the nickname stuck."

"You miss her," Lecie observed.

"Aye, she is a wee little thing and is bound to be twice the size next I see her."

"It must be hard to be away from your home for so long."

"Wherever you are is my home." Albin smiled. "You blush most becomingly when complimented in any fashion."

"You appear to have that effect on me," Lecie said. "I only wish things would work out so well for Sir Talan and Mylla."

"They do indeed have a rough road ahead of them. If the lord justice is intent on wedding Mylla, I see no way to deter him."

"Do you think Talan will walk away?"

"Hard to tell," Albin said. "When it comes to honor Talan is unyielding. He sees things in either black or white. There is no shade of gray. In the end, he will do what he believes to be the right thing."

"But they love each other. Surely that will outweigh any sense of honor he feels?"

"Though we are friends, I have never been privy to Talan's innermost thoughts," Albin said. "Whilst I am often paired with Fulke, Gervase is close to Guy, and Warin has Osbert. Talan has always been considered the loner of our band. From their time spent together at court he has her ladyship's confidence but more often than not keeps to himself."

"I know Talan has always thought highly of his lordship," Mylla said. "He has said as much."

"He all but worships the ground Fulke walks on." Albin chuckled. "Atween us, I think it makes Fulke uncomfortable."

"How so?"

"Fulke feels that he has to be the better man in all things in order to deserve such adoration. Trust me when I say, tis trying for Fulke at times to be the better man. He would have gladly slain Reynold if not for the dire consequences our family would have faced."

"Well it sounds to me like you balance each other out." Dreading he would leave her for any amount of time, Lecie asked the question uppermost in her mind. "When will you return to Castell Maen?"

"I am scheduled to meet with the master builder on the morrow to ascertain a more accurate time frame for the date of completion." Albin studied her anxious mannerisms before adding, "Then we all shall journey to Castell Maen for a spell afore returning here."

"By all, do you mean the children as well?" Lecie could not keep the hope from her voice.

"Lecie." Albin shook his head as if she should know better. "You are my wife. Your family is now mine. I have already informed the children that I have no intention of replacing their father, yet will stand in his stead for as long as they have need of me."

Tears slipped from Lecie's eyes and she opened her mouth to tell Albin how much she loved him.

"Well, isn't this cozy," Gunilda's harsh voice called from the darkness.

Albin stiffened while Lecie hastily brushed away her tears. "Where have you been, Gunilda?"

Strolling into the garden, Gunilda's eyes swept the table before coming to rest on Lecie. "What do you care? From the looks of things you replaced both me and Hamon."

"If I had my way, I would see you gone along with your lover," Albin said with narrowed eyes. "You remain by the grace of my lady wife so I suggest you watch your tone."

"Sir Albin was kind enough to hire additional staff." Lecie calmly faced Gunilda. "They are kind and work hard so mayhap you will learn something by their example."

"I make board well enough." Gunilda ran her hand along Albin's arm as she strolled away. "And you should count yourself fortunate that I choose to remain. A quarter of the men who patronize this place only come to bed me."

"No accounting for taste," Albin grumbled.

"Speaking of which," Gunilda called without turning around. "I suggest you stifle your swiving tonight. Your rutting by the falls earlier this day was loud enough to wake the dead."

Her eyes flaring wide in stunned surprise, Lecie gasped.

Chapter Thirteen

It was well after dawn when Albin woke Lecie by caressing her face. "I must depart for the tower, lass."

Stretching, Lecie made to rise when Albin restrained her with a kiss. "Go back to sleep. After keeping you up half the night you deserve the rest."

Lightly touching her kiss-swollen lips, Lecie smiled. "I am not the only one who needs more sleep."

"I am a battle trained warrior, I can handle anything." Wiggling his eyebrows, Albin grinned. "Besides, I have ulterior motives for allowing you to be a layabout this morn."

"Oh?" Rising on an elbow, the linen sheet slipped to expose Lecie's breasts. "What might they be?"

"I shall give you one guess." His eyes drawn to the tempting sight, Albin bent his head to suck on a pert nipple. Reluctantly pulling away, he met her passion filled gaze. "Hold that thought for my return."

"Oh, I shall." Watching him slip naked from the bed, Lecie settled back to admire the view. "Do not tarry over long."

Splashing water on his face from the basin on the dresser, Albin raked wet fingers through his tousled curls. "Keep looking at me like that and I shall be tarrying here longer."

"I would not be opposed to that," Lecie said with a tempting smile.

In response, Albin glanced toward the ceiling with a grin.

"What was that about?"

Sitting on the edge of the bed, Albin glanced over his shoulder at her. "I was merely thanking God above for gifting me with such a lusty wife."

"Albin," Lecie scolded. "I am sure the good lord has better things to do than listen to you rave about my wanton behavior."

Grabbing his crumpled tunic off the floor, Albin began to dress. "I still believe he would approve of my gratefulness."

"Albin..."

"Aye my love?" He paused in the process to look at her.

"You are an amazing and beautiful man," Lecie said solemnly.

"It pleases me greatly that you think so."

With a tender smile, she plopped back on the pillow. "Now be gone with you so you can return to me all the more quickly."

♥

Albin knocked on Talan's door and grinned in the darkened passageway to hear his friend stumbling from the bed to answer his summons.

"Good morn, layabout," he said when the door swung open to present a scowling Talan.

"There is nothing good about being rousted from a pleasant dream." Talan glowered.

"Ahh, I see." Albin nodded knowingly. "The fair and tempting Mylla paid a nocturnal visit, did she? In that case, you have my deepest apologies for disturbing your slumber."

"What do you want, Albin?"

"Since I have been lax of late, I am on my way to the tower to meet with the master builder."

"Give me a trice to dress."

About to close the door, Albin pushed against it. "No need. You have recently filled the gap left by me and I would like to make it up to you."

"If that were the case, you would not have rousted me," Talan grumbled. "Tis not oft of late that I have pleasant dreams."

Instantly sobering, Albin noticed the strain of late had taken its toll on his friend. "The justice will not be swayed?"

"I know not since Richard will not hear of defying the man," Talan said. "He believes all we can do now is pray that the justice turns his attention toward another."

"What are the odds of that happening?"

"Slim to none." Talan averted his eyes. "The justice sent a messenger to the sheriff's requesting the sum of Mylla's dowaire. Leofrick advised his father to say that they could not afford to put one aside for her. Again, Richard would not hear of it, nor would the surly Edmund for that matter."

"The lord justice is one of the wealthiest men in the realm," Albin said in disbelief. "Surely Mylla's dowaire would be considered a pittance to such as he?"

"It speaks volumes about his character, does it not?"

"Well, do not give up hope. Oftentimes these things have a way of working themselves out." Albin gripped Talan's shoulder. "When you wake, enjoy a day of leisure with your fair lady. I have but one favor to ask of you."

"What is it?"

"Lecie confirmed that Hamon threatened harm to the children."

"I knew as much." Talan stiffened. "The lowborn knave shall be held accountable for the harm he has brought to Edric's family."

"Agreed, but first we must find him."

"If you are going to root him out, I shall go with you."

"No, my plans this day remain unchanged," Albin said. "I shall see to my duty first. We shall search for Hamon in earnest on the morrow."

"What favor do you ask?'

"Would you include Lecie and the children in your plans for the day?"

"You believe Hamon still intends to carry out his threats?"

"He is a coward but I have no intention of taking any chances where my family is concerned."

"Nor I so consider it done," Talan said. "Be ever vigilant. Cowards tend to strike from the back."

"He would not be fool enough to come after me," Albin said in parting. "Sorry I disturbed you."

"Wait, did you just apologize to me?"

"It slipped out." Albin was still laughing when Lecie came rushing out of the master chamber. Seeing the panicked look on her face had him instinctively reaching for his sword. "Where is he?"

"I am so glad I caught you."

Albin felt her tremble when she threw her arms around him. "What is wrong, my love?"

"Please do not go to the tower today." Easing back, she looked up at him. "Send one of the recent hires to accomplish the task or wait another day."

"Why? What happened? I only just left you."

"I cannot explain it." Lecie shook her head with tears glistening in her eyes. "I just have a foreboding that something bad is going to happen to you."

"Which is why I spoke to Talan," Albin soothed. "He is planning on spending the day with Mylla and I have asked him to include you and the children. I cannot leave you in more able hands."

"You believe Hamon will attempt to follow through with his threats to harm the children?"

"Tis merely a precaution to keep me from worrying." Lightly capturing her lips, Albin kissed her until she relaxed against him. "Feel better?"

"No." Shaking her head, Lecie clung to him. "Tis you I am worried about. Cannot Talan go to the tower with you? I shall promise to remain here with the children."

"The lord justice seems intent to lay claim to Mylla," Albin confided. "I cannot ask Talan to give up the little time he has left with her."

"Then swear to me you will be careful."

"I swear it on my life."

"Do not say such things," Lecie said, "tis bad luck."

Kissing her soundly, Albin attempted to lighten the mood. "I do not believe in luck."

♥

After a morning spent with the master builder, Albin felt anxious to return to the inn.

"Baron Erlegh will be pleased to hear of the progress," Albin cut the master builder off mid-sentence. "I shall be sure to pass along how precise your accounting has been."

Accustomed to the curtness of the Erlegh knights, the harried elder builder said, "Until next time."

Intent on easing Lecie's mind, Albin spurred his horse into a gallop.

Rounding a forested bend in the road, he found his way blocked by four burly looking men brandishing crude makeshift weapons. "Let me guess," Albin said slowing his horse to a walk, "Hamon sent you."

"You took something that belongs to our companion." Wielding a pickax, a dark-haired man wearing a threadbare tunic and hose moved closer. "We are here to get it back for him."

"I am assuming that you are referring to my wife." Casually dismounting, Albin's hand slipped to the hilt of his broadsword. In his peripheral he tracked the movement of two of the men as they attempted to surround him. "And just how do you wretched band of lackwits intend to take her from me?"

"Ain't it obvious?" A heavyset man with thinning blond hair and rotten teeth spoke up. "She will be free to wed again once she is a widow."

On the contrary, if you plan to kill me, you should have brought more men." Surveying the dense foliage on both sides of the road, Albin slapped his horse on the rump. The battle trained destrier galloped to a distant spot to await further signal. "Where is your fearful leader?"

"You mean fearless," the man closing in on Albin's back hissed. "Once the tavern is his, we shall all have the run of it."

"Is that what the churl promised you?" Throwing back his head, Albin laughed. "Can you not see the arms I bear? In the unlikelihood you were to succeed in slaying me, my liege and brothers-in-arms will arrive to even the score afore your scrawny arses pass through the door."

The men shared an uneasy look before the heavyset man said, "Free drink and victuals for life is a risk well worth taking." Lumbering forward, he raised the iron bar he held to strike. "Get em!"

Calmly whisking his sword from its scabbard, Albin whirled around in place to cleave the man's head from his body.

The remaining trio of attackers gasped while they watched their comrade's headless corpse crumple to the ground with a loud thud.

Bellowing his battle cry, Albin thrust his sword into one man's throat before driving it into the chest of another. Kicking the dying man free of the blade, his sword dripped blood and gore when he turned to face the sole survivor. "I told you, you should have brought more men."

The dark-haired man surveyed the carnage of his friends before resting on a place within in the trees.

"I take it that is where the coward is hiding." Adjusting his grip on the hilt, Albin smiled. "Let us finish here first, shall we?"

Backing away, the dark-haired man prepared to flee. "I have no desire to fight you."

"Tis far too late for you to decide such a thing," Albin said shaking his head, "so you have two choices afore you. Die like a man or face your judgement in the boots of a coward. Either way, you shall not leave this place to bring future harm to my family."

Shaking uncontrollably, the man extended his arms above his head and charged. The pickaxe was descending when Albin drove his sword in an upward thrust that had the weapon entering beneath his opponent's ribs and out his back.

The pickaxe fell harmlessly to the ground as the man helplessly clawed at the blade impaling him.

"You should have picked better friends." With a somber look, Albin pulled his sword free.

Blood ran from the dark-haired man's mouth when he attempted to speak. His eyes unseeing, he collapsed on the ground at Albin's feet.

Rage had Albin stalking toward the tree line. "When I get my hands on you, I vow you will not have such an easy death, you coward." Brandishing his sword, he stood listening for any sign of Hamon's location. After some time, he gave up. "We shall meet one day soon, count on it."

Whistling for his horse, Albin cleaned his blade on one of the fallen men's tunics before sheathing it. With a last long look at the tree-line, he grabbed the reins and mounted intent to return home.

He had not ridden far when a piercing pain in his upper back and chest nearly unseated him. Spurring his destrier's flank, he reined around to face the threat. "Hamon, you spineless piece of shite," he raged. "It will take more than a quarrel to the back to bring me down."

The sound of disturbed brush had Albin scanning the tree line for some sight of the tapster. About to ride into the trees after him, his vision began to blur. "There is no rock big enough for you to hide under long."

His tunic sticking to his skin from the blood flowing from the wound, he let loose with his battle cry before spurring his horse around in the direction of home.

By the time he reached the inn, he was slumped over his horse struggling to remain conscious.

Joseph came running from the stables only to draw up short at the sight of him. "I shall fetch help with all haste, Sir Albin."

His horse dutifully returned to its stall while Albin heard a commotion from far away. The last thing he heard was Lecie screaming, and the last thing he saw was her reaching for him.

♥

"Lift him down gently." Her heart pounding in fear, Lecie instructed William and Merek. Eyeing the blood staining Albin's horse and tunic she struggled to remain focused. "Joseph, fetch the leech at once."

Without a word, Joseph took off running.

Preceding the two gangly men as they struggled with Albin, Lecie prayed all the way to the back door. "If you cannot manage to lift him above, lay him in the kitchen."

"We can manage, M'lady," Merek murmured. "He will be more comfortable in his own bed."

Winifred assessed and took charge of the situation the moment they entered. "Anne, find Mary. Sir Talan and Mylla took the children on an outing and she knew where they went. Summon them back at once. Betta, fetch water and clean linens to bind the wound." Speaking to no one in particular, she eyed Lecie's ashen face. "Has the leech been summoned?"

"I sent Joseph for him." Lecie heard her voice and wondered why it sounded so distant. "This is my fault. I knew something bad was going to happen and I still let him go."

"He is a man with a mind of his own, M'lady," Winifred said. "Now we must tend him and have faith that he will recover."

"Someone needs to summon the sheriff," Merek said adjusting his grip on Albin's legs. "I wager this was no accident."

"I shall do it myself as soon as we have him settled," William huffed from his place at Albin's shoulders.

Wrapping her arm around Lecie's shoulders to steady her, Winifred cleared a path to the steps.

The few early patrons consisting mainly of overnight lodgers grew silent when the group slowly passed.

"Go on up and prepare the bed," Winifred gently urged Lecie. "I shall lend assist to the men."

"Winifred…" Lecie found she could not voice her fears. Hiking up her skirts, she fled up the steps.

Completely pulling the coverlet off the bed, Lecie's hands shook when she adjusted the pillows against the headboard. Stepping aside as the men struggled through the door, tears flooded her eyes when Albin moaned weakly.

"Gently now, lay him on his side." Winifred directed the men. "The tip is protruding from his chest so try not to jostle the quarrel."

Relieved of their burden they stepped back to catch their breath.

Oblivious to everyone else in the room, Lecie knelt beside the bed closest to Albin.

"I shall summon the sheriff now." William rushed from the chamber.

"Is there aught else you need, Winifred?" Shifting from foot to foot, Merek could not take his eyes from the quarrel sticking out of Albin's back.

"The iron tip must be cut before the quarrel can be removed," Winifred said. "The armorer will have the proper tool. Tell him what happened and return with all haste."

Casting a worried glance at Lecie, Merek hurried out.

"I need shears to cut away his garb." Perched on the edge of the bed, Winifred glanced up when Lecie did not respond.

"He cannot afford to lose so much blood," Lecie said on the verge of panic. "I cannot lose him. My heart will not survive it."

"M'lady," Winifred snapped, "you must get a hold of yourself."

"You are right. I shall fetch the shears." Fleeing the chamber, Lecie bumped into Betta holding linen to be used as bandages. "Fetch shears for Winifred. I have something else to attend to."

"What could be more.." Betta rushed to warn Winifred the instant she realized where Lecie was headed.

Flinging open the door to Gunilda's chamber it banged against the wall.

Startled, Gunilda shot upright on the bed. "What the bloody—"

"Shut your mouth!" Seizing Gunilda's shoulders, Lecie began to shake her. "Where is he?"

"Have you gone mad?" Gunilda shoved against Lecie in an attempt to loosen her hold.

"You ungrateful whore," Lecie swore. "My parents should have left you in the gutter from whence you sprung."

"Then who would have tended to your father's needs when your mother was too fat with child to see to them?"

Slapping Gunilda hard across the face, Lecie came within inches of her foul smelling breath. "Know you this, if my husband dies, I will not rest until I drive a dagger through your blackened heart."

Lightly touching her discolored cheek, Gunilda glared her wrath. "Tis a pity he still lingers."

"Get out," Lecie snarled, "afore I slay you here and now."

"What is the ruckus all about?" Rubbing red watery eyes, Harsent stood in the doorway.

"You heard her," Gunilda whined. "Lecie threatened to kill me."

Pushing past Harsent, Lecie snapped, "Lend the bitch assist in removing her things for I will not be held accountable for my actions if I see her again."

In her absence, Winifred and Betta had managed to cut away Albin's tunic and chainse to fully expose the entrance and exit wounds.

"Betta here was concerned about your welfare," Winifred said when Lecie reentered. "Your husband needs you now, M'lady."

"I know that," Lecie said, "but this was no accident. Hamon is behind it and Gunilda is his lover. If she remains, Albin is in danger."

All three women focused on the door when Dr. Rayburn entered. Acknowledging Lecie with a cursory glance, he moved to the bed.

His color an alarming ashen color, Albin lay unmoving.

"He was struck in the back," Betta said giving the doctor room.

"I can see that for myself. If he were a lesser man, he would have fallen dead on the spot." Dr. Rayburn ignored Albin's rumble of pain when he rolled him to examine the entrance wound.

"Can you save him?" Brushing the tracks of tears streaming from her eyes, Lecie forced the words out.

With a non-committal grunt, Dr. Rayburn dug through his leather satchel for a set of iron tongs.

As he moved to grip the end of the quarrel, Lecie stepped forward in alarm. "You are just going to rip it out of him?"

"Would you have me leave it instead?" Dr. Rayburn spoke without pause.

"I have sent to the armorer for a tool to cut the quarrel," Winifred said. "Merek should be back any time now."

"The longer the shaft remains the higher the risk of infection," Dr. Rayburn impatiently explained.

"Wait." Sliding on the other side of the bed, Lecie clasped Albin's limp hand to her cheek.

"Normally I would advise against that," Dr. Rayburn said, "but since you feel you are better at doctoring than I, do what you will."

"I shall," Lecie responded unperturbed. "Winifred, please be ready to staunch the flow of blood that is sure to follow."

"The blood needs to flow to cleanse the wound." Dr. Rayburn settled a stern gaze on Lecie. "Will you again ignore my advice and stain your soul with another man's death?"

Ignoring him, Lecie met Winifred's shocked gaze. "Please be at the ready."

Without further preamble, Dr. Rayburn gripped the quarrel with the tongs and yanked it free from Albin's chest.

Lecie's cry of pain when Albin clamped down on her hand was lost to his scream of agony.

Feeling him go limp again, Lecie anxiously scanned Albin's face.

Covering the wound with fresh linen there was a slight tremble in Winifred's hand. "Will he live?"

Dr. Rayburn shrugged with a look of disapproval. "So long as the wound does not fester, he has a chance."

"Is there aught else you can do for him?" Willing to do anything, Lecie humbled herself. "Please, I beg of you."

"I told you the wound must be cleansed by blood flow."

"But he has lost so much already," Lecie said uncertainly.

"Heed me or not, I have given you my advice," Dr. Rayburn said on his way out.

Lecie ran a hand along Albin's brow to ease his strained features. "Winifred, mayhap he is right."

"Begging your pardon, I think not," Winifred said firmly pressing the linen against the wound.

"You are right, of course," Lecie acknowledged close to tears. "I am not thinking clearly."

A commotion on the steps preceded Talan bursting into the room ahead of Leofrick, Edmund, and Sheriff Richard.

One look at Albin's deathly pallor had Talan's jaw clenching. "We were returning Mylla home when William reached us. What happened?"

"Twas Hamon," Lecie said. "I know it was. He must have ambushed Albin on his return from the tower."

"Did Albin confirm this?" Spotting the bloodied quarrel on the dresser, Talan picked it up.

"He has not spoken at all," Lecie managed.

"Retrace Albin's route to the tower and see what you can find." Sheriff Richard instructed Leofrick. "I would know what we are dealing with here afore we leap to any conclusions."

"Worry not, Lecie," Leofrick said with a determined expression. "We will not rest until we find out what happened."

"I have already told you what happened." On the verge of hysterics, Lecie came close to shouting. "Hamon ambushed him. Who else but a coward would strike from behind?"

"Hamon is known to every villager in Rochester." Richard attempted to soothe her. "If twas him, he cannot have gone far without a horse. Do you know if he is in possession of a crossbow?"

"I know not if he has one," Lecie said, "but the surly lot of men he runs with most surely do. You should be looking for them as well."

"I will speak to the armorer and send a messenger to Castell Maen." Edmund spoke low to his father. "Baron Erlegh will want to know what happened here."

"Albin is Fulke's closest friend," Talan interjected. "He and her ladyship will not want to hear this from anyone but myself."

"Then I suggest you depart at once." With a meaningful look at Albin, Richard retrieved the quarrel for evidence.

"Shall I stand guard?" Edmund asked when his father prepared to leave.

"If twas Hamon and his band they would not be foolish enough to come here so soon after," Richard said. "Go home and ask you mother to prepare poultices for Albin."

"Aye, Father." Edmund appeared displeased by the menial task.

"You have my word we shall get to the bottom of this," Richard said to Lecie. "I shall return later to check on you."

After Edmund followed his father out, Lecie knelt beside the bed to take Albin's hand. "He cannot die." She met Talan's gaze with brimming eyes. "He cannot."

"There is a lady from Cornwall who visits Castell Maen with her husband. She is a skilled healer beyond even her ladyship's capabilities. I pray Lady Bronwyn is there for I know she will lend us assist." Straightening to leave a feeling of foreboding settled over Talan. "Will you be alright until we return?"

"I am not the one to be worried about," Lecie said without taking her gaze off Albin.

Clasping Albin's forearm, Talan bent his head in prayer.

"Please make haste," Lecie implored with a sense of urgency. "I shall do enough praying for us all once you depart."

Standing quietly beside the window, Winifred made her presence known when Lecie broke into soft sobs. "We shall do everything we can for him until you return, Sir Talan."

With a last long look at his friend, Talan rushed out.

Chapter Fourteen

Sitting vigil for the remainder of the day, Lecie stood at dusk to light the tallows. "Thank you for keeping me company, Winifred. You should seek your rest now."

"You must rest yourself, M'lady." Rising from her chair, Winifred frowned. "At the very least you must eat something to keep up your strength."

"I shall eat a bite later." Resettling herself on the bed, Lecie looked for the slightest sign of improvement in Albin's condition. "He is so pale and still."

"Yet is breathing is sound and steady." Winifred consoled her. "He just needs rest to build up his strength."

"If only he would say something."

"Sir Albin would not approve of you worrying yourself so," Winifred said. "I have never seen a man so enamored with his wife."

"I love him." Tears fell unchecked down Lecie's cheeks. "More than I ever believed possible. I have not yet told him and now it may be too late."

"Begging your pardon, M'lady, but I tend to think he heard you just now."

"Do you really think so?"

"With all of my heart." Gently squeezing Lecie's shoulder, Winifred stepped back. "I shall return shortly with your supper."

"Please, my love. Do not leave me." Curling on her side, Lecie lifted Albin's hand to her cheek. "I could not bear it."

Giving into tears, Lecie startled when Tugger came bounding into the room followed by Winifred a short time later. Drying her eyes, she sat up to order the dog from the room.

Whining low, Tugger nudged Albin's foot where it hung over the edge of the bed. His soulful brown eyes then shifted to Lecie as if wanting an explanation.

"Very well," she conceded. "You may stay. I will not even tell your young master of your traitorous change in allegiance."

With a soft whimper, Tugger lay beside the kindled hearth to keep an eye on Albin.

"I brought you some salted pork, bread, and a cup of cider." Winifred broke into Lecie's troubled thoughts. "When I collect the tray in the morning, I would like to see it empty."

"You sound a lot like my mother," Lecie said with a sad smile. "Thank you, Winifred. I do not know what I would have done without you this day."

Pleased by the compliment, Winifred smiled. "Summon me at once should you have the need."

Her throat dry, Lecie rose to take a long swallow of cider. Tossing the food to Tugger, she said, "Guard him well, and I shall reward you thrice over."

Resuming her place beside Albin, she draped her arm across his torso and fell into an exhausted uneasy slumber.

♥

Startled awake in the early morning hours by Tugger's low warning growl, Lecie sat up and spotted him pacing beneath the window with his hackles raised.

"What is it, boy?" Slipping from the bed, she threw open the shutter.

Growling in earnest now, the dog ran to the door. The instant Lecie opened it, Tugger darted out. Not far behind, she heard him bounding down the steps and his claws scrambling for purchase in the common room on his way to the kitchen.

"Fetch, and hold," Lecie commanded when she threw the bolt and pulled open the back door.

With a yip, Tugger charged into the darkness toward the thick copse of trees behind the stables.

Winded from trying to keep up, she scanned the dense tree-line for any sign of movement. "I know tis you, Hamon," she shouted into the predawn silence. "I shall be better prepared for you next time!"

Sticking two fingers into her mouth like her Da had shown her, a piercing whistle rent the air. Tugger barked in response from a distant spot before he came bounding out of the brush.

His tail wagging, he came and sat dutifully by her side.

Scratching him behind the ears, Lecie said, "Good boy. The next three rabbits you catch are all yours."

Rising, Lecie glanced toward the trees with narrowed eyes.

♥

"His color looks better this day, M'lady."

Blinking awake, Lecie waited for Winifred's words to penetrate her sleep-deprived mind. Once they did, she sat straight-up to observe Albin.

His chest rising and falling in an even sleeping pattern his face was indeed a shade lighter than the ashen gray of yesterday.

Lightly holding her hand to Albin's cheek, Lecie willed him to open his eyes to assure her all would be well. "He still feels cool to the touch and has no color at all in his cheeks."

"Still, he is strong, M'lady," Winifred said. "I have the poultices from the sheriff's wife to apply to the wound and given rest, he will be up and about afore you know it."

"You heard what the village leech said. He still needs the medicine Sir Talan spoke of to ward off infection."

"Would you happen to know how far a ride it is to Castell Maen?"

"Albin told me owing to good weather tis over a full day's journey with little by the way of rest," Lecie said glancing out the window. "By the looks of it we are in for a storm. They are bound to be delayed if the weather turns foul."

"We cannot turn our minds to such things," Winifred said. "You are still wearing your bloodstained kirtle. Go refresh yourself and get something to eat whilst I keep an eye on Sir Albin."

"I would feel better after a quick bath." On her way out Lecie noted Tugger's absence and paused by the door. "Where is the dog?"

"I let him out when I came in." Inspecting Albin's wound Winifred glanced up. "He seemed quite pleased to get out this morn, no doubt to chase an early rabbit or two."

"I believe he was after larger prey," Lecie said half to herself.

"I beg your pardon, M'lady?"

"When Tugger returns, he is allowed in here. Actually, I prefer it," Lecie said. "I would also like someone to stay with Albin at all times. Regardless of what the sheriff may think, what happened to my husband was no accident."

"Are you of a mind this Hamon fellow will return to do Sir Albin harm?

"I would not put it past him."

"Then I shall warn the others to be vigilant and we shall take shifts in order to complete our other tasks."

"In so short a time, I have come to find that I would be lost without you, Winifred." With a last worried glance at Albin, Lecie headed for the bathing room.

Dressed in a gold linen kirtle and white chemise, Lecie combed her wet hair and left it to dry as she peered in to check on Albin.

"Do not tell me you have already broken your fast?" Winifred chastised her. "You were not gone long enough."

"I am going now," Lecie assured her. "I just wanted to check and see if there was any change."

"I will summon you at once if he stirs even a wee bit," Winifred said. "Do try not to worry so much, M'lady. Sir Albin knows what he is fighting for."

"I pray you are right."

"Anne is taking a turn in the kitchen and is waiting for you. Do not come back until you have eaten."

"Are you sure you are not a mother? You have all the qualities of one."

"It pleases me beyond all measure that you allow me to mother you," Winifred said with a pleased smile. "Now be off with you."

William was tending the few early morning patrons in the common room when Lecie entered. "On the off-chance, has any word come from Castell Maen?"

"Not as of yet, M'lady." Tall and wiry with a fringe of gray hair and full white beard, William's kind brown eyes were filled with regret. "Can I get you a cup of mead or mulled wine to go along with your breakfast? Cider or ale perhaps?"

"Nothing right now," Lecie said. "Please find me if there is word."

"At once, M'lady, and might I say, we are all praying for Sir Albin."

"Thank you, William." Acknowledging the few villagers she knew with a dip of her head, Lecie entered the kitchen.

Mary had the children seated around the worktable rolling out dough in shapes of animals to bake. Dusting off her hands on her apron, she stood to greet Lecie. "Good morn to you, M'lady."

"Good morning to all."

"Good morning, M'lady." Removing a tray of rolls from above the fire, Anne gestured for Lecie to take a seat beside the children. "I am not near as skilled as Winifred, yet managed a decent enough porridge this morn."

"It was very tasty," Clayton affirmed as Lecie slid onto the stool beside him.

"Why thank you, Master Clayton," Anne replied with a smile. "That is very kind of you to say."

Accepting the bowl of steaming porridge, Lecie discovered she was famished and began eating before it had time to cool.

"Is Alby going to be alright?" Sabina leaned past Osana to catch her older sister's eye. "I am very fond of him."

"Me too," Clayton piped in. "I do not even mind that Tugger has taken a liking to him."

"I already told you, he will be fine," Osana spoke up. "A giant like Alby cannot be felled by only one arrow."

"Well there you have it." Lecie forced a smile. "He just needs some time to heal."

"You look weary this morning, M'lady." Anne slid a glass of cider in front of Lecie and proceeded to clear away the children's bowls. "If you do not mind me saying, you need to be taking better care of yourself."

"You sound like, Winifred," Lecie said scooping up the last bite of porridge. Downing the cup of cider she stood. "I cannot tell you how grateful I am that you and Mary are seeing to the children."

Acknowledging with a smile, Anne called after her, "Will you at least try and get some rest?"

Lecie met William's eye half hoping he had heard something in the short time she had been in the kitchen. His compassionate gaze had her trudging up the stairs with a dejected look.

Her eyes immediately went to the bed upon entering the master chamber only to let out a gasp of surprise and joy when Albin turned his head to look at her.

"Why did not you summon me?" Chastising Winifred, Lecie rushed to the bed. "How are you feeling?"

"Do not be vexed with Winifred, twas my doing." His voice a hoarse shadow of its usual baritone, Albin drew Lecie down beside him. "Have you eaten?"

"I consumed a full bowl of porridge." Kissing his brow, she leaned back to look at him. "You frightened me near to death."

"I shall do my utmost not to do so again."

"Begging your pardon," Winifred said with an embarrassed flush. "With your permission, I shall return to my normal duties now."

Without taking her eyes from Albin, Lecie said, "Take some free time aforehand. You deserve it."

Crossing herself for answered prayers, Winifred pulled the door closed behind her with a relieved smile.

Once they were alone, tears filled Lecie's eyes. "I thought I was going to lose you."

"Not if I have any say in the matter." Reaching up, Albin brushed away a tear with the back of his finger.

"Twas Hamon, was it not?" Her eyes darkening with rage, Lecie propped herself up on an elbow. "The sheriff would not take my word for it but they are searching for him as we speak."

"I cannot say for certain," Albin said with a frown, "yet I would wager all I have twas he."

"Rest with me a while." Yawning, Albin's eyes began to droop. "I do not like the shadows I see beneath your eyes."

Curling up beside him, Lecie met his tender gaze. "I love you, Albin."

"Tis about time you said it." Holding her tight against him, Albin fell asleep with a contented smile.

Lecie woke when the sun began to set with her cheek burning hot. Rising from her place on Albin's shoulder, her heart began to pound.

Panic stealing the breath from her body, she managed a choked, "Albin?"

Moaning in response, Albin opened his eyes without locking on her.

"Winifred," she shouted loud enough to carry below. "Winifred!"

Pounding on the steps preceded Winifred rushing through the door followed closely by Mary, William, Merek, and Anne.

"He burns with fever," Lecie said as all eyes focused on Albin.

Ushering the rest of the group out with a sweep of her hand, Winifred asked Anne to remain. "We need cloths and water to cool him."

"I know of something better," Lecie said. "His lordship's page, Warin, told me of how her ladyship saved a young lad's life stricken with fever." Her eyes darted to Albin when he moaned. "Lady Reina cooled the fever by soaking the lad in a cold stream.

Winifred, call the men back. We need to get Albin into the bathing chamber. Anne, fill the tub with as much water as it will hold."

"Aye, M'lady." The two women chimed in unison and jumped into action.

"We shall make you well again, my heart." Lecie was placing a kiss on Albin's fevered brow when William and Merek came rushing back in with Winifred on their heels.

"Sir Albin, we are trying to help you," William said when Albin slapped away their hands.

"Tis alright, husband," Lecie soothed. "We need to get you into the bathing room to cool your fever."

Mumbling incoherently, Albin relaxed the instant Lecie touched him.

Instructing the men to proceed, she said, "Have a care not to jostle the wound."

Oblivious to Albin's nakedness, Lecie slowly led the way down the narrow passageway while the men struggled to keep a grip on Albin's sweat-soaked skin.

Winifred was waiting with Anne when they finally made it into the bathing chamber.

"Gently now," Winifred urged when the men strained to lift Albin over the high lip of the tub.

Slipping into the cold water, Albin moaned in relief.

"We shall have you better afore you know it," Lecie said bathing his fevered brow with a cloth.

"Is there anything else you need, M'lady?" Merek spoke softly from behind Lecie.

"I shall summon you if there is." Her eyes resting on Albin's unshaven face, Lecie wrung out the cloth.

"Anne," Winfred said as the solemn group filed out, "assist me in changing the sheets afore you go below."

"I love you, Albin." Lightly running a fingertip along his jaw line, tears filled Lecie's eyes. "The first time you spoke to me I knew I was lost."

"What did I say?" Albin whispered without opening his eyes. "Something nonsensical I am sure."

"After I had to ask you twice if I could get you something, you simply said, 'Ale would go down nicely after such a tedious journey.'"

"I was obviously flirting with you," Albin jested. "How could you possibly have feelings for me after such a lame first impression?"

"Twas the way you said it, and the tender way you looked at me."

"Tell me more."

"I did not take you for a knight who enjoys romantic stories," she teased. "For I thought that was more of Sir Guy's leanings."

"Wife."

"Very well." Pleased he was once again responding to her, Lecie drew up a stool to perch on. "When we received word his lordship was coming to Rochester the entire village was abuzz." Lecie smiled in remembrance. "My father had to turn away some folk at the door for fear there would be no room when he arrived." Wringing out the cloth, she held it to the back of Albin's neck. "I had just come from the kitchen when you entered. Whilst all other eyes rested on Baron Erlegh, I had eyes only for you." Taking a deep unsteady breath, she felt relieved to find his half-open eyes resting on her. "You were jesting about something with Sir Gervase and did not even notice my regard."

"Not true." Reaching up, Albin captured her hand to hold it against his flushed cheek. "You were wearing an amber kirtle that so matched your eyes I was held spellbound by your beauty."

"You remember?" Surprised and pleased, Lecie smiled.

"Aye, I remember." He closed his eyes. "More so I remember the crushing disappointment I felt when Gervase informed me you were Edric's wife."

"Twas Sir Gervase who told you I was married?"

"Aye, twas he." Albin chuckled. "I should have known better than to trust the word of such a rattlebrained man-child."

"You still sound fond of him."

"I am."

Picturing Gervase with his handsome looks and fine manners, Lecie said, "He certainly seems to have a way with woman. Gunilda and Harsent spoke of little else after his visits here."

"Had he known you were not Edric's wife, he would have wooed you himself," Albin replied anxiously waiting for her reaction.

Pleased by his jealous tone Lecie feigned interest in Gervase to tease him. "If he were to learn a sonnet or two from Sir Guy twould be hard for a maiden to resist his courtly charms."

"Are you saying you would have fallen for the dolt if he showered you with flowery speech?"

"I was not a maiden to be wooed by mere words."

"Are you making light at my expense?" Albin appeared appalled by the very idea.

"What kind of wife would I be if I did such a thing?" Lecie dabbed his brow. "If you recall correctly, Sir Gervase also happened to be present the first time you came here, and still, I had eyes only for you."

"Well…good. I would hate to call out a man I consider brother even if he is an addlepate."

"You really should be kinder when you speak of him," Lecie said. "He has only ever spoken well of you."

"I shall keep that in mind the next time he does something that vexes me."

"The water has loosened the linen," Lecie observed. "I shall have to fetch more to bind the wound after I cleanse it."

"No." Albin clasped her hand to stop her. "Have Winifred see to it."

"I will do no such thing." Lecie straightened away from him. "You are my husband and I shall tend you."

"Lecie," Albin said sternly, "send for Winifred."

"Fine." Hurt by his rejection, Lecie stood to shake out her skirts.

"Thank you."

"No thanks are required," Lecie snapped on her way out the door, "as your wife, I am honor bound to obey you."

Saucy wench," Albin called after her.

♥

Albin pasted a smile on his face until he recognized Winifred in the doorway with an arm full of clean linen.

His features slipping into a grimace of pain, Albin nodded for her to enter. "I fear I cannot act the able-bodied husband for my wife any longer."

"How bad is it, Sir Albin?" Kneeling beside the tub, Winifred peeled back the bloodied linen to expose the infected pus filled lesion on his shoulder. Streaks of red had begun its deadly trail from the center of the oozing wound.

"Aye," he answered Winifred's unspoken question. "It festers. I would spare my wife the grisly sight so soon after losing her father."

"Sir Albin." Winifred eyed the wound with dread. "I must summon Dr. Rayburn at once if you are to stand a chance."

"No." Albin refused with a shake of his head. "The leech would drain the last drop of blood from me and still not heel what ails me."

"What would you have us do?" Winifred nervously wrung her hands. "This is beyond anything I have ever seen afore."

"My last hope is on her Ladyship Reina." Albin grimaced when Winifred tugged on the linen that had adhered to the wound.

"Then I shall pray her ladyship arrives in time, Sir Albin." Tossing aside the soiled bandages, Winifred gently washed the encrusted blood away.

Dipping his head in acknowledgement, Albin pushed against the bottom of the tub to expose more of his shoulder. "Bind the wound afore my wife sees it then send for the men to lend assist in returning me to my bed. I doubt I can make it on my own."

"I know I am overstepping," Winifred said, "but I feel M'lady has a right to know."

"She will know soon enough." Albin briefly blacked out when Winifred lightly bound his shoulder. The next thing he remembered was William and Merek helping him out of the tub.

He leaned heavily on the two men and fought against the darkness on the way to the master chamber. Visibly shaking from the effort, he closed his eyes after managing to climb into bed.

"Rest now, Sir Albin." Winifred opened the shutters to allow the cool breeze to enter the room. "Lecie will no doubt be in soon to check on you."

"Tis unlikely," Albin responded without opening his eyes. "My wife is in a fit of temper at the moment."

"That she is," Winifred admitted. "She is also beset with worry about you, as we all are."

"I have far too much to live for to die now," Albin said before slipping into unconsciousness.

Chapter Fifteen

Passing through the full common room during the evening meal, Lecie lit a tallow in the kitchen and headed straight for the brewing shed. A place she had always gone to be alone, she nearly pulled the door from its leather hinges before storming inside.

"By all that is holy, Lecie, you gave me a fright." Clutching her chest, Betta dropped the lid to a barrel of hops.

"My apologies," Lecie murmured. "I thought I would make myself useful and check on the stores of barley."

Eyeing Lecie with worry, Betta gestured to the full barrels lined against the wall. "The men Sir Albin hired are seeing well to the stores."

"I am glad to hear it." Not in the mood to talk, Lecie turned to go. "I am going for a walk."

"I am praying for your husband's recovery," Betta said softly.

"You know me so well. I fear I am deeply distressed by his condition despite his assurances."

"Begging your pardon," Betta said, "if that is the case, perhaps taking a walk is not what you should be doing right now."

"You are right, of course. Despite the fact that I am wroth with him my place is beside my husband." Glancing over her shoulder, Lecie smiled. "Thank you for reminding me of that fact."

"I am not such a lost soul as some might think."

"A lost soul is the last thing I would ascribe to you."

Pausing in the kitchen, Lecie poured a cup of ale and grabbed a loaf of fresh baked bread to bring to Albin.

The common room was at full capacity when she passed through. Stopping only long enough to ask Simon if a messenger had arrived from Castell Maen, she acknowledged the negative reply with a weary nod and headed up the steps.

Tugger anxiously scratching and growling at the closed master chamber's door had Lecie's heart pounding. Dropping the cup and bread, she rushed forward. She felt the fine hairs on the back of her neck stand on end when Tugger turned soulful eyes upon her as if pleading with her to hurry.

Twisting the latch on the door, Tugger lunged inside ahead of her.

Time appeared to stand still for Lecie while her mind tried to make sense of what she was seeing. Hunched over the bed, Hamon held a pillow poised inches above Albin's face. A flashback image of the pillow she picked up from the floor on the day of her father's death nearly overwhelmed her. Fixated on the pillow, rage consumed her. "You lowly fiend, you murdered my father, and now you are attempting to kill my husband!"

With hackles raised, Tugger growled and gnashed his teeth waiting for Lecie's command.

Inching away from the dog, Hamon's look of surprise switched to one of malice and he again lowered the pillow over Albin's face. "This time, I shall not fail."

"Tugger, attack," Lecie called when she leapt on the bed to protect Albin.

Snarling, Tugger surged forward to clamp down on Hamon's boney calf. Blood oozed from the puncture wounds as the dog's paws scrambled for purchase on the polished wood flooring.

With a bellow of rage, Hamon hefted the stoneware pitcher on the nightstand to smash it against Tugger's head and side. Yelping in pain, the dog refused to loosen his grip until after repeated blows broke the pottery.

With a last loud whine of pain, Tugger took several faltering steps to fall unmoving beneath the window.

"No," Lecie screamed throwing herself off the bed on top of Hamon. Pummeling him on the back with her fists, she cried out for help.

"Enough of this," Hamon hissed, elbowing Lecie in the stomach.

Buckling from the winded blow, she lost her grip and felt herself falling backward. Tensing for impact, she slammed into the dresser striking her head before tumbling face-first to the floor.

"I shall deal with you shortly," Hamon ground out. Scooping up the discarded pillow, he returned to the bed.

Dazed and winded, Lecie pulled herself up to grab Albin's sword. Barely able to lift the heavy weapon, she struggled to slide the steel blade from its wooden sheath.

"You always did enjoy playing the man." Amused by her attempts to stop him, Hamon chuckled. "I shall soon show you how a real man treats his woman."

Albin began to flail on the bed when Hamon pressed his full weight upon the feather pillow cutting off his air supply.

In desperation, Lecie spotted Albin's silver dinner knife on top of the dresser and dropped the sword with a clatter.

Snatching up the blade by the intricately carved handle, she flung herself forward. "Get away from him!"

Hamon inhaled sharply when the knife entered his back to the hilt. Staggering away from the bed, he attempted to remove the blade embedded between his shoulder blades. After several futile attempts his arms fell to his sides and he turned to face her with a look of disbelief. "I always knew you were a bitch." With his mouth spurting blood, he dropped to his knees before pitching forward dead at her feet.

"You slayed him!" The high-pitched screech from the doorway had Lecie spinning around. "You murdered my Hamon." Her chest heaving, Gunilda stood staring in shock at her lover's life-blood staining the wood beneath his prone body.

Ignoring her, Lecie shoved the pillow away from Albin's face. "Albin, speak to me." Tears slipped from her eyes as she gently cradled his head. "Please, my love, say something."

So focused on the steady rise and fall of Albin's chest, Lecie was unaware of Harsent rushing into the room followed by a host of other people.

"Let him go, M'lady."

Winifred's soothing tone broke through Lecie's shock bringing her into the midst of the chaotic scene happening around her. "He tried to kill my Alby."

"He shan't have another chance to hurt anyone, M'lady." Winifred gently wiped the tears from Lecie's cheeks with the edge of the bed covering. "Sheriff Richard and his sons are below. They have already taken Gunilda and Harsent's statements and would like to speak to you now."

"The sheriff is here?"

"You were not yourself for a wee bit, M'lady," Winifred said with a concerned look. "The sheriff was in here for quite some time to assess the scene. He is waiting below to hear your accounting of what happened."

"I will not leave my husband."

"There is nothing you can do for him right now. The fever is making him delirious. He has been holding one-sided conversations with his mother, and keeps calling out to someone named Glenbard."

"Then he is dying." Lecie broke down. "His mother has passed on, and he is estranged from his eldest brother. He must be trying to make amends afore he leaves me."

"You must not think such a thing, M'lady."

"You do not understand." Clasping Albin's hand, Lecie brought it to her cheek." Afore she died, Albin told me that his mother had pleaded with him to reconcile with his brother. That is what he is attempting to do so he can die in peace."

"People utter all sorts of nonsensical things when fevered, M'lady. Come away now afore the sheriff sends someone up to bring you down."

Allowing Winifred to lead her away, Lecie hesitated. "How long will it take?"

"I know not but afore we go down, I must warn you. Gunilda has accused you of slaying Hamon. Twould be my guess she has set about convincing Harsent to back her story."

"I did slay him," Lecie said with a faraway look when they entered the hallway. "I had no choice."

"And that is exactly what you need to tell the sheriff."

"Tugger," Lecie spoke so softly, Winifred could barely make out the name.

"He is hurt but alive. Betta is tending to him."

"I need to see him. He fought so bravely."

"You must remain focused now to clear your name, M'lady. Simon closed the tavern and Mary took the children for a walk by the river until this mess is sorted out. Once Gunilda is discredited, you can check on the dog and return to Sir Albin's side."

"What if—"

"Please, M'lady. I vow Sir Albin will come to no further harm."

Seated at a table beside the hearth, the sheriff glanced up when Lecie and Winifred entered. His sons Leofrick, Edmund, Caine, and Frederick were standing silently along the wall behind him.

"You should clamp her in irons and drag her to the tree," Gunilda spat from the corner.

"Silence yourself or be gone with you," Sheriff Richard barked.

Glaring her wrath at Lecie, Gunilda held her tongue.

"Please have a seat." Extending a hand to the chair across from him, the sheriff observed Lecie's pallor and trembling hands. "You have no need to be frightened, my dear. By all accounts it appears to be a clear cut case of self-defense."

"So I am to be discredited, is that it?" Enraged, Gunilda stepped forward. "I saw her with my own eyes stab my man in the back when all he wanted to do was make amends with Sir Albin."

"I suppose his trio of cohorts were also trying to make amends when they waylaid Albin on his way home," Leofrick scoffed.

"Most likely they were," Gunilda spat. "Why do not you summon them here to give testimony to that affect?"

"That would be impossible—"

"Leofrick!" Having silenced his son, Sheriff Richard eyed Winifred. "If the wench speaks out of turn again, lock her in her chamber."

"Aye, Sheriff." Winfred situated herself beside Gunilda. "I will do so gladly."

"Now then," the sheriff said to Lecie, "could you walk me through the events leading to the tapster's death?"

Clasping her shaking hands together, Lecie looked Sheriff Richard in the eye. "Hamon was about to murder my husband the same way he murdered my father so I did what I had to do to stop him."

The sheriff shared a perplexed look with his sons. "Your father was not murdered, Lecie. He died of the withering disease."

"Tis true my father was dying, yet twas Hamon who hastened his passing."

"You know this for a fact?"

"Aye, I do," Lecie said. "The wretch smothered my father with a pillow and was about to do the same to my husband when I interrupted him."

"You lie," Gunilda hissed. "Sheriff, she will say anything to protect her neck from the noose. Can you not see that?"

The sheriff locked eyes on Winifred.

"Take your hands off me." Pulling her arm free of Winifred's grasp, Gunilda plopped down into a chair. "I vow to hold my tongue but I have a right to be here."

Sheriff Richard returned his attention to Lecie. "If you believed such a thing about your father, why did you not bring it to my attention?"

"I did not realize what Hamon had done until I saw him holding a pillow above Albin's face," Lecie murmured. "When I confronted him about my suspicions, he took delight in admitting the truth of it."

The eldest of the sheriff's sons, Edmund, observed the rapt staff surrounding them and said, "Mayhap we should continue this particular talk in private, Father."

"I have no doubt the gossipmongers have already spread the news of what happened here far and wide," Leofrick said. "They may as well hear the truth."

"Edmund is right," Sheriff Richard said. "Facts often become twisted into innuendo and rumor and our good names shall not be dragged into it." Turning his attention to the staff, he added, "After I speak to your mistress, I will have additional questions for you all so please wait in the garden until summoned."

"I did not warrant such kind consideration from you or your sons," Gunilda griped as she shoved back her chair to follow the others out. "You questioned me as if I were the one who plunged the knife into my dearly departed Hamon's back."

"Owing to your immoral profession, you are not entitled to such consideration." Eyeing Harsent with a calculating gaze, Sheriff Richard said, "Make sure you heed my words and remain on premises. I am not through with you yet."

Harsent's frightened eyes flew to Gunilda.

"With my man murdered, where else would we go?" Pulling Harsent along, Gunilda called, "Besides, unlike Lecie, we have nothing to hide."

Winifred held back when the room cleared to speak to the sheriff. "My Lady is still beside herself after what has transpired. May I please have permission to serve her something to ease her discomfort afore I go?"

"Aye, see to your lady." Sheriff Richard dipped his head. "And if you would be so kind, serve us all. We may be here for some time."

Sheriff Richard kept the topic to the mundane until Winifred returned balancing a tray filled with cups of ale, a round of rye bread, and crock of goat cheese. "With all that has happened preparations for supper were halted midway. This is the best I could do at the moment."

"Twill suit us well enough," Sheriff Richard assured her.

"Sheriff, might I be so bold to ask a favor?"

Surprised by the request coming from a servant, Sheriff Richard waited for Winifred to continue.

"In lieu of joining the others in the garden, I would like to tend Sir Albin. I know twill ease M'lady's mind to have someone with him."

"It appears Sir Albin has hired an able staff," Sheriff Richard said with a look of approval. "Permission granted."

Dipping into a curtsy, Winifred squeezed Lecie's shoulder on her way out.

"Now then." Sheriff Richard eased back in his chair. "What say you to being less formal, my dear?"

Politely declining the cup of ale Frederick held out to her, Lecie said, "Whatever you think best, Sheriff."

"You have had so much to deal with of late and I am sorry for your trouble. Rest assured, we shall soon put this matter to rest so that you have one less thing to..." He broke off when the front door opened to admit Justice de Glanville in his somber black garb.

Followed by his harried clerk hunched over by the weight of the leather pack he carried, the justice's dark eyes assessed the scene. "Your son Caine informed me that I would find you here, Sheriff."

"Justice de Glanville." The sheriff jumped to his feet. "What an unexpected pleasure this is."

"I was fortunate to conclude the king's business in a timely manner." Waving him back into his seat, Justice de Glanville strode forward. "I assumed your daughter and wife would be with you since neither is at your home."

"My wife's widowed uncle has fallen ill in Faversham." Intent to keep his daughter from the lord justice's unwanted attention, Sheriff Richard outright lied. "Mylla accompanied her mother for an extended visit."

"Nothing contagious, I hope?" Clearly displeased, the justice pulled off his black woolen cap.

"I would not have sent them if it were, Lord Justice."

"Did I not inform you of my intention to return to Rochester with the chief purpose of calling upon your daughter?"

"The man is an elder and the illness sudden. Being the important man you are I knew not when you would return, Lord Justice."

Slightly pacified, the justice said, "Now that I am here, you know. Send a messenger with instructions to have her return at once."

Hiding his disappointment by dipping his head, Richard glanced at his son Caine. "See it done."

"Aye, Father." With a crestfallen expression, Caine was in no hurry to leave.

"Bring in my satchel," Justice de Glanville ordered his clerk. "It appears we will be boarding in this hovel. That is, unless you have room to spare, Sheriff."

"Unfortunately, I do not, Lord Justice."

"I figured such with your brood." The justice glanced around with a look of repugnance. "I need to piss."

"The garderobe is in the back and down the hall, Lord Justice," Frederick said.

With a cursory glance at Frederick, Leofrick, and Edmund, the lord justice huffed on his way past.

"I told you that your plan would not work," Edmund whispered to his father. "You took a great risk to the detriment of us all. If the lord justice knew you were lying—"

"Cease your never-ending prattle." Leofrick spoke in a hushed tone. "Twas worth the risk to keep Mylla safe from him."

Lecie snapped out of her brooding to listen intently.

"She could do no better, and you know it," Edmund said. "He could find positions of importance for us all."

"And all we would have to do is offer up our little sister as sacrifice, aye Edmund?"

"Shut up the both of you," Frederick hissed. "He is coming back."

"You must have had an arduous journey," Sheriff Richard said when the lord justice returned. "Can I offer you and your clerk refreshment?"

"Is this hovel not properly staffed?"

"It is," Sheriff Richard said, "only you arrived whilst I was conducting an investigation so the staff is waiting in the garden."

"I will take a cup of wine, if indeed there is any, which I doubt."

"The wine will not be up to your standards, Lord Justice," Edmund said. "However, if you would like some twill be an honor to serve you."

"Then do so." The justice waved a hand.

Ignoring Leofrick's scowl, Edmund rushed to comply.

"An investigation you say, how intriguing." Taking the empty seat beside Lecie, Justice de Glanville eyed her shrewdly. "So we meet again, witch eyes."

"I was not aware you were acquainted with Lady Lecie." Sheriff Richard appeared confused.

"One does not forget a woman bearing unnatural–did you say lady?" The justice turned on Lecie. "You did not introduce yourself as such when we were introduced at the festival."

Fidgeting under the justice's intense gaze, Lecie murmured, "I have only been recently wed, Your Lordship."

"I see." Justice de Glanville eyed his clerk when he returned. "Bring a parchment and prepare to record."

Scrambling to obey, the clerk sat at an adjacent table and prepared to take notes.

"Tell me more about this investigation of yours, Sheriff." The justice leered at Lecie. "Surely, the lady here did nothing wrong?"

"She has been cleared of any wrongdoing, Lord Justice."

"Yet she was the accused. Of doing what, pray tell? Witchcraft?"

"Most assuredly not," Sheriff Richard said taking offense. "Her father and I were friends from boyhood, and I was present the day Lecie was born. I look upon her as a daughter and can personally vouch to her impeccable moral character."

"In that case, I suggest you monitor your tone and tell me what you are investigating."

"I certainly meant no offense, Lord Justice. We are looking into the death of the former tapster from this establishment. There appears to be conflicting stories as to what transpired yet I fully back Lady Lecie's account and have concluded the death to be an unavoidable case of self-defense."

"The only thing conflicting is your interest in the matter. Did you not say you liken her to your daughter?" Taking a sip of wine, Justice de Glanville set the cup down with a look of distaste.

"I am a man of God, King, and country, Lord Justice. I am sworn to uphold the laws of all three and that is what I shall do so long as I have breath in my body."

"How very noble of you," the lord justice drawled, "and how preordained that I arrived when I did. This way, no one can accuse you of partiality."

"I have never been accused of such, Lord Justice, nor do I ever expect to."

"Then we are in accord. What were the so called conflicting stories?"

With a look of resignation, Sheriff Richard said, "Two lowly tavern wenches have sworn that they witnessed Lady Lecie stab the tapster in the back without provocation."

Feeling betrayed by Harsent, Lecie's startled gaze flew to the sheriff.

"Surprised there were witnesses to your foul deed, My Lady?" Justice de Glanville smoothly interjected. "Bewitching as they may be, your eyes quite clearly give your wicked thoughts away."

"I was thinking that there were no witnesses present until after the fact." Lecie bravely met the justice's penetrating gaze. "The entire time Hamon was attempting to smother my husband I was calling out for help."

"Your husband was involved? Then why is he not here to clear this matter up?"

"Sir Albin is gravely ill after being struck by a crossbow quarrel somewhere on the road atween here and the tower, Lord Justice." Sheriff Richard spoke to spare Lecie. "Lady Lecie realized the attack was premeditated. After locating three deceased individuals near the scene of the attack, we concluded she was right."

"I banned them all from the tavern not long ago," Lecie put in softly.

"What does any of this have to do with the tapster?"

"He was acquainted with the men found on the road," Sheriff Richard said. "Sir Albin managed to dispatch the threat prior to being struck in the back by who we now believe to be the deceased tapster."

Hearing the men were dead, Lecie's look of relief did not go unnoticed by the lord justice.

"Sir Albin you say?" Justice de Glanville smirked. "You say he is near death?"

"He will not die," Lecie vowed. "Sir Talan will return soon with medicine from Castell Maen."

"His wound has become infected," Sheriff Richard said. "As we speak he burns with a fever that shows no signs of abating."

"Sir Albin has a great number of enemies who would not grieve his passing." Justice de Glanville's smile turned malicious. "In fact, my dear friend Baron Reynold will be most pleased to hear of this latest turn of events. From what he has told me, he had a most unpleasant encounter with this lady's husband in the palace's corridor."

"Your pardon if you please, Justice de Glanville," Sheriff Richard spoke with a worried glance at Lecie. "Are you saying that Sir Albin deserved what happened to him?"

"Certainly not." Justice de Glanville's smile did not reach his eyes. "Where would the justice be in that?"

"My thoughts precisely," the sheriff said with a skeptical look.

"It truly is fortuitous that I have arrived at such a time." Justice de Glanville reached for his cup. "Whilst we await the return of your wife and daughter, I shall hold a court of justice to decide this lady's fate."

Chapter Sixteen

"Lord Justice," Sheriff Richard said, "with all due respect I must protest. The evidence clearly exonerates—"

"You forget yourself." The justice examined his filed nails with a bored look. "I can strip you of your position on a whim. Go against me on this, and I shall."

Refusing to allow such a thing to happen, Lecie stood when Sheriff Richard opened his mouth to protest. "May I have permission to see my husband aforehand?"

"You may." Justice de Glanville's gaze slid to her. "Enjoy what remains of this day with him. We shall convene court in the village square at dawn on the morrow."

With a look of regret the sheriff placed his hand on Lecie's forearm when she moved past him. "I shall join you in a trice."

"No, you will not," the justice said. "You and I have much to discuss and I will not risk you colluding with the accused."

"My father is far more respectable—" Leofrick's next words were lost when Edmund elbowed him hard in the gut.

"Leofrick," Sheriff Richard said to diffuse the sudden tension, "return home and inform your mother that I will be detained here for some time."

"Aye, Father." With a last look at Lecie, he left.

"Please excuse me." Lecie briefly met the sheriff's worried gaze before she lifted her skirts to ascend the steps. Come what may, her fate was out of her hands now.

Relieved someone had removed Hamon's body from the master chamber she eyed the blood soaked flooring.

Trembling uncontrollably, she realized her body was not reacting to any feelings of guilt or remorse for slaying Hamon. It was relief that she had arrived in time to save Albin's life.

Tears flooded her vision as she turned her eyes heavenward to give thanks.

Albin's low moan brought her back to the present. Burning with fever, his lips had become white and cracked.

Perched on the edge of the bed beside him, Winifred was trickling water into his open mouth. "M'lady, is all well with you? Betta seems to think otherwise."

"She is more oft right than not." Lecie braved a smile. "Justice de Glanville has arrived and tis obvious he does not think very highly of me."

Both women glanced up when Anne came rushing in. "Leofrick just told Merek in the yard that the justice is trying you in the square on the morrow, M'lady. Is it true?"

"Aye, tis true," Lecie said fighting back tears. "If I am found guilty… if I am…I want you both to promise me that you will look after Albin and the children."

"Justice is on your side, M'lady," Winifred said. "Sheriff Richard said so."

"It matters naught what the sheriff said. The justice is bent on revenge for a past slight so I do not expect it to go well for me. Please promise me. I need to know my family will be looked after so I can face what is to come with my head held high."

"I promise, M'lady," Anne said. "I will look after them like they were my own."

"And you have my word," Winfred said, "but there must be something we can do."

"I am afraid all we can do now is pray." Smoothing a curl away from Albin's temple, Lecie added, "Would you please leave me alone with my husband for a time?"

"Send for me if you need anything at all." With a sympathetic look, Anne hurried from the chamber and promptly burst into tears.

"Betta will be in soon to scrub the floor. She did not want you to see it." Pausing at the door, Winifred turned back. "The lot of us would do anything for you and Sir Albin, anything at all."

"Thank you," Lecie managed in a broken whisper. A whimper had her rushing toward a slow moving Tugger when he slipped past Winifred before she could close the door. Dropping to her knees she resisted the urge to throw her arms around the injured dog. "You will have a life of leisure till the end of your days for being so brave." Pulling a blanket from a trunk, Lecie placed it at the foot of the bed for Tugger to curl up on.

Lying on the bed facing Albin, she felt hot tears slip into her hair. "Come what may on the morrow, I shall never stop loving you. Wherever it is that I may be."

♥

Winifred stormed down the steps intent on confronting Gunilda and Harsent. Justice de Glanville supping alone beside the hearth gave her pause when she entered the common room.

Glowering at the pair of loose women perched on stools at the bar, she briefly met Merek's gaze and jerked her head toward the kitchen.

"Has Mary returned with the children?" Winifred startled Simon who was adding wood to the hearth's fire when she entered.

"The children are beside themselves with worry so she took them to look for berries in the forest and they have yet to return."

Simon straightened. "The sheriff instructed us to see about our duties. Whatever is going on with the mistress?"

"I shall tell you when we are all gathered." Pulling out a stool by the worktable Winifred perched on it. "Where is William?"

"After we moved the tapster's body to the stables, he was in need of some fresh air. I think he went for a walk by the river."

"The stables? Whyever did you bring him there instead of the churchyard to be buried?"

"The king's man ordered it," Merek whispered from beside the door. "I overheard him say that he wants the body to be presented on the morrow as evidence against our lady."

"He is going to do everything he can to see our lady convicted," Winifred said. "That means, we are going to have to do everything we can to stop him."

They fell silent when William entered through the back door. "Why is everyone gathered in here?"

"The justice is hell-bent on hanging our lady," Winifred said, "and we are going to stop him."

"Hush woman or he will hear you," Merek chastised his wife. "We cannot very well help her if we are strung-up alongside her."

"What would you have us do?" Simon wanted to know.

Lowering her voice, Winifred said, "Gunilda and Harsent intend to bear false witness against our lady. We need to find a way to make them recant their testimony."

"Gunilda is out for blood," Simon said. "Even if we were to combine our savings twould not be enough to buy her off."

"No way would they do such a thing." William shook his head. "The justice would hang them for lying."

"They could say they misconstrued what they witnessed," Winifred persisted. "It happens all the time."

"You do not know this man." William eyed the door. "He accused our lady of having the eyes of a witch."

"That is ridiculous," Winifred scoffed. "Our lady may not attend mass on a regular basis but there is a valid reason for it."

"You did not let me finish," William said. "I heard him boasting to the sheriff's eldest son how many witches he has drowned. He takes delight in it."

"So what can we do?" Simon asked.

"The only thing we can do," Winifred said, "stick to the original plan. We do not need the women to change their testimony if we can get Harsent to admit the truth."

Merek crossed his arms. "And just how are we going to do that?"

"Harsent is a lush," Winifred said. "I have seen her in the morn after an eve of overindulgence. It takes far too much ale to bring her low so this night, you will ply her with wine."

"Wine is costly," Simon said. "Should we not ask M'lady's permission?"

"I will cover the cost myself," Winifred said turning to her husband. "Just make sure she doesn't stop drinking until she passes out."

"I can do that easy enough."

"Then have at it, husband." Winifred smiled. "I shall thank you properly another time."

"Do you really think Harsent will speak the truth?" Simon appeared unconvinced. "It seems to me Gunilda has a tight hold on her."

"Not as tight as the drink does." Winifred spoke with determination. "On the morrow you and Mary keep the children away from the village. I would have them nowhere near the square."

"Consider it done," Simon said. "We will pack some food and head upriver for a spot of fishing."

"Also, M'lady will rest easier knowing Sir Albin is being looked after. Have Anne tend him. If he stirs, send Joseph to summon me from the square. Mayhap he will be well enough to testify as to what really happened."

"Do you think such a thing possible?"

"I believe anything is possible," Winifred said. "Sir Talan is bringing medicine and he should have arrived by now. William, at first light will you take the road south in search of them? The rain has eased, yet if they travel by wagon it could be bogged down somewhere along the way."

William dipped his head. "Consider it done."

"Not to sound pessimistic," Simon said, "but if the justice is intent on finding our lady guilty, what makes you think anything we do will change his mind?"

"Think about it," Winifred said. "Every villager from miles around will be in the square to watch a woman they know and love stand trial. If we can get Harsent to recant, Gunilda's testimony is worthless. Even the justice could not be so brash as to ignore irrefutable proof of her innocence."

"I can see why Merek leaves the planning to you," Simon said with a smile. "I shall see to it Anne and Mary are informed."

"You forgot about me," Betta said as she entered. "I have known Lecie far longer than any of you. She is more of a daughter to me than one of my own would ever be."

Sharing an uneasy look between them, Winifred decided to trust her. "Do you think you can speak to Harsent about recanting when Gunilda is not about?"

"I will do my best," Betta said. "Gunilda plays on Harsent's fears of being cast into the streets when she is no longer able to support herself. I have no doubt a few assurances to the contrary will go a long way."

"How could she even think M'lady would cast her out?" Winifred asked.

"There was a time Harsent knew otherwise," Betta said. "The drink has addled her mind."

"Then make whatever assurances necessary," Winifred said. "Our lady's fate depends upon it."

Chapter Seventeen

The next morning dawned clear and cool. Dressed in a dark brown woolen kirtle with linen cream chemise, Lecie pinched her cheeks to add color to her ashen face. Braiding her hair into a single plait, she coiled and pinned it at the crown of her head.

"Tis wise of you to keep the hair off your neck." Strolling into the master chamber, Gunilda's lip twisted into a snarl. "The hangman will prefer it that way."

"I ordered you to be gone from here," Lecie ground out as she whirled to face the gloating woman. "Leave now or by all that is holy I vow to earn the title you have falsely laid against me."

"You no longer have authority here. The king's justice has ordered me to remain so that I may testify against you."

"Then I suggest you remove yourself from my sight."

"By day's end I shall see the end of you." Flicking her dark eyes to Albin resting fitfully on the bed, Gunilda smiled exposing her rotted and missing teeth. "Do not overly fret. Your knight is sure to follow you into death."

Crossing the chamber in three strides, Lecie slapped Gunilda hard across her cheek. "You conniving whore. Even in death I will end you if my husband dies."

"You speak of witchery," Gunilda gasped.

"Aye, I do," Lecie spat with a bitter smile. "By my blood and the heart that pumps it, I curse you, Gunilda. Come what may by the end of this day, I shall not rest in my grave until you have repented and paid for your crimes against my loved ones."

Gunilda crossed herself and slowly backed toward the door. "Your words do not scare me."

"Do they not?" Clapping her hands together, Gunilda's shriek brought a satisfied smirk to Lecie's face. "Confess your lies to the justice and I shall remove my curse. Fail to do so and your death will be a violent one, mark my words."

"You murdered Hamon and deserve to die for it." Her eyes wide with fright, Gunilda's voice shook.

"Very well." Closing her eyes, Lecie held her hands out, palms up. Do not say I did not warn you."

"No, you cannot."

"Get you down below, Gunilda," Winifred snapped from the doorway. "The Justice is requesting your presence."

Startled, Gunilda shrieked. "Lecie has gone mad and sold her soul to the devil."

"With you bearing false witness against her, who could blame her?" Winifred hissed.

"She cursed me."

"As will I, if you do not remove your loathsome self from my sight." Winifred slammed the door before fully Gunilda cleared it.

Gunilda's cry of pain preceded her footsteps running down the hall.

"I know tis against God's will to carry hate in our heart," Winifred said, "yet I feel some people are deserving of it."

"Some people are beyond redemption," Lecie said losing all hope of clearing her name. "I do not suppose there has been any word from Sir Talan or Castell Maen?"

"Not as of yet, M'lady, yet we remain hopeful."

"I am not a witch you know." Lecie changed the subject. "There is a baron by the name of de Wrotham to the north of here.

There is a rumor his daughter is a witch. It gave me the idea to scare Gunilda into confessing the truth."

"You need not explain to me," Winifred assured her. "I would vouch to Gunilda being a witch far sooner than I ever would you."

"Winifred, I have a favor to ask of you." Her eyes resting on Albin, tears slipped down Lecie's cheeks. "Would you hold a message in confidence for my husband?"

"Twill not be necessary, M'lady. You can tell him yourself after all this is over."

"Forever an optimist you are." Lecie smiled despite the lead weight resting in her belly. "You do so remind me of my mother."

"And like her and your father the rest of us will be with you in spirit this day." Squeezing Lecie's hand, Winifred solemnly met her gaze. "No matter what happens, you must be strong to the end. You are the lady wife of a knight of the realm. Do us all proud."

"I shall." Lecie inhaled a deep calming breath. "I have done nothing wrong and the king's itinerant justice shall see no weakness on my part. I vow it."

"Then take some time to yourself, M'lady. I shall await you below."

Perched on the edge of the bed, Lecie's resolve faltered when she gazed down at Albin. Shadowing the last days of her father, dark circles beneath his eyes stood out in stark contrast to his sickly pallor.

"You must fight, husband." Taking his hand, she clasped it tight between hers. "I can bear anything that befalls me this day so long as I know you live on."

As if in reply, Albin moaned low.

"I love you. I always have, and I always shall." Rising, she bent to kiss his heated brow. "Always."

With a last look at her beloved, Lecie held her head high and left the chamber to face her fate.

Chapter Eighteen

Justice de Glanville was giving instructions to his clerk when Lecie entered the common room.

Standing silently beside his sons, Sheriff Richard lowered his eyes in shame after she acknowledged him.

From his place behind the bar, Merek kept a watchful eye on the occupants.

Holding her head high, Lecie looked down her nose at the lord justice. "I am prepared to depart at your leisure."

"Lord Justice," he coldly corrected her.

"Lord Justice," she repeated.

Steepling his fingers, Justice de Glanville slowly ran his eyes over her apparel. "Do you not wish to break your fast afore we depart?"

"I am not at all hungry."

"Troubling thoughts perhaps?" Picking up his gold hilted dinner knife the justice speared a slice of cold fowl. "I, however, am not afflicted by such."

"Then with your permission, I shall await you in the kitchen."

"No, you shall not." The justice's refusal drew Lecie up short. "I will not risk the chance of you fleeing."

"Lord Justice," the sheriff interjected, "I cannot fathom such a thought ever entering Lady Lecie's mind."

"I shall gladly accompany her," Leofrick added.

"This is the second time I have had to remind you that tis I who am in charge here, Sheriff." Justice de Glanville spoke around a mouthful of meat. "You will not approve of what happens if there is a third."

The sheriff dipped his head with a remorseful look directed at Lecie.

Pulling out a chair at the next table, Lecie sat facing away from the justice. Inwardly fighting the temptation to fidget, she clasped her hands and waited.

The silence grew palpable while the justice took his time eating. Calling for more ale, he studied Lecie until she felt his regard and flushed with color.

Briefly meeting his unwavering gaze, she focused on the door willing Sir Talan to walk through it with Albin's medicine. When it actually opened inward, she came out of her chair with a small gasp.

Escorted by her mother, Emmaline, Mylla rushed to embrace Lecie. "We heard the most awful rumor..." Spotting the justice she trailed off.

"Ah, Mistress Mylla." Justice de Glanville stood with a look of satisfaction. "What a pleasure tis to see you again."

"I trust your journey home was uneventful?" Sheriff Richard formally greeted his wife.

"Twas unexpected to be called back so soon yet our journey was uneventful." Nervously eyeing the justice, Emmaline moved closer to her husband.

"Pardon my impetuous summons, my sweet." Justice de Glanville approached Mylla. "In my desire to see you again, twas at my behest your bedside vigil was cut short. I trust your ailing family member can make do without you."

Too petrified to speak, Mylla nodded.

"Who was it you were tending to again?" The justice eyed the sheriff. "Your father told me but alas, I forgot."

Having been informed of her father's lie, Mylla swallowed convulsively before saying, "My Uncle John."

"Very good." Presenting his arm, he added, "Allow me to escort you to the square."

Leaving her no choice but to accept, Mylla nervously met her father's helpless gaze.

Justice de Glanville flicked his eyes to Lecie when she stood to take Leofrick's extended arm. "I look forward to having you watch me dispense the king's justice."

On the way out Lecie glanced toward the back wall where Winifred stood weeping softly beside her husband. Forcing a smile for the pair, she kept her head high.

"God be with you, M'lady," Winifred bravely called after her.

Following Justice de Glanville and Mylla, Lecie, and Leofrick heard the sheriff and his wife speaking in angry hushed tones behind them.

Noting Lecie's interest in the conversation, Leofrick leaned close to whisper. "Mother believes father should intercede on your behalf."

"He already has to no avail. Were he to do so again, your family would suffer along with me."

"You do not blame him?"

"Of course not." Eyeing the despicable justice walking beside her gentle and beautiful friend, Lecie added, "Promise me you will find a way to keep Mylla from him."

"I know not if I can," Leofrick replied grimly. "We are at the whim of the man on both accounts."

"Then there is no justice in this world," Lecie whispered in a broken voice.

"So twould appear." Gently squeezing Lecie's hand they walked on in silence.

Lecie ignored the sympathetic and curious gazes directed her way when they entered the teeming village square. Small children stood in the back of wagons to be afforded a better view and basket lunches could be seen everywhere in preparation for the long day ahead. Instead of the usual jeers and catcalls that normally greeted the accused, the crowd remained uncharacteristically silent.

Frowning in clear disapproval at the show of respect, the justice led Mylla to a row of benches up front.

The ancient oak dubbed the hanging tree rested on a rise off the square. A cart pulled by two mules was set beneath a thick branch that held a rope noose swinging ominously in the brisk autumn wind.

"Why would he do such a thing?" Lecie's step faltered when she spotted Hamon's body propped-up in a coffin for all to see.

"Because he is sadistic," Leofrick said grinding his teeth.

"We are all here in support of you, Lecie," Frederick spoke softly in her ear. "The villagers respect you and will act accordingly."

"Thank you," Lecie murmured, "although being pelted with rotted food is the least of my concerns."

"Assist her into the cart," Justice de Glanville instructed Leofrick.

"Pardon me?" Leofrick drew to a stunned halt. "I must have heard you incorrectly, Lord Justice. The cart acts as a deterrent for those pondering ill will and awaits only those found guilty of the crime for which they have been charged. Surely it would send out the wrong message to the crowd were you to change this tradition?"

Justice de Glanville's dark eyes narrowed while he waited for Leofrick to comply.

Lecie took the decision from Leofrick by hiking up her skirts to climb the sloping rise. "I need no assistance." Hoisting herself up into the back of the cart, she stepped around the noose. "I await your pleasure, Lord Justice."

"Oh, I have every intention of being pleased this day. By day's end I declare you will not be so arrogant." With a sneer the justice turned to address the crowd. "Good people of Rochester, you are gathered here today to hear evidence of murder."

"Lady Lecie freely gives to those who have nothing," a disembodied voice called from the crowd. "She would do harm to none without just provocation."

"Aye," another called. "If she did wield a blade against Hamon, he most rightly deserved it."

The crowd began to murmur in agreement when Gunilda stood from a bench reserved for witnesses. "I saw her murder Hamon with my own eyes," she shouted, "as did Harsent seated beside me. Think what you will of us but we still have eyes and are here to swear by what we saw."

Pale and sweating profusely, Harsent twisted the ends of her threadbare shawl.

"Good people," Justice de Glanville called. "We have more than two witnesses to prove that Lady Lecie stabbed an unarmed man in the back. We also have an unimpeachable witness who overheard the lady threatening the life of the man called Hamon mere days prior to his death."

"Lord Justice," Sheriff Richard spoke up. "At the time Lady Lecie believed Hamon posed a credible threat to her younger siblings. She spoke out of fear and anger and I would not have mentioned it had I known twould be used against her."

"Nevertheless, you did mention the fact that the lady threatened a man who is now dead by her hand," the justice said with a warning look. "Misguided or not, I see no better motive for murder than that."

His tall frame sagging in defeat, Sheriff Richard remained silent.

Resigned to her fate, Lecie closed her eyes and sent up a prayer for Albin's recovery.

"Behold!" Withdrawing Albin's costly silver dinner knife, the justice held it up for the crowd to see. "Gunilda of Rochester, do you recognize this blade?"

"Aye," Gunilda responded loudly, "I most certainly do. Tis the very blade Lecie drove into poor Hamon's back when he was paying his respects to Sir Albin."

"Harsent of Rochester, do you likewise recognize this blade?" When Harsent failed to respond, the justice's gaze bore into her. "Well, do you?"

Cringing at his booming voice, Harsent's gaze rested on Winifred where she stood between Simon, and Merek.

"Harsent of Rochester," the justice thundered when he came to stand before her. "Know you the penalty of rescinding previous testimony given to the king's itinerant justice?" Leaning closer to the terrified woman, he hissed, "Tis death."

"I saw her," Harsent mumbled low.

"You saw who, do what exactly?" the justice called loudly.

"I saw what Gunilda said I saw," Harsent whispered.

"Louder!"

"Lecie slayed Hamon," Harsent yelled.

"You heard for yourselves good people of Rochester," the justice continued. "Two witnesses testifying to the fact that Lady Lecie is guilty of murder."

"Lord Justice," the sheriff could not keep himself from protesting, "tis obvious the woman has been coerced."

Closing the distance between them the justice spoke so only the sheriff could hear. "Interfere once more and I shall see your position stripped and your family tossed into the street by day's end."

When Sheriff Richard defiantly refused to back down, Lecie spoke for the first time. "Sheriff, please. Rochester needs you."

Breaking eye contact with the justice, Sheriff Richard faced Lecie. "Then I would ask your forgiveness for the injustice done to you this day."

"There is nothing to forgive." Tears slipped freely down Lecie's cheeks. "Please see the children are taken care of if my husband does not make it through."

"I give you my word." Forced to clear his throat, he added, "Your parents would be as proud of you as I am, my dear."

Irritated by the heartwarming scene the justice brought the restless crowd to order. "Good people of Rochester, I can see where you can have an emotional attachment to Lady Lecie. Nonetheless, justice must be upheld or the kingdom will fall into anarchy."

"Let Lady Lecie tell us what happened," a female voice called.

Searching the crowd for the speaker, the justice scowled when cries of agreement rang out.

"If you have nothing to hide, you have nothing to lose," the female voice taunted. "Let the lady speak."

"Aye," the crowd chorused. "Let the lady speak."

"Very well," the justice snapped, "I am nothing if not fair."

Lecie searched the sea of faces until she located Winifred. Afraid the justice would punish her loyal friend, she shook her head to deter further interference.

In defiance of Lecie's wishes, Winifred held her head high.

"Speak, woman," the justice ordered regaining Lecie's attention. "Let us hear what you claim transpired afore smiting down an unarmed man."

Unnerved by so many gazes on her, Lecie focused on a distant spot to retell her story. In a calm clear voice, she relived the moment where she walked in on Hamon about to smother Albin. She explained her feeble attempts to stop him and Hamon's subsequent confession to having murdered her father. After recalling what happened to Tugger, she described how the knife came to be in her hand and how she was forced to stab Hamon to keep him from killing Albin. "My hand to God," Lecie said after she had concluded, "I did what I had to do to save my husband."

A slow clapping broke the silence of the square when the justice jeered, "A tale well told." With a mock bow, he continued, "You should have been born a troubadour so adept you are at creating a scene to cover your crime."

"I spoke the truth." Lecie addressed the crowd. "I did no less than any one of you would have done in the same situation."

Murmurs of agreement raced through the onlookers as Justice de Glanville once again took charge of the situation. "You claim your victim murdered your father?"

A warm breeze swirled around Lecie when she opened her mouth to reply. Closing her eyes, she felt her parents calming presence with a sense of wonder.

Determined to fight for her life, she met the justice's unflinching gaze with her head held high. "I swear my life on it."

"How apropos since your life depends upon it." The justice chuckled harshly. "You stated that Hamon attacked you, yet you bear no marks to prove such a thing happened."

"That is not true," Lecie said. "There is a large bump on the back of my head where I struck the bureau."

"You could have harmed yourself to give credence to your lie," the justice scoffed. "Where is the village physician?"

Dr. Rayburn stepped from the crowd without looking at Lecie. "I am here to serve you at your will, Lord Justice."

"You heard this woman's story?" Justice de Glanville pointed at Lecie.

"I did indeed."

"What say you about her father being murdered? As I heard tell, he died of a lingering illness."

"That he did." Facing the crowd, Dr. Rayburn called, "Many of you are aware of the fact that Lecie of Rochester banned me from saving the life of her father. I attended his body after death and can attest to the fact that there was no foul play involved."

"Tis no secret Lady Lecie is opposed to bloodletting." A male voice shouted. "It does naught else than make the body weaker."

"Who dares proclaim such a thing? Step forward," Dr. Rayburn demanded. "Bloodletting drains the poisons from the body and purifies the soul." Met by silence, his narrowed gaze skimmed over the crowd. "The accused may as well be answering to three murders this day, instead of one."

Lecie gasped at the accusation while the crowd broke into confused chatter.

"Good people of Rochester," Justice de Glanville shouted to gain order. "Here is a man who has treated your ills, delivered your babes, and delivered ease to your dying loved ones as they departed this world. Yet you doubt him?" Searching the front of the crowd, the justice pointed at a heavyset blond balding man with a mustache. "Alan of Rochester, stand and face the accused."

Laboring to his feet, Alan grunted and clutched the underside of his ponderous belly as if in pain. "Lord Justice?"

"Do you recognize this woman?"

"I do," Alan whined uneasily, his shifty blue eyes moving no higher than Lecie's skirts.

"And did you not approach me at the inn a day past with information pertinent to this case?"

"I did."

"Speak up man! What did you hear with thine own ears, Alan of Rochester?"

"I happened to be in the tavern when I overheard Lecie threaten the life of her father so I felt the need to confess it to you since I believe her to be a murderer...Lord Justice."

Murmurs raced through the crowd at this bit of scandalous news.

"Alan is naught but a deceitful liar," an angry male voice yelled. "Everyone here and beyond knows he is not to be trusted."

"Aye," another cried. "If he tells us the sun is shining, we prepare ourselves for rain!"

"Enough," Justice de Glanville shouted. "This man has no reason to be deceitful in this matter and you will hear him out." Scanning the crowd for anyone who would defy him, he once again faced Alan. "What did you hear the accused say immediately prior to her father's death?"

Loudly clearing his throat, Alan spat a wad of phlegm into the dirt at his feet. "I was sitting in the common room when Lecie came from the kitchen. I heard her say she was going to put an end to her father's suffering."

"Aye, tis true," Lecie cried when the crowd erupted into shouted denials. "I said it as I carried medicine given to me by the Lady Reina in order to ease my father's pain."

"So the village liar speaks a single truth and tis twisted into something else entirely," a male voice called. "He seeks attention like always, naught else."

"Be that as it may, my good people." Dr. Rayburn waited until the chatter died down to add, "I pleaded with the accused to allow me to treat her father and yet she refused. He is now dead." Casting a contemptuous gaze at Lecie, he once again faced the crowd. "She has also refused treatment for her husband who as I speak lay dying in yonder inn. Aye, good people," he called louder. "Lecie of Rochester stands accused of one murder, yet she should be held accountable for the other two as well."

"Lady Lecie," she corrected. "If you are going to accuse me of being a murderess, I would ask that you address me properly."

"Lady Lecie." Dr. Rayburn mockingly bowed his head.

"And after my husband is treated with proper medicine, he will not die."

"Silence you," Justice de Glanville sprayed spit as he whirled on Lecie. "You have had your chance to spout falsehoods."

"This trial is not only a farce, tis a travesty of justice." A feminine voice carried above the rising din of the crowd.

Stunned intakes of breath from her family preceded Justice de Glanville's surprised expression when he faced Mylla. "I beg your pardon?"

People craned their necks in an attempt to see the slight woman who dared confront the king's itinerant justice. Her light blonde waist-length locks stirring in the gentle breeze, Mylla opened her mouth to repeat herself.

"Lord Justice," Lecie spoke up to protect her friend. "If you have finished presenting the evidence against me I would hear my sentence."

Silence reigned as the crowd waited for Justice de Glanville to speak. Appraising Mylla, he darted a cold glance at Lecie before addressing the sheriff. "I would suggest you remove your daughter from these proceedings. It has become apparent to me her fondness for the accused has clouded her sound judgment."

"Aye, Lord Justice." Sheriff Richard stepped forward. "I shall have one of my son's escort Mylla and her mother home."

With a look brooking no disobedience, the sheriff presented his arm to Mylla. "Come, daughter."

Accepting his arm, tears filled Mylla's blue eyes when she looked at Lecie. "God be with you and grant you peace, my dearest friend."

Lecie brushed at the tears on her own cheeks. "Have faith and live a blessed life for me, Mylla. The life you are meant to lead."

Breaking into sobs, Mylla wrapped her arms around her mother's waist when Caine escorted the pair away.

His eyes following Mylla's progress, Justice de Glanville resumed, "You heard the accused. She wishes for the proceedings to be at an end afore more evidence can be brought against her." Scanning the crowd, his eyes dared defiance. "What say you good people? Are you prepared to hear the king's justice brought against this woman?"

The crowd remained silent aiming looks of disapproval at the justice.

"Condemn her," Gunilda screamed into the silence. "She is in league with the devil and deserves to die for what she did to my Hamon."

"Most honorable Lord Justice," Dr. Rayburn shouted, "we are prepared to hear your just verdict."

"Very well." Justice de Glanville dipped his head. "The people of Rochester have spoken." Turning to face Lecie, he stared coldly up at her. "Lady Lecie of Rochester the evidence has proven your guilt. For your willful murder in opposition to God's and King Henry's law of the land, I find you guilty." After a dramatic pause, he added, "In King Henry's name, I sentence you to death by hanging to be carried out post-haste."

Chapter Nineteen

"Albin, you must wake!"

Hearing the tone his mother used when she was vexed with him, Albin made an attempt to rise only to realize he was pinned to the ground. Had his horse fallen on him? Fighting to pull air into his burning lungs he tried to recall what battle he was in. Fulke. The thought of leaving his best friend's back unprotected gave him the surge of adrenalin he needed to remain conscious. Focusing on the soft neigh of his horse, he opened his eyes to discover the neigh was a persistent whine, and it was coming from Tugger.

"Saints be praised, we thought you were breathing your last," Betta murmured. "Sir Albin, can you hear me?"

"Lecie," he managed in a hoarse whisper.

Betta slid her arm behind Albin's head to prop him up. "Drink."

The instant he felt the cool water on his tongue Albin wanted more.

"You must take it slow, Sir Albin, or you will not be able to keep it down."

When he had his fill Albin winced from the pain in his shoulder when Betta eased him back onto the pillows. "Lecie?"

"First things first, I must know if you recall Hamon assaulting you."

His heart pounding, Albin feared the worst. "Where is my wife?"

"She walked in on Hamon attempting to smother you," Betta said in a rush. "Hamon is dead by her hand and her trial is commencing in the square as we speak. Can you remember anything?"

"No." Albin shook his head trying to wrap his mind around the idea of Lecie on trial for slaying Hamon. "Why would Sheriff Richard accuse her of murder when by your own account twas justifiable?"

"The sheriff has nothing to do with it, Sir Albin. The king's itinerant justice is here and he is determined to find Lecie guilty."

Lurching into a sitting position, Albin fell back when the room began to spin. "Summon men, I need assist."

"The men are all gone, only Joseph remains behind."

"Get him."

"Are you cer—"

"Get him, damn you! We may already be too late!" Breathing heavy, Albin fought through the pain to swing his legs over the edge of the bed after Betta ran from the room.

He fell to his knees on his first attempt to stand. Using the bed to gain leverage he made it to his feet when a commotion in the hallway caught his attention.

Her Ladyship Reina followed by a woman unknown to him with long dark hair and silver eyes stopped short at the sight of him.

"Sir Albin, get back into bed." The dark-haired woman made it to Albin's side before he could respond.

Ignoring the woman, Albin weakly gripped Reina's hand. "Where is Fulke? My Lecie is in danger."

"I am Bronwyn, Sir Albin." The dark-haired woman spoke while Lady Reina motioned to the bed. "We were met on the road by a man named William. He said he works here and told us everything that happened. Fulke is with my husband, and Sir Talan. They are headed for the square as we speak. Now please, if you stand a chance, I need to treat you."

"Tis too late for me." Albin blinked rapidly to banish the dark spots consuming his vision. "Save my wife." His knees buckling under him the last thing he remembered was the soft touch of Reina's hand on his forehead.

♥

Scanning the group of men standing beside the wagon, Justice de Glanville's gaze rested on a heavyset man dressed all in black. "Executioner, attend your duty."

"There shall be a higher reckoning for the injustice done this day, Justice de Glanville," Winifred called from the crowd.

His face a mottled red the justice demanded silence.

"Question the woman Harsent, Lord Justice," Merek called. "I have no doubt her story will change."

"Who said that?" Justice de Glanville shouted. "I command you to step forward."

"You are not the king," another anonymous speaker called from the crowd. "I say Lady Lecie is innocent."

"As do I," cried another followed by more shouts of innocence.

"I am an extension of King Henry's arm. Dare to oppose my command and I shall have each and every one of you strung up beside the convicted."

Forced into remaining silent the crowd expressed their displeasure with looks of anger and disbelief.

"Executioner, you may proceed," Justice de Glanville called ignoring the hostility of the crowd.

Winifred's soft sobbing was the only thing heard when the hooded executioner climbed into the cart beside Lecie.

Tying her hands behind her back, the executioner leaned close. "I beg your forgiveness for this lawless deed, Lady Lecie."

Recognizing the voice as a local she had known all her life, Lecie managed a tremulous smile. "There is nothing to forgive, Walter. You have no more choice than I."

"Thank you, My Lady." Reluctantly slipping the noose over Lecie's head, Walter gently adjusted the knot at the back of her neck. "God be with you."

"And also with you," Lecie said in a tremulous voice.

Jumping down from the back of the cart, Walter moved to stand beside the mules. "I await your command."

Justice de Glanville frowned at Walter's insolent tone yet moved to stand directly before Lecie. "Have you any last words, Lecie of Rochester?"

"I do." Lecie cleared her throat when her voice cracked. Her eyes on the back of Winifred where she huddled against Merek, she called, "I am Lady Lecie and innocent of the charges laid against me this day. I ask only that you pray for the health of my beloved husband. If tis God's will that he should follow me in death, I ask you all to look after my younger sisters and brother. I would not have this travesty be held against them." Redirecting her gaze to Justice de Glanville, she continued, "Seek your revenge. I am prepared to die with the knowledge that you cannot escape God's judgement."

Narrowing his eyes, the justice flicked his hand. "Proceed."

With his hand on the reins, Walter hung his head and led the mules forward.

Fighting panic, Lecie began to feel the wagon slide beneath her feet. When she cleared it, her body lurched forward to dangle from the end of the rope.

A collective gasp filled the silence and many turned away from the horrid sight of her flailing limbs.

Deprived of oxygen, Lecie's body bucked uncontrollably and she began to lose consciousness. A vision of her mother came to her and an overwhelming sense of peace enveloped her.

"What madness is this?" The shout came from a trio of riders galloping into the square. Villagers scrambled out of the way of the mighty destriers hooves as they churned up clods of turf on their way past. "Talan, cut her down!"

"Lordship Fulke." The murmur raced through the crowd as all eyes locked on the imposing blond warrior.

Talan rode up the slope to grab Lecie around the waist. "I got you."

With the pressure off her neck, Lecie was able to draw air into her burning lungs.

Guiding her knee around the pommel, Talan sliced through the rope with his dagger. After pulling the noose off and tossing it aside. He cut the rope from her hands. "Are you alight?"

Unable to speak, Lecie collapsed gasping against his chest.

"You are safe now," Talan soothed. Wrapping his arm around her, he spurred his horse around to join Fulke and Euric. "She is understandably frightened yet appears otherwise unharmed, My Liege."

"Baron Erlegh," Justice de Glanville bellowed in rage, "you are defying a command given in the name of King Henry."

Sizing up the justice, Fulke's blue eyes turned glacial. "As you well know, I am on familiar terms with our good king. I have no doubt he will grant the delay after I explain this is naught but a sham trial masquerading a vendetta against my house."

"You are no longer his favorite," the justice sneered with contempt. "Whilst I am on familial terms with him."

"Nonetheless, I wager he would still lend me an ear." Fulke shrugged. "After all, he overruled you when you were the loudest calling for my head."

"You drew your weapon in the king's presence! If I had my way, more than your pretty head would have been decorating a spike that day."

A collective gasp rolled through the enthralled crowd to discover the rumors were true. Baron Erlegh had drawn his sword in defense of his baroness.

"Yet here I am, and I remain a baron nonetheless." Fulke grinned. "I hear Baron Reynold did not end his tenure at the palace so favorably."

Justice de Glanville concealed his rising temper by clasping his hands behind his back. "Yon woman has already been given a fair trial and found guilty of murder. Your interference is only prolonging her death."

"The trial was a farce, Your Lordship," Winifred shouted. "I beg you to hear the evidence and judge for yourself."

"Aye," another called. "This is a travesty of God and king's law."

Cocking a chiseled brow at the justice, Fulke dismounted. "You heard the people, let me hear the evidence for myself."

"I have passed sentence," Justice de Glanville spat.

"Let me make myself clear," Fulke said towering over the slighter man. "Restart the trial or I shall take Lady Lecie and ride to London this day in order to put the matter to the king. Once he is reminded of your close association with Baron Reynold, I am sure he will see this absurdity for what it is."

"I have disassociated myself from Reynold, and the king knows it."

"Shall we put it to the test?"

"Whether it be this day or another," Justice de Glanville hissed for Fulke's ears alone, "I will have my revenge." Waving a hand in Lecie's direction, he called for all to hear, "By all means feel free to proceed. I have no doubt my verdict will stand."

"Thank you." Fulke bowed mockingly before approaching Talan's horse. "I would have liked to extend my congratulations to you on your recent nuptials under different circumstances, My Lady. However, things being what they are, I would like to wish you a long and blessed life with my chosen brother."

"Albin." Her voice a raspy whisper, Lecie placed her hands on Fulke's shoulders when he assisted her down.

"My wife and one more skilled than she are tending to him now," Fulke assured her. "Let us clear this matter up so we may join them."

Tears of relief flowed from Lecie's eyes and she lowered her head to conceal them.

Fulke called for drink as he brusquely waved Harsent and Gunilda off the bench with a flick of his hand. Moving the bench to the base of the rise, he motioned for Lecie to have a seat while a villager passed her a cup of water.

After she took several swallows to quench her thirst, Fulke moved to sit beside her. "Now then, why do not you start at the beginning and tell us once again what happened?"

Emboldened by his reassuring smile, Lecie began, "I went to check on Albin and found our dog whining and scratching at the door. I knew something was wrong since he is so fond of Albin and had been keeping vigil." Her voice cracking, she took several swallows of water. "When I opened the door," she continued, "I saw Hamon standing over my husband with a pillow in his hands. Twas then that I realized he had killed my father the same way. When I accused him of such, he confirmed it."

"Twas justifiable," a villager shouted from up front.

"Silence yourselves!" Justice de Glanville faced the crowd with a menacing look. "The next person who speaks out of turn will be flogged!"

"What happened next?" Fulke gently coaxed Lecie.

"After confessing to my father's murder, Hamon attempted to smother my husband so I sicced Tugger on him." Lecie fell silent reliving the terrible event. "Hamon snatched up a pitcher from the nightstand and repeatedly struck the poor dog. I thought he had killed him."

"Tis alright, you are doing well," Fulke said to Lecie before facing the onlookers. "Someone needs to fetch the dog from the inn."

Justice de Glanville threw his head back and laughed. "Do you plan on questioning the animal, Baron Erlegh?"

"Lying whore!" A villager jeered when Gunilda joined in the laughter.

"In a way," Fulke said. "Surely I do not have to tell you that if a dog were struck with such brutal force, twould bear proof of the assault?"

Sharing a relieved smile with Winifred, Merek broke into a brisk jog to fetch the dog.

"Carry on, Your Lordship," Sheriff Richard said when Justice de Glanville remained silent.

"Thank you, Sheriff." Fulke turned back to Lecie. "Who was in charge of cleaning the chamber?"

"Tis I, Your Lordship." Winifred made her way to the front. "I am Winifred and a recent hire at The Wounded Stag."

"Twas you catcalling! I recognize the voice!" Justice de Glanville moved to seize Winifred.

Following Fulke's signal, Euric and Talan blocked the justice's path to Winifred.

"Do you dare hinder me from carrying out my duty?" His face a mottled red, the lord justice seized hold of Talan's tunic.

"Twas done on my instruction," Fulke said standing. "I am now in charge of these proceedings and any witness I call has the full immunity of the court. Henceforth, I expect you to remain seated and silent unless otherwise called upon."

"You have no idea what I am capable of," the justice seethed.

Turning his back on the enraged justice, Fulke winked at Winifred. "After the attack did you happen to remove any crockery from the floor of the master chamber?"

"I did indeed, Your Lordship. A pitcher broken into several pieces just like M'lady stated."

"Did you also happen to see the dog after the incident?"

"No, I did not," Winifred said. "There was quite a commotion so I tended to M'lady whilst another took charge of the dog."

"Thank you. You may return to your place."

Dipping into a curtsy, Winifred smiled at Lecie before blending back into the crowd.

Fulke's eyes widened when he finally spotted the wagon bearing Hamon's covered body. "By god, why is the man not buried?"

"The guilty must bear witness to the evil they have wrought," the lord justice responded.

"Do you honestly believe the stench and sight of decay would force an innocent to plead guilty?"

"Dare you question how the king rules his kingdom?"

"By all appearances you do not resemble the king." Fulke tilted his head. "If anything, you have a remarkable likeness to Baron Reynold. If I did not know any better, I would swear you were his kin."

"Get on with it," Justice de Glanville snarled.

"Dr. Rayburn, attend me if you will."

"Your Lordship?" Rising from his seat, the arrogant doctor approached.

Striding over to the body, the crowd gasped when Fulke removed his dagger to slit both legs of the bloodstained breeches Hamon wore from ankle to knee.

"What is the purpose of defiling a murder victim?" The justice demanded to know.

Ignoring him, Fulke beckoned the doctor over. "Do you see any visible signs of an animal attack?"

Examining each leg, Dr. Rayburn glanced toward the justice.

"Well," Fulke snapped, "do you?"

"It appears both legs have been set upon by an animal," Dr. Rayburn replied softly.

"Louder," Fulke said. "You have besmirched this good woman's name since I have been coming to Rochester. Now is the time to redeem yourself in the eyes of your patients."

Nodding stiffly, Dr. Rayburn looked over the crowd. "There is evidence giving credence to Lady Lecie's account."

"What is all this for?" Gunilda seized hold of the lord justice's cloak. "You are the authority here, not his lordship."

Slapping her hard across the face, the lord justice backed away with an appalled expression. "Keep your hands to yourself, gutter filth."

Before Gunilda could get over the shock, Fulke was speaking to her. "Thank you for reminding me of your presence. Since you are aware of the penalty for what you have done, I have no doubt you will stick to your story til the very end." Stopping before the terrified Harsent, he waited in silence until she felt compelled to look at him. "Care you to have a turn at the truth?"

"She made me," Harsent blurted. "After Hamon slayed Sir Albin, he was going to force Lecie to marry him so he and Gunilda could have control of the inn. They swore I would never be turned out if I went along with their plans."

"If Lady Lecie had any intention of turning you out, she would have done so some time ago," Fulke said. "How low you must have fallen to repay her kindness in such a way."

Harsent turned pleading eyes upon Lecie. "Please forgive me."

"What of the scene you claimed to have witnessed?" Fulke continued.

"Gunilda told me what to say."

"She lies." Gunilda threw herself at the feet of Justice de Glanville. "She is so often befuddled by drink she knows not what she says."

Kicking Gunilda away from him, Justice de Glanville hissed, "I shall have your neck for embarrassing me."

"Make way!" Merek slowly made his way through the crowd. "I have brought the dog as requested, Your Lordship."

Pulling the leash out of Merek's hand, Tugger went bounding up to Lecie the instant he spotted her. Nearly knocked over by the weight, she threw her arms around the loyal dog and fought the urge to cry. "Good boy," she whispered in his ear.

Fulke strode up to them when Tugger sat dutifully by her feet. "It has been far too long since I had a friendly mauling." Patting the dog's flank in greeting, Tugger whimpered and backed into Lecie whenever Fulke touched his head and snout.

"Further proof backing up Lady Lecie's account." Fulke pinned Justice de Glanville with his gaze. "Despite the fact it should not be needed."

"Are you through?" Justice de Glanville ground out angrily.

"Do you require additional proof?"

Glaring his wrath, Justice de Glanville turned his back on Fulke to address the crowd. "After further consideration, I find Lady Lecie innocent of the charges laid against her. In her stead and by command of King Henry, I order the hanging of the fallen women Gunilda and Harsent."

Lecie leapt to her feet. "No, you——"

Fulke gripped Lecie's forearm to silence her. "They have earned their punishment," he whispered. "You cannot undo it."

Lowering her eyes, she nodded.

"Seize the wench," Justice de Glanville ordered when Gunilda attempted to flee.

Ignoring her screams, two hulking village men roughly seized Gunilda by the arms to drag her to the cart.

Angry now at the injustice nearly done, the crowd hurled insults at the two fallen women. Without rotted fruit to throw, they began to toss whatever was close at hand.

Seeing Harsent get struck in the face with a rock, Lecie turned beseeching eyes upon Fulke. "Must I stay?"

"It is required of you," Justice de Glanville responded without taking his eyes off Gunilda. "These two women spoke falsehoods that nearly cost you your life. Now you will witness what befalls those who bear false witness against another in Henry's kingdom."

"When the time comes do not look," Fulke whispered to Lecie.

Hauled into the cart, the two men held Gunilda still while a third man secured a rope to the branch above her head. Tying her hands behind her back, they slipped the noose around her neck.

"Gunilda of Rochester," Justice de Glanville began, "you have been found guilty of collusion and bearing false witness against the wife of a knight. By King Henry's command, I sentence you to death by hanging." Pausing to look around at the villagers anxious to see the deed through, he smiled. "Have you any last words, harlot?"

"Aye," Gunilda shouted. "With my last breath, I curse you all."

"Proceed afore I have her skinned alive," Justice de Glanville ordered.

Lecie closed her eyes when the mules began to move. Feeling the noose around her own neck, she felt on the verge of fainting when Fulke reached out to steady her.

"Deep breaths," he whispered.

Gunilda's curses abruptly cut off when the cart slipped from beneath her feet. Her body bucking wildly the roar of the crowd was deafening.

Unable to bear hearing such joy at the death of another, Lecie covered her ears with her hands.

After what seemed an eternity, Fulke touched her arm. "Tis over."

Lecie opened her eyes to find the justice glaring at her.

"You will watch the next whore die unassisted or with assist," he said. "Tis your choice but by God, you will bear witness."

Without responding, Lecie turned her attention to the men escorting a sobbing Harsent to the cart. "I forgive you," she called. "May God have mercy on your soul."

"I did not mean any harm," Harsent wailed oblivious to everything going on around her.

"You should have thought of that afore spilling your foul lies," Justice de Glanville spat. "Let the deed be done, I am famished."

Once Harsent was in place, Justice de Glanville stepped forward to announce sentence. Noting the fact that Harsent had wet herself, he stepped back with a satisfied smile. "Have you any last words?"

"God forgive me," Harsent cried brokenly.

The second Harsent's feet slipped from the cart, Lecie closed her eyes. Her breath hitching, she fought to contain the sobs threatening to overwhelm her.

Fulke laid a calming hand on her shoulder until men stepped forward to cut down Harsent's body. Once it rested in the wagon beside her conspirators, Fulke addressed the justice. "Now that the matter has concluded, I will take Lady Lecie home."

"So be it," the justice said. "I will be journeying to the palace posthaste to inform the king of your interference this day."

"Whilst there, do give my regards to Reynold and his lovely wife, Arabella. Oh, wait." Fulke shook his head. "What was I thinking? Reynold has gone missing. Odd that happened so soon after embarrassing the king. Do you not agree?"

"You lowborn churl," the justice snarled turning his attention to other matters. "Sheriff Richard, King Henry is moving court for the winter and has requested my presence. I shall return in the spring to discuss the matter of your daughter. Until then, you are not to entertain other offers."

Lecie turned horrified eyes on the justice. "Mylla…"

"That is a calamity for another day," Fulke murmured leading her away.

Chapter Twenty

Assisting Lecie up before Talan, Fulke tipped his head toward the third rider. "My Lady, I would like to introduce you to an old friend of mine, Sir Euric. He and his lady wife have traveled with us from Tintagel. Bronwyn is the skilled healer I mentioned earlier."

"My liege and lady were away from Castell Maen which is why my return was delayed," Talan said to explain his late arrival.

"I am grateful to you all for coming." Her throat still raw, Lecie strained to be heard.

"My beloved is skilled in the healing ways," Sir Euric said with a reassuring smile. "If anyone can heal Sir Albin tis she."

Nodding in acknowledgement, Lecie felt the lead weight in her chest lessen.

Spurring their horses, they left the gawking crowd behind.

Tugger broke away from Merek's hold to come bounding down the cobbled lane after them.

The strain she had been under finally caught up to Lecie and she began weeping from the sheer relief of having survived the day.

"It pains me that I was unable to arrive afore this dreadful day," Talan said holding her gently against him. "How fortunate you are so strong."

"Twas not your fault," Lecie murmured, "and I am not as strong as you think."

"After the ordeal you were put through, I would wager next to her ladyship, you are the strongest woman I have ever met."

"Mylla was there until she was ordered away." Lecie changed the subject. "She outright defied the justice so tis she who deserves such praise."

The mention of Mylla had Talan staring off into the distance.

"She is in love with you, Sir Talan," Lecie confided. "Twould sadden me greatly to see her forced to wed the justice."

"Nothing has been declared, and if I have any say in it nothing ever shall be," Talan swore.

"What can people like us do against someone so powerful?" Lecie shifted slightly to look at him. "The justice boasted about having a familial association this very day. Is he related to the king?"

"He was wed to Lady Kaylein," Talan said. "Her mother was cousin to King Henry twice removed."

"Did she die?"

"She was wise enough to flee him," Talan said. "Shame had King Henry declare her dead so de Glanville could take another wife to produce an heir."

"Mylla."

"She and I are intent to be together at all costs." Briefly meeting her worried gaze, Talan slowed his horse to a walk behind the others when they reached the inn.

"It gladdens my heart to hear it," Lecie said. "If there is anything you ever need, you have a friend in me."

"Thank you." Talan looked away when Fulke approached.

"Come," Fulke said assisting Lecie down. "I know you are as anxious to see Albin as I am."

Tugger charged into the inn and up the steps ahead of the small group.

The men greeted an elder woman named Hylda who was cradling a baby beside the open window.

Seated quietly at a table with untouched food before them, the children cried out in delight at the sight of Lecie.

The first to reach her, Clayton flung his arms around her waist. "We heard the most horrible things from passerby and begged to return home."

Her lower lip trembling, Sabina added, "The shearer said they were going to hang you for killing Hamon."

"Well you can see how wrong he was." Lecie reached out to smooth Sabina's golden hair.

"Why do you sound so—your neck," Osana said with a horrified expression.

"I shall explain all to you after I see Albin."

"Her ladyship and another lady are with him," Mary said. "We heard Sir Albin shouting several times over the course of the morning."

Relief had Lecie smiling. If he was shouting, he was alive.

Extending his hand for Lecie to precede him, Fulke grinned. "Shall we see what the great oaf is complaining about?"

Leading the way, Lecie addressed William behind the bar. "I warrant the whole of the village is on their way here. Please send them away the inn is closed until further notice."

"Gladly, M'lady," William said rushing to bolt the door.

Her heart hammering, Lecie entered the master chamber to find Anne and two women she had never seen before intently tending to her husband.

The woman with long silken ebony hair and striking silver eyes looked up at her approach. "I am Bronwyn, and you must be Lecie. Your husband has been calling for you."

The second woman with golden-red hair and brilliant blue eyes made room for her.

"Albin?" Lecie grasped his hand.

"I am afraid I had to lance the abscess to drain the infection and the pain was too much for him to bear in his weakened state," Bronwyn said with a grimace. "He passed out a short while ago."

"Passed out?" Never having heard the expression, Lecie grew anxious.

"He fell unconscious from the pain," Bronwyn revised, "tis the body's way of protecting itself."

"Will he live?"

"Worry you not. I have no intention of allowing him to die." Bronwyn motioned to her husband. "I am in need of a strong stomach and sharp blade."

Withdrawing his dagger from its sheath, Euric moved to the side of the bed. "Show me what needs to be done."

"First you must sterilize the blade in the fire and then I need you to cut away all of the infected flesh. He is going to have a wicked scar but there is no helping it." Holding her finger above the gruesome wound, Bronwyn showed him the area to remove. "Once that is done we shall cauterize it with the fireplace poker."

The room swayed when Lecie focused on the wound Albin had concealed from her. "He told me twas healing."

"He would," Fulke said, "so as not to worry you."

Deaf and mute after a childhood illness Reina clasped Lecie's hand while mouthing words to Fulke.

"My wife said that if the sight is too much for you, she will take some air with you in the garden."

Squeezing Reina's hand, Lecie smiled. "I thank you for the offer, Your Ladyship, yet my place is beside my husband."

Nodding in approval, Reina shared a pleased look with Fulke.

"Do you know what needs to be done?" Bronwyn spoke softly from behind Euric. "There can be no sign of infection left."

Bending close to examine the wound, Euric glanced over at her. "I shall see to it. Why do you not wait by the window?"

"Forgive me," Bronwyn said to Lecie after perching on the sill. "After all I have seen in this time, there are still some things I cannot stomach. Tending to an infection is one thing, cutting into someone's flesh quite another."

Once again confused by her odd choice of words, Lecie's brows drew up in question. "In this time, My Lady?"

"I am afraid my story is quite a long one. If you would like to hear it, I promise to tell it to you one day on one condition."

"What might that be?"

"Call me by my given name, Bronwyn."

Instantly at ease, Lecie said, "Gladly, if you call me, Lecie."

"Deal." Bronwyn held out her hand.

Puzzled, Lecie held out her hand where Bronwyn firmly clasped it to pump it up and down a few times. "I have a feeling we are going to be great friends, Lecie."

"I believe so as well."

To avoid looking at what Sir Euric was about to do, Lecie began to study Reina. Beautiful and petite with golden-red hair, her delicate features gave her an angelic air. Hovering over Euric should he need assist, kindness radiated in her every action. Lecie could see what had drawn the towering baron standing loyally beside her and she was happy for them both.

"I shall properly introduce you when we are once again blessed by Albin's robust laugh," Fulke said noting her regard.

Her cheeks flushed from having been caught staring, Lecie met Fulke's calm blue gaze. "I look forward to it, Your Lordship. And if you do not mind my saying, her ladyship is most beautiful."

"And just as kind," Bronwyn said. "I am so pleased to say I can finally communicate with her."

"I hope I can do so as well one day," Lecie said. "Albin—"

"Bloody hell!" Albin bucked halfway off the bed at the first cut of Euric's knife.

Fulke moved with lightning speed to hold Albin's arms immobile while Talan pinned his legs to the bed should he inadvertently lash out at the healers.

"Albin." Kneeling on the floor opposite Euric, Lecie cradled her husband's face. "Can you hear me?"

His eyes wide and rolling, it took a while for Albin to recognize her. "Am I dreaming or dead?"

"Neither, husband. You are here with me." Her tears splashed onto Albin's cheek and she smoothed them away. "Her ladyship has brought Lady Bronwyn to make you well again."

Grimacing in pain, the cords of muscle in Albin's neck strained as he struggled to keep still. "I feared you were lost to me."

"I have no intention of going anywhere without you." Lightly kissing his forehead, she added, "You must brace yourself now. Sir Euric must cut away the infection."

"Aye." Albin's eyes rested on Fulke above him "Tis about time you made an appearance."

"I would have come for the nuptials had I been invited, and they had not been so hastily spoken."

"Cocky as ever." Albin managed a slight grin.

"You will not have an easy time of it," Fulke said in all seriousness. "Are you ready?"

"Just get it over with."

Placing a thick strip of leather between Albin's teeth, Fulke nodded at Euric.

Albin bore down on the leather strip the instant Euric touched him with the blade. Guttural moans of pain followed each deep cut.

Unable to bear his pain, Lecie's hand shook when she soaked up the blood to keep the wound visible to Euric.

After what appeared to be an endless time to the chamber's inhabitants, Euric straightened to toss the putrefied leavings into the fire. "Bronwyn, I am confident that I removed it all."

"Right," she said with a worried look toward Albin, "now for the fun part." Removing the poker from the glowing embers of the hearth, Bronwyn added, "I am afraid this is going to be very painful, Sir Albin."

"I thought you said it was going to be fun?" Albin's lighthearted attempt at teasing fell flat.

"To stave off further infection it must be done." Bronwyn positioned herself beside him for a last inspection of the wound.

"I have seen it done many a time on the field of battle to no affect, yet if it gives me a chance to make a proper life with my wife, have at it."

"I know a little more than archaic butchers on a battlefield," Bronwyn said. "Let us get to it, shall we?"

Reluctantly pulling his attention from Lecie, Albin looked at her strangely. "I am as ready as I shall ever be."

Spitting out the leather Fulke had again given him, Albin let out a stream of curses when Euric laid the hot iron on his flesh.

The sizzle and smell of burning flesh against hot metal had Lecie on the verge of fainting.

"You have done well." Bronwyn spoke to her husband when she inspected the wound. "It should heal well now."

Relief spread through the group and everyone visibly relaxed knowing Albin would not have to be put through the ordeal again.

"I do not know about you but I could sure use a cup of ale," Fulke said. "I would rather it be me laying there than Albin."

Reina elicited a slight chuckle from Fulke when she replied to him.

"Aye, my love," Fulke said. "Apart from a few occasions, he likely would say the same about me."

"Get me a cup of ale and I will even overlook those few occasions," Albin said.

"You need broth," Fulke said, "not ale."

"Saints bones," Albin swore. "Knocking at death's door and I am denied one of my comforts."

"I shall now see to him," Lecie said smoothing the damp hair away from Albin's temple. "I know you must all be weary and famished. Please consider this your home whilst you are here."

"When is the last time you have eaten, Lecie?" Fulke spoke at Reina's behest. "You are far too pale. There are others who can tend Albin whilst you see to yourself."

"I do not wish to leave my husband, Your Lordship."

"Go," Albin encouraged her. Reaching up to cup her cheek his eyes widened on her neck. "What the—"

"Mayhap a quick bite afore I return." Lecie abruptly stood. "I shall see that the ale is brought up along with your broth."

"Lecie, I know the telltale sign of a noose when I see one."

"All that can wait until you are feeling better." Kissing him on the forehead, she smiled. "Get some rest now."

Unappeased, Albin looked to Fulke.

"Your wife is right, my friend. All you need to know is that she is safe. The rest can wait."

"I have a feeling that I am not going to like what I hear," Albin said, "but glad I am that you arrived when you did."

"We all have reason to give thanks on that account." Fulke gripped Albin's forearm "And if you ever cause us such a fright again you will answer to me."

"I shall stay with him" Anne spoke for the first time from her place beside the hearth.

"No," Albin said. "Please send Betta up. I was overly curt with her earlier and would like to apologize."

"With your permission," Talan said to Fulke on the way out. "I would like to pay a visit on the sheriff."

"I am sure Mylla would like an update as well," Fulke said. "Take all the time you need."

Chapter Twenty-One

After a full meal complete with a brace of hares thanks to Tugger, the group relaxed with their favorite drinks of choice.

Her eyes slipping to the steps every so often, Lecie listened to stories of Castell Maen with interest.

"He will be alright you know." Bronwyn interrupted her troubled thoughts. "All he needs now is rest."

"How can you be so sure?" Lecie searched Bronwyn's silver eyes. "Are you a wicce?"

"What would make you think that?" Bronwyn's gaze briefly flashed to Euric. "Do I act like one?"

"Please forgive me." Lecie hesitated. "Only at times you speak strangely, and I have yet to see a woman so skilled in the healing arts."

"No offense is taken on my part." Leaning close, Bronwyn whispered, "In truth I do practice the old ways. I hope that is not something you take offense to."

"You saved my husband's life and I am forever indebted to you." Lecie reached for Bronwyn's hand. "I care not how twas done. Only, I must warn you, the justice accused me of being a witch. Please be ever weary of him as I would not see you hurt."

"I knew we were going to be great friends." Bronwyn squeezed Lecie's hand. "Do not worry about me. I am well aware of the rumors swirling about de Glanville."

"M'lady." Anne rushed down the remaining steps. "Sir Albin is insisting he see you. Oh, and he would like more ale."

"If he is asking for his two favorite things," Fulke said with a chuckle, "he will most assuredly pull through."

Lecie stood with a grateful smile. "If you will excuse me, I shall see to my husband."

"I shall follow directly with the ale," Anne called to her back.

The tears pooling in Lecie's eyes slipped free when she entered the master chamber to find Albin calmly looking at her. "I woke and found that I could not bear another trice without you by my side."

"You gave me quite a scare, husband," she scolded perching on the edge of the bed. "Pray you never do so again or I shall be in line behind his lordship to take you to task."

"I shall do my best," Albin said pulling her down beside him. "My intent was to discover who hurt you but at the moment I would gladly settle for a kiss."

The first light touch of their lips had them straining against each other for more.

"Is this a private audience or can anyone take part?" Holding a cup of ale, Fulke grinned from the doorway.

Albin groaned when Lecie broke away to stand.

"Do come in, Your Lordship."

"Your timing leaves a lot to be desired," Albin griped. "One would think you are paying me back for a past offense."

"I was merely saving Anne a trip to deliver your ale," Fulke said with a smirk. "Make of it what you will."

"Since you are both here, I would know what happened at the sham of a trial."

"Shall I?" Fulke addressed the question to Lecie. "I have experience with Albin's temperament and feel I can do justice to the tale."

"By all means, please do, Your Lordship."

Filling Albin in on all that had transpired, Fulke ended with his arrival at the inn.

"I am indebted to you," Albin said. "Had it not been for your timely arrival I would have lost my Lecie."

"You owe me nothing." Fulke brushed it off. "You have saved my skin countless times twas nice to return the favor."

"I am not a fit husband," Albin declared. "I cannot even protect my wife."

"Nonsense, you shall not say such a thing again." Lecie gripped Albin's chin between her thumb and finger to stare intently into his eyes. "Promise me."

"Aye, lass," Albin conceded softly. "I vow it."

Fulke cleared his throat to dispel the intimate scene. "I fear we have not heard the last from de Glanville."

"Do you think he will inform Henry of what went on here?"

"Highly unlikely," Fulke said. "After reminding him of his close association with Reynold I believe in this particular instance the score is settled."

"In this instance," Albin said. "You speak of Talan and Mylla?"

"The future does not bode well for them."

"He loves her and will not willingly let her go." Albin frowned at the implications.

"She feels the same way about him," Lecie said. "Even if it were not so, I could not see Mylla with such a vile man as the justice."

They looked up at a knock to find Reina, Bronwyn, and Euric standing in the doorway.

"Can anyone come in, or is this a private gathering?" Euric was the first to speak.

"Aye, come in," Fulke called. "We are in need of a change of subject."

Bronwyn examined Albin's wound with an approving nod. "I am pleased to see some color in your cheeks, Sir Albin."

"You have my deepest thanks, My Lady. I owe you and her ladyship a boon."

"Your gratitude is enough for me," Bronwyn assured him.

From her place beside Fulke, Reina observed Albin and Lecie with a beaming smile.

Albin took note and returned the smile. "Care to tell what amuses you so, Your Ladyship?"

"Lecie is worthy of you, Albin." Reina mouthed the words slowly. "I myself could not have chosen a finer lady for you."

"I beg to differ." Albin gazed at Lecie with all the love he felt for her shining in his eyes. "I shall have to work my entire life to be worthy of her."

"Albin, no." Lecie pressed a hand against his good shoulder when he struggled to rise from the bed.

"Euric, lend me assist if you will." Albin swung his legs over the edge of the bed. "There is something I must do."

Euric shared a worried look with Bronwyn. "Albin, you need not leave the bed. There is a chamber pot beneath it."

"Lad, if I felt the need to relieve myself, I would have already cleared the room."

With Euric's support, Albin stood to allow the vertigo to pass. To the puzzlement of all, he stepped up to Fulke only to slowly drop to his knees.

Understanding had Fulke crossing his arms with a satisfied look.

"My dearest friend, you were right." Albin looked up with shining eyes. "And I thank you."

Assisting Albin upright, Fulke guided him back to the bed. "You know I would not have rested until you were as happy as I."

"Aye," Albin chuckled. "You are stubborn in that way."

"Get some rest. There is time enough for me to gloat later."

"That is what I am afraid of," Albin grumbled closing his eyes.

Ushering everyone out, Reina paused in the doorway. Her eyes briefly resting on Lecie once again snuggled in Albin's embrace she closed the door with a smile.

"Her Ladyship approves of you," Albin observed once they were alone.

"She is everything I believed her to be," Lecie said gazing up at him.

"And you are my everything," Albin whispered. "My Lecie, my lady, my life."

Chapter Twenty-Two

Rochester, England

Spring 1128

The sun had just made its first appearance when Albin returned to the common room in search of Lecie. "Did I not tell you to wait for my assist afore descending?"

Slowing her pace on the last few steps, Lecie ran her hand over the growing swell of her abdomen. With a beaming smile, she reached up to plant a kiss on Albin's cheek. "Tis sweet that you worry so about me."

"Do not attempt to placate me. I am vexed with you."

"Alby, I have been treading these steps since I could stand on my own two feet. In fact," she teased, "I vow I could find my way down them in my sleep."

"That may very well be, however, prior to now you were not carrying my child."

"Your child?" Pulling away from him, Lecie planted her hands on her hips. "Would you care to rephrase that statement?"

"It is true, is it not?" Clearly puzzled, Albin sought to pull her back when she stepped further out of his reach.

"I do not believe you are the one carrying our child for months on end. Nor do I believe tis you who will endure the pain of childbirth when the time comes."

Snatching her into his arms, Albin grinned. "You are a feisty one, my love, but anything that pains you pains me doubly so."

"Why is it you always know what to say?"

"Words come easy to a man in love, and I love you beyond measure."

Snaking her arms around his waist, Lecie lifted her face for his kiss. "You do not play fair."

"Not when it comes to you." Seizing her lips, Albin lifted her up against him. He groaned when Tugger's loud barks carried to them from outside. "It appears the children are not the only ones anxious to set off. Once we arrive at Castell Maen, I expect you to mind me about the step rule."

"I would never dream of being a disobedient wife." She burst out laughing when Albin bent a sarcastic look upon her. "Oh alright, I promise to try and be more obedient."

"I suppose that is a start," he teased. "Are you certain about going? We can just as easily make our home here."

"There are too many bad memories that need to be dispelled from this place," Lecie said taking a last look around. "Besides, now that it is being managed so well there is no reason to remain."

"Then let us go and make some new memories," Albin said holding open the door for her.

The staff stood alongside the wagon bidding their farewells to the children.

Spotting Mylla standing beside Talan, Lecie rushed over. "I was hoping to see you afore we left."

"I shall miss you ever so much." Embracing her, Mylla stepped back with a warm smile. "The babe is growing by the day."

Tears burned Lecie's eyes when she noted the sadness her friend was struggling to conceal. "This is not goodbye. We are leaving the inn in able hands and after the baby is born, we shall return for a visit to see how things are faring."

"If I am still here, I shall look forward to your visit."

Her heart breaking for her friend, Lecie kept the topic light. "In the meantime, my husband has vowed to keep me busy going over building plans for a fortified manor house of our own. After tis completed, you shall have to come for a lengthy visit. Promise?"

"I promise to try," Mylla said softly.

Embracing Mylla again, Lecie held her extra tight. "You must have faith in Talan. What is meant to be will always find a way."

"Regardless of what happens, I shall not waver in my devotion to him."

Joining the men, Lecie bid farewell to Talan. "Will we be seeing you at Castell Maen soon?"

"It all depends." Talan glanced over at Mylla.

"Talan…" Lecie searched for something to say.

"No words are needed but keeping us in your prayers would not be amiss."

"You both shall never leave them," Lecie vowed. "Surely, there must be something that can be done?"

"Short of dishonoring Mylla's entire family and incurring the wrath of the crown by running away together I fear there is not."

"I am so sorry for you both." Lecie reached out to touch his forearm.

"Are you ready, wife of mine?" Securing his horse to the back of the wagon, Albin strode over. "If we delay any longer, the children will set off without us."

"I was just bidding her a safe journey," Talan said. "See you soon, my friend."

"If there is anything—"

"Thank you," Talan cut him off.

"Do you have a message for Castell Maen?"

"Wish them all well for me."

Feeling helpless, Lecie embraced Talan.

Awkwardly patting her on the back, Talan waited for Lecie to release him.

"Do not even think about it," Albin called when she hiked up her skirts to climb onto the bench seat of the wagon.

"Whatever pleases you, husband." Releasing her skirts, Lecie waited with a mischievous look. "After all, I am a most dutiful wife."

Sweeping her up into his arms, Albin planted a kiss on her lips. "I shall tell you in private what pleases me most."

Running a hand along her belly, Lecie smiled. "I think I know well enough already."

Laughing, Albin situated himself beside her. Excited to be off, Tugger barked and the children began waving.

Picking up the reins, he clucked the mules into motion.

Bursting into tears, Mary walked alongside the wagon waving at the children.

"We shall see you soon, Mary," Clayton called to soothe her.

Casting a last glance back at Talan and Mylla, Lecie leaned into Albin. "It breaks my heart to see them so in love and so unhappy."

Albin clutched the reins in one hand to wrap his free arm around her. "If loving you has taught me anything it is that where there is love, there is a way."

"Do you really believe that?" Gazing into his eyes, the love she felt for him nearly overwhelmed her.

"I do," he whispered, capturing her lips.

THE END

Knight Series Book 3

A KNIGHT
OF VALOUR

CANDACE C. BOWEN

About the Author

Candace C. Bowen is the award-winning author of the Knight Series. Born in a suburb of Chicago, Candace moved to South Florida with her family at an early age. A writer of full-length historical romance fiction, she has broadened her scope to creating tales of modern day horror and historical adventure.

Candace resides with her teenaged son and adopted cat in South Florida. If you have any questions or comments, she would love to hear from you.

Email: ccbowen@knightseries.com

Web: www.knightseries.com

Twitter: @candacecbowen